Straight Talking

What are you supposed to say when you are sitting opposite the man you love, the man you are not in love with but the man you love, and you are feeling his pain as if it is your own.

When you would do almost anything to stop his pain, but the one thing you could give him, the one thing that you know would surely make it go away, is the one thing you just can't give.

I look at Adam and I want to put my arms around him. I want to cuddle him and tell him that it's all going to be OK, but I can't do that. I have to be cruel to be kind, I can't give him a teaser, a taste of what he will be missing in the future because then he will collapse, and if he collapses I don't know what will happen to me. Really, I don't.

Jane Green is a journalist, she lives in west London.

Jane Green

Straight Talking

ARROW

Reprinted in Arrow Books, 1998

11 13 15 17 19 20 18 16 14 12

This edition first published in the United Kingdom in 1997 by Mandarin Paperbacks and reprinted 4 times

Arrow Books
The Random House Group Limited
20 Vauxhall Bridge Road, London SW1V 2SA

Random House Australia (Pty) Limited
20 Alfred Street, Milsons Point, Sydney,
New South Wales 2061, Australia

Random House New Zealand Limited
18 Poland Road, Glenfield,
Auckland 10, New Zealand

Random House (Pty) Limited
Endulini, 5a Jubilee Road, Parktown 2193, South Africa

The Random House Group Limited Reg. No. 954009
www.randomhouse.co.uk

A CIP catalogue record for this book
is available from the British Library

ISBN 0 7493 2439 2

Papers used by Random House are natural, recyclable products made from wood grown in sustainable forests. The manufacturing processes conform to the environmental regulations of the country of origin.

Printed and bound in Denmark by
Nørhaven A/S, Viborg

To my wonderful parents . . . for
proving there is such a thing
as a happy ending.

'What is love? As far as I can tell,
it is a passion, admiration and respect.
If you have two, you have enough.
If you have all three, you don't
have to die to go to heaven'

William Wharton

– One –

I was never supposed to be single at thirty years old. I was supposed to be like my mother, wasn't I? Married, a couple of kids, a nice home with Colefax and Fowler wallpaper and a husband with a sports car and a mistress or two.

Well, to be honest I would mind about the mistresses, but not as much as I mind being single. What I'd really, really love is a chance to walk down that aisle dressed in a cloud of white, and let's face it, I'm up there at the top, gathering dust.

It can't be that unusual, surely, to be thirty years old and to spend most of your spare time dreaming about the most important day of your life? I don't know, perhaps it's just me, perhaps other women redirect their energies into their careers. Perhaps I'm just a desperately sad example of womanhood. Oh God, I hope not.

It's not as if I haven't had relationships, although, admittedly, none of them have come close to proposing. I've come close to thinking they were my potential husband. A bit too close. Every time. But hey, if you're going to go into it you may as well go into it thinking this time he might be Mr Right, as opposed to Mr

Right-for-three-weeks-before-he-does-his-usual-disappearing-act.

Sometimes I think it's me. I think I must be doing something wrong, giving out subliminal messages so they can smell the desperation, read the neon lights on my forehead . . . 'KEEP AWAY FROM THIS WOMAN, SHE IS LOOKING FOR COMMITMENT', but most of the time I think it's them. Bastards. All of them.

But I never quite lose hope that my perfect man, my soulmate, is out there waiting for me, and every time my heart gets broken I think that next time it's going to be different.

And I'm a sucker for big, strong, handsome men. Exactly the type my mother always told me to avoid. 'Go for the ugly ones,' she always used to say, 'then they'll be grateful.' But she landed up with my handsome father, so she's never had the pleasure of that particular experience.

And the problem with small men is they make you feel like an Amazonian giant. At least they do if you're 5′8½″ and a size twelve, or thereabouts, the product of constant dieting in public, and constant bingeing in private.

Big men are far better. They put their arms around you, their head resting on yours and you feel like a little girl; safe from the big bad world; as if nothing could ever go wrong again.

So here I am, and for your information I am neither fat, ugly, nor socially dysfunctional. Most people think I'm twenty-six, which secretly annoys the hell out of me, because I like to think of myself as mature and sophisticated, and I'm generally thought of as strikingly attractive.

I know this because the men – when they're still in the stages of being kind to me – say this, but unfortunately I've always longed to be strikingly pretty. I've tried being pretty, painting on big eyes and looking coyly out from under my fringe, but pretty can't be attained. Pretty, you either are or you aren't.

I'm successful, in a fashion. I earn enough money to go on shopping binges at Joseph every three months or so, and I own my own flat. OK, it's not in the smartest part of London, but if you closed your eyes between the car and the front door, you might, only might mind, just think you were in Belgravia. Apart from the lingering smell of cat pee that is.

Of course I have cats. What self-respecting single career woman of thirty who's secretly desperately longing to give it all up for the tall, rich stranger of her dreams doesn't have cats? They're my babies. Harvey and Stanley.

They might be stupid names, but I quite like the idea of cats having human names, particularly ones you don't expect. The greatest name I ever heard was Dave the cat. A cat called Dave, brilliant isn't it? I can't stand Fluffys, or Squeaks, or Snowys. And then people wonder why their cats are arrogant. I'd be supercilious, too, if my mother had called me Fluffy.

Luckily she didn't. She called me Anastasia, Nasty to my enemies, Tasia, pronounced Tasha, to my friends, of which I have many.

Because just in case you're reading this and you happen to be happily married with other couples as friends, doing cosy couply things together, let me tell you that when you're a single girl, friends are vital.

I always thought the women's magazines were talking a load of crap when they told you to forget about men, crack open a bottle of wine and sit around with your girlfriends cackling about sex, but it's true.

I still can't quite believe it's true because it's only

recently, well, within the last three years, that I've discovered this group of female friends, but that's exactly what we do, once a week, and just in case you're thinking it's sad and lonely, it's not. It's great.

There's me, naturally, Andrea, commonly known as Andy, Mel, and Emma.

And I suppose, much as I hate the term 'ladettes', that's exactly what we are, except we all despise football. Actually Andy says she loves football, and she claims to support Liverpool, but she only says it for two reasons: she fancies Stan Collymore, and she thinks it impresses men.

They are impressed, but they don't fancy her because Andrea is everything I dread. She's more blokeish than most of the 'blokes' I know. If a guy's drinking beer, Andrea will instantly challenge him to a drinking competition, and she usually wins. Attractive? I don't think so. They all think she's a great laugh but they wouldn't want to wake up next to her.

You think I'm bitter? If you'd been dumped from a great height by what feels like practically every single man in London, you'd be slightly bitter. But bear with me and you'll discover I'm not quite as bitter as I sound.

In case you're wondering how I earn my money, I'm a television producer. A bit of a joke, isn't it? Me who leads such an exciting glamorous life, producing a daytime television show, me who rubs shoulders with the stars every day of her life, me who can't find a bloody man.

But I've had some fun on the show, I grant you. I remember one time an actor came on as a guest – can't tell you who he is, much as I'd like to, because he's very famous, and very famously married to an equally famous wife. The night before the show I had to go to his hotel to brief him, you know, just to check my researcher had got the right stuff, and there we were, drinking gin and tonics in the hotel bar, with him rubbing my leg under the table.

I can't deny I fancied him rotten and I followed him upstairs to make sure we 'hadn't left anything out'. Gave him the blow job to end all blow jobs. I'll admit it didn't do a lot for me, but then again, I've dined out on that story for nearly four years. I would tell you too you understand, but we're not exactly close friends, and I haven't decided whether or not I can trust you.

But what I have decided is to tell you about my life, and for all this hard, career-type stuff, I'm a real softie inside. The classic scratch the surface and you'll find marshmallow stuff. You've got to be hard in television, I didn't make it this far just by dishing out the odd blow job, but put me in a room with a man I could love, a man who could take care of me, and I'm jelly, bloody jelly.

That's my problem you see. They meet me and think I spell danger, glamour, excitement, and then two weeks down the line, right about the time I'm trying to move my toothbrush into their bathroom cabinet and my silk night-dress under their pillow, they realise I'm not so different after all.

And after I've cooked them gourmet meals, because I'm an excellent cook, and added a few flowers and feminine touches to their bachelor pads, they know I could make a good wife. Actually I'd make a bloody superb wife, and they're off, like shit from a shovel.

I'd love to take you back over my whole life, but you probably wouldn't be that interested. Two parents, middle-class, comfortable, even wealthy I suppose, and not very interested in me.

I was the classic wild child, except I think I probably

could have been a bit more wild, a bit more crazy, but underneath the good girl was always fighting to get out. Maybe that's why people think I'm a bitch now. I spent so many years trying to be good, being walked over by everyone, when I decided to stand up for my rights, people started getting scared, and what do people do when they're scared of you? Exactly. They call you a bitch. But my close friends know that's not true, and I suppose they're the only ones that really matter.

Hang on, the doorbell's ringing. God I *hate* people dropping in unexpectedly. This guy I used to fancy, Anthony, once came over when I was in a grubby old bathrobe with legs that were booked in for a leg wax the following week. I looked a state, and I had to sit there and talk to him, trying to hide my gorilla legs. We never got it together, unsurprisingly.

It's OK though, it's Andy. She probably wants to hear about the last one, the three-monther, bit of a record for me. For all her faults, Andy's great, always makes you feel better. Every time I get dumped I turn first to Mel to ease the pain, and then to Andy to cheer me up, and inevitably I leave feeling the world's a better place. Good job she joined us now, before I get seriously depressed.

You may as well join us, sit down, kick your shoes off and don't worry, it's a smokers flat. Beer or Chardonnay, which would you prefer?

The presenters of my show are the biggest pair of assholes I ever came across. I used to fancy Him before I worked here, but as soon as I met him I realised he fancied himself more than anyone else ever could, and that was that, turned my stomach.

Whether it's fortunate or unfortunate, he likes

blondes. Being blonde, albeit a Daniel Galvin special that costs me a small fortune and has to be redone every six weeks, he likes me. He doesn't actually flirt overtly, doesn't David, just gives me the odd wink when he thinks no one's looking.

And I play up to him, as long as She's not around; his on-screen partner, the woman who plays wife, mother, sister, daughter to the macho inanity he spouts every morning from ten twenty to twelve noon.

She's not crazy about me, but Annalise Richie, the female star of *Breakfast Break*, knows I'm good and she knows David likes me, not to mention the editor of the programme, who, for what it's worth, I slept with on and off for about two years.

Oh, and by the way, don't get these two confused with the other presenters. They're not the sickly sweet pair on the BBC, who paw each other all morning like a pair of rampant lovebirds, nor are they the married couple on the other side who, granted, are as slick as they come.

David and Annalise, you know the ones. He's the one with the perfect looks, if you're into Ken dolls, and she's the dyed blonde who looks like she needs a bloody good scrub with carbolic soap.

Off camera of course, because on camera she's poured into a chic little number from wardrobe, and Jesus, wouldn't I love to tell her adoring public that underneath the silk Equipment shirt is a Marks & Spencer bra that's gone grey. Horrible.

And this morning I need her whining voice like a hole in my head, sitting in the gallery above the studio, trying to turn down the earpiece so her nasal tones sound halfway bearable.

'Tasha, I'm not sure I like these questions, I don't understand what point we're trying to make here.'

'Annie,' I say, gritting my teeth until I practically grind them down in one easy movement, and calling her by the nickname she prefers because it makes her feel like a friend to the crew, 'Annie, we're back on air in three minutes, the woman's an expert on relationships, she's a good talker, just press play and she's off.'

From the monitors above me I see Annalise visibly relax. Stupid cow. Every time a guest comes on who's a pseudo-intellectual, Annalise gets in a panic, quite rightly, because she hasn't got the brains to cope.

The guest is Ruby Everest, larger-than-life stand-up comedienne who specialises in degrading men. My kind of gal. She also happens to have a first from Cambridge in psychology, and dealing with hecklers is her forte. I met her earlier in the green room, and immediately warmed to her.

'Vain bastard, isn't he?' are her first words to me, gesturing at David, preening himself in a pane of glass that happened to have a shadow behind it at the time.

'Isn't that the bloody truth,' I respond, suddenly blushing as I remember my vow not to swear in front of guests, or people I don't know well, which I suppose includes you so I'll try to mind my Ps and Qs. But Ruby just grins, so I grin back.

You can always recognise a fellow member of the sisterhood. Not all women belong, only those who have been prone to a little rough and tumble – they've been treated roughly and then they tumble. Once upon a time, in their twenties, the sisterhood were men's women. All their friends were men, they'd go out, get drunk, shag some bloke and kick him out in the morning. It was fun in your twenties, you knew you'd settle down eventually, and you just wanted to do as much as possible while you still could.

But now in your thirties you've changed. You've

become women's women. There's a weary air about you, you're resigned to the fact that the knights in shining armour disappeared with the round table, and if married men are as good as you're going to get, then that's as good as you're going to get.

Ruby's like me, I can see it immediately. She's a woman who's had enough, a woman who's forced herself to be happy with her cats and her girlfriends, with the odd one-night-stand, with the men who treat her like shit and don't come back for more.

But you see the problem with the sisterhood, with women like Ruby and me, is that we still have hope. We can't help it. We pretend we're happy with our lives, and when we see couples kissing in public places we make mock vomiting expressions, but we long for love. We believe in love. We sit in darkened cinemas and watch *Sleepless in Seattle* and *While You Were Sleeping* with tears streaming down our faces. Even when we know they're all fuckers, we still hope for the one fucker who will rescue us from single life.

Maybe I'm wrong, but I'm assuming you're a member of the sisterhood, otherwise we wouldn't be talking, but then again, we're still in the getting to know you phase. Stick around, you might learn something.

Sitting in the gallery I see Ruby being led into the studio and placed on the sofa facing Annalise and David. Annalise smiles her sickly smile, and they both shake hands with her, making the facile small talk they usually make. This time it's about the weather, how hot it is, and I smile broadly as I hear Ruby say, 'I can't cope with this heat at all, I had to take my knickers off in the green room.'

Annalise looks shocked, while David visibly perks up. Sad bastard, I notice his eyes immediately flick to her crotch for a split second. When they return to meet her eyes, she has one eyebrow raised, and he actually manages to look embarrassed.

And then the floor manager counts them down to being on air, the cameras zoom in, and here we go again, another twenty minutes of bullshit.

'Hi and welcome back to *Breakfast Break*,' says Annalise, grinning into the camera.

'For today's phone-in we're looking at Betrayals in Love,' says David, trying to look as sincere as he possibly can. 'Has your boyfriend ever had an affair with your best friend? Maybe your girlfriend ran off with your brother? Or perhaps you've been the betrayer. Whatever your story, we want to hear it, so call us now on 01393 939393.'

I know what you're thinking, who writes this shit, and you're right, it is shit but show me someone who thinks daytime television is intellectually stimulating and I'll show you a bloody liar.

Of course it's rubbish, but what the public wants, the public gets. So back to David spouting my crappy script.

'Joining us in the studio today is Ruby Everest, the brilliant comedienne who waxes lyrical on men and their foibles. But Ruby,' he says, turning to her with a fake smile, 'surely women can be as bad.'

'Of course,' she says, leaning towards him, 'but women generally only betray when they've been severely hurt emotionally.'

'But your new show,' continues Annalise, '*Hit Him Where It Hurts*, is all about men who treat their women badly. Has that been your experience?'

'Look,' says Ruby, 'I'm thirty-five, I've been out with more men than you've bought new clothes, and I'm still single. If I found a man who was as good as my women friends, I'd be in there like a shot, but I haven't. All the men I've been out with, without exception, have been screwed up.'

David tries to interject, panicking at her 'swearing', but Ruby's on a roll. 'They either don't want sex, or they want it so much they're shagging all your friends as well. They want you to be their mummy, but the minute you try taking care of them they suddenly feel all claustrophobic and can't wait to find the exit route.

'They meet you and tell you you're wonderful, and within three weeks they're telling you that you'd be that bit more wonderful if you lost a few pounds, or wore mini-skirts, or dyed your hair.'

She sighs deeply. 'I'm so fed up with it I'm thinking of turning gay.' Yes! This is what I've been waiting for. She's only saying what all my friends have been joking about for years, but they're not famous and they don't say it on live television. This means big headlines tomorrow, I can see them now, RUBY COMES OUT; RUBY RUNS TO WOMEN; LESBIAN LAUGHS FOR RUBY. The tabloids will have a field day.

The first call comes in. Some sad woman from Doncaster whose husband has been having affairs all their married life. But she loves him and she doesn't want to leave him. Why do so many women put up with this treatment? Why do so many women not think they deserve any better? But Ruby tells her you either put up with it or get out, and, harsh as it sounds, I suppose she has a point.

And then I fall silent as I hear the next call is Simon from London. It couldn't be, I tell myself, he knows I work here, but of course Sod's law is working and it is. It really is.

His well-spoken vowels dipped in a bucket of sarcasm fill my ears through the headphones as he says hello to the presenters, and I can't breathe. I think, in fact, I'm going to throw up.

I haven't spoken to Simon for three years. Not since the bastard dumped me out of the blue after nine months. And I loved him, Jesus how I loved him. It wasn't love of course, even I can see now that it was infatuation, but at the time it near enough killed me.

I know exactly what you're thinking, how could she have loved him after nine months, but occasionally, or not so occasionally if you're me, a nine-year relationship can be condensed into nine months, or even nine weeks, and sometimes nine days.

They're so passionate, so intense, so painful, that even years afterwards you still feel the hurt when you hear their name. This is how it was for me and Simon.

I'm so wrapped up in memories I don't even hear what he's saying, and when finally I pull myself together I hear him say, 'I didn't mean to have an affair with Tanya, but my girlfriend was so dynamic and exciting when I met her, and then she changed. She was this vital successful career woman, but by the end all she wanted to do was shop for the flat and iron my shirts.'

Excuse me for running out the gallery with my hand clapped over my mouth, but this is all a bit too much for me. I *am* going to be sick.

– *Two* –

I remember that night clearly because I didn't want to go. It was a party, some friends of Andy's, couple called Matt and Kate. I couldn't be bothered. Couples invite other couples, with a few single friends thrown in for good measure, and all the couples have a great time and all the singles are bored stiff.

All I wanted to do was put on a big sloppy jumper, order a Chinese takeaway big enough for four people, and watch hopeless American sit-coms.

But don't feel sorry for me, I just have nights when I have enough of people, enough of small talk, enough of make-up, enough of worrying that every hair's in place. I have nights when all I want to do is slob out and eat. Got a problem with that? Good.

So this was one of those nights, but Andy wouldn't let me stay in. I tried everything. I told her I was working, I told her I had a headache, I told her my period was coming and I felt like a fat pig, but she wouldn't listen.

Sometimes that's a good thing with Andy. You know that when you go out with her she'll always bring at least three people you've never met before, but sometimes you're just not in the mood. Sometimes you just want it to be the two of you, quietly chatting about life, the universe and sex. Sometimes you don't want to have to make the effort.

In the end I looked in the mirror and decided I could do without a Chinese meal for four, and I knew if I stayed in I wouldn't be able to fight the temptation for longer than about two minutes, so I thought what the hell, I'll go and I'll leave after an hour.

Because every now and then you have to do things you don't want to do, and this wasn't a night when I secretly hoped that because I didn't want to go, I'd meet the man of my dreams.

Because isn't that how it usually happens? The nights when you make an effort, the nights when you spend hours slapping on make-up, blow-drying your hair, wearing your expensive new outfit are the nights when you never meet anyone. Not even the ugly ones.

I know I don't have to tell you that you only ever meet men when you least expect it, but I swear, this wasn't one of those nights, it really wasn't.

So there we were at this party, and out of habit I'd already sized up every man in the room and decided none of them were worth talking to. It was the kind of party I usually hate anyway. I long for parties from my student days, when the room was lit in the murky glow coming from one lamp in the corner, when music was turned up, when no one gave a damn, when you could get drunk, stoned, dance, forget about yourself.

But when you're a grown-up, parties change. Now you walk into a flat, or a house, with stripped wooden floors and proper champagne glasses, none of that plastic stuff any more, and you sip kir royales as you pretend to be interested in what some sad geek does for a living.

And I miss student food: hundreds of pieces of thick, doughy french bread, with hunks of cheese still in its wrapper and a few pâtés with a jar of Branston pickle being the most sophisticated thing at the party.

Doesn't matter how much you eat, you can't fill up or pig out or chow down on Marks & Spencer canapés. But they look pretty, so people think they're being so clever and smart by serving them.

And this was a Marks & Spencer, cheap-sparkling-white-masquerading-as-champagne-and-mixed-with-cassis kind of party. The boring kind.

Andy was getting over-excited – full of piss and vinegar as usual – because there were men around. It doesn't matter whether she fancies them or not. So I was standing in the corner getting more and more pissed off, and dreaming of Chinese takeaways.

I remember looking at my watch thinking, if I can get away within half an hour, I can stop at the takeaway and quench my hunger. You think it's an emotional hunger? Really, tell me something else I don't already know. I haven't been in therapy that long, but even I know that when the food cravings overtake me, it's not to fill my stomach, it's to fill that big empty space inside my heart.

Oh I'm sorry, I didn't mention therapy before, but to be honest I haven't decided how much I want to say about it. If you must know, I've gone because of this lack of relationship business, but it's very private, it's my time, my space, and I pay a hell of a lot for it – £40 an hour. I might tell you later, we'll see.

So there I was, planning a binge, when Simon came over, only I didn't know it was Simon then, did I? I just thought it was some ugly bastard with glasses, although they were Armani, those little round numbers, and actually he wasn't ugly, my mood was ugly.

He had a funny face. He looked like a little wise owl with sticky-up black hair and his suit – which was black and trendy, worn over a crisp white T-shirt – was at odds with his face. He looked like a little boy pretending to be a grown-up. I know that at that point I should have realised that my maternal instincts would kick into play very shortly, but I didn't, I honestly didn't, I swear, I just thought he was an ugly boffin.

I was waiting for him to say something incredibly naff, something like 'Would you like a drink?' or 'How do you know Matt and Kate?', but he didn't, he just stood there and looked at me, not from a great height I might add. In my three inch heels we were more or less the same height. Possibly he was even shorter, but time and memory have added a few inches. Don't they always?

And he looked at me and he looked at me and he looked at me. And I, Miss Tough, Strong, Television Producer, blushed. And then he opened his mouth and said, 'Would you like a drink?'

And I smiled sweetly and said, 'I'd love one,' but he didn't do anything, he just stayed there and looked at me, very seriously, very intently, as if I could be the woman he was searching for.

And as he stared, six words went through my head: 'Uh oh, here we go again,' and my stomach lifted up and did a very short twist, the kind of twist that means I'm going to fall for them.

'You're the best-looking bird in this room,' he said finally, and after a long pause I replied with, 'But you're not the best-looking bloke.' Sorry, I'm almost embarrassed to tell you that now, but it was the best I could come up with at the time.

'Ah, but I am the cleverest.'

'Using a word like cleverest I very much doubt it.'

'But I am, Anastasia, I'm clever enough to stop you making the great escape.'

I smiled broadly, couldn't help myself. 'How did you know?'

'Which bit? Your escape or your name? I decided you look like an Anastasia, although I could have had a bit of help there, and I can always tell when someone's about to do a disappearing act, and you were about to make a run for it. Crap television on tonight though. I already checked.'

I laughed, amazed that this bloke, this bloke with a funny boffin face was onto me, and that's when I decided we would make a great couple, and even while we talked, even that first evening, I was wondering what my life would be like with him.

We'd live in Islington, I decided. In one of those ramshackle Georgian houses which we'd do up ourselves. Simon would be great at DIY I thought, and together we'd sand the floorboards and paint the walls white.

We'd have a bohemian wedding, because Simon, although he must have been successful – the editor of a men's magazine – Simon didn't look the type for a big, flashy, smart affair. We'd each choose a poem and a song for each other, something that would mean everything. I'd already chosen it, Ray Charles, 'Come Rain Or Come Shine'.

And as he talked, as he made me laugh, over and over again in my head I could hear *I'm gonna love you, like no one loves you, come rain or come shine. Happy together, unhappy together, wouldn't it be fine. I guess when you met me now, it was just one of those things, ah but don't you ever bet me now, because I'm gonna be true, if you let me.*

Jesus, Simon was funny. He was sarcastic, brilliantly intelligent, and almost as cynical as me.

'Load of ponces,' he said, looking around. 'What I could really do with is holing up in a dark cosy pub, with a few bottles of ice cold beer and a lovely Anastasia by my side.'

I hate pubs, hate them. Working-class hovels smelling of beer and cigarettes, and while I like beer and cigarettes, I hate pubs. But what did I say? As if I need to tell you.

The pub was exactly the kind of pub I hate, but it had one redeeming feature, a real fire, a fire to feed my fantasies, to make it look as if we were in a film, not a sad daytime television film, a Hollywood love story, a *Sleepless in Seattle*.

And when all the chairs were on the table and the staff were huddled behind the bar glaring at us and daring us to leave, we stood up, and walked out, with Simon's arm draped casually over my shoulders as my heart pounded so hard I couldn't talk.

Neither one of us needed to say come back for coffee, it was left hanging in the air, an unspoken agreement that tonight, even if only for one night, we would be together.

Jesus, I sound like a romantic novel, but that night was amazing, it was so, I don't know, special. He was so special. He made me feel like the only real woman in the world. We got outside the pub and turned to face one another and he put his finger to his lips, took his glasses off and bent to kiss me.

A soft, warm, strawberry-beery kiss. He kissed me on the lips again and again, and I tentatively licked the inside of his mouth, before it became a great big passionate snog. No other word for it, I was finally acting like the student I wanted to be at the party. We stood on a street corner, with people walking past and making vomiting noises, and we snogged for minutes and minutes and minutes.

We climbed into his beautiful old dark blue Citroën, and he drove to his flat in Belsize Park. I remember driving past the Screen on the Hill, past Café Flo, already planning our breakfast of coffee and croissants with the Sunday papers, sitting on the pavement outside in the sunshine.

And we drove home and we made love. It wasn't shagging, or fucking, or screwing. It was slow, tender, beautiful. It felt like the kind of making love you do when you've built a relationship, when you know the ins and outs of someone's body, when you really care about them.

God, he was a brilliant lover. Behind those boffin glasses and mismatched clothes he was a funny, selfless, experienced lover. I should have known then, I should have known, but me being me, I wanted to believe I was different, I wanted to think that he'd never made love with anyone like this before.

There was nothing awkward about that first time. Even that moment when he crawled between my legs and propped my knees up, licking and sucking my clitoris, sending me into spasms of pleasure, while occasionally raising his head and meeting my eyes, even that wasn't awkward.

It was delicious, the whole thing was delicious, and after he'd led me to the peak of excitement, when he finally pushed his lovely thick cock into me, he showered my face with kisses, murmuring, 'My Anastasia, my beautiful Anastasia.'

I couldn't help myself, I cried, didn't I? It was so beautiful I lay there with tears streaming down my cheeks and Enigma playing in the background, and

Simon propped himself up on one elbow and licked the salty tears off my face.

'We're going to be good together you and I,' he said. 'I wish I'd known you for ever. I wish I'd seen you as a little girl, I bet you were gorgeous, tumbling dark curls and those big brown eyes. Mmm delicious,' he said, as he bent to kiss my right nipple.

Neither of us slept that night, but that first night, when you're not used to sharing a bed, to sharing your space with a body you're unfamiliar with, you don't care do you? You lie there replaying every touch, every lick, every kiss, and you lie awake the whole night with a huge bloody smile on your face. Well I do anyway.

Every time I tossed and turned, Simon would lay a hot, sticky hand on my stomach, or plant a soft kiss on my shoulder, or fling a big, hairy thigh over mine.

'Good morning,' he finally said, at six, when neither of us could pretend that we had slept, or were going to sleep, or wanted to sleep.

'*Good* morning,' I replied sleepily, and what I hoped was sexily. It worked though, I felt his hand slowly move up my leg, brushing over my pubic hair and lazily circle my stomach, moving further and further down while he flicked his tongue expertly over my nipples.

I watched him as he was doing it, a mixture of feelings going through me, not least because there's a hotline directly from my nipples to my clitoris, and I was becoming more and more excited. But he looked like a little boy, and I'm not trying to be sick or anything, don't get me wrong, but at that moment, despite getting bloody turned on, I wanted to look after him, I wanted us to look after each other.

So we made love again and I can't tell you it was

better than the first, because although you're meant to say that, it was about the same, maybe even a bit worse because I wasn't so keen on the kissing, I was sure my breath smelt like a coffin.

And afterwards he stood up, stretched and while he was absent-mindedly messing about with his cock, he told me was taking me out for breakfast.

I should have been repulsed, I mean I know he wasn't having a wank or anything which, don't get me wrong, I wouldn't have minded, actually I find it a big turn-on, but it was so intimate, and I was so touched he was already that relaxed with me.

I know now it wasn't a big deal. I know now that all men are relaxed about their bodies, whenever, wherever, whatever. They don't care if they've got paunches, or droopy asses, or small cocks because when they look in the mirror they see Mel bloody Gibson.

He went to the bathroom and I stretched in his big grown-up bed, scissoring my legs out to either side of the bed, smiling up at the ceiling. Not my taste, I thought, looking around, but things can be changed. The rickety wooden shelves are a bit naff, but they can go, and all it needs is a good tidy up.

There's nothing quite like lying in a new lover's bed by yourself the morning after you've first had sex, just at the time when you determine what your future's going to be together, whether in fact, there is a future.

When they wake up in the morning and kiss you and cuddle you and screw you before disappearing to shave, then you know it's a one-night-stand.

When they wake up in the morning and kiss you, and cuddle you, and want to take you out for breakfast, then you know you could be onto a winner.

It's exhilarating, exciting, it makes you tingle all

over. You assess their bedroom, their belongings, decide whether you'll be staying at their flat, or whether they'll be staying at yours. You look around the room, at the sun streaming in through filthy windows and you think, I could be happy here, I could be happy with this.

And when Simon came back from the bathroom he jumped on top of me, squashing me until I begged, and he bit my nose. Yeah it sounds stupid, but I just grinned, and I couldn't stop grinning. I didn't even care when I had to get out of bed with no clothes on. I still sucked my stomach in, I'm not that stupid, but I didn't give a damn about my cellulite, my unsupported tits, my ass. I knew he was watching and I knew he liked what he saw. What a great feeling.

'Has anyone ever told you you look beautiful when you come?' he said, in a very loud voice as I was biting into my toast in Café Flo, because, you clever readers, they'd run out of croissants.

What do you say when someone asks you a question like that? You can't say yes, which may or may not be true (actually it is true, three blokes have said it to me but not because I *do* look beautiful, because they think it's something they ought to say. Only problem is I never believed it. Until now.), because then they start getting paranoid and jealous of all the men you've ever had sex with, and you can't say no because it sounds, well, it just sounds prissy if you ask me.

So I shook my head while Simon carried on, in an equally loud voice, 'You do, you look really wild and abandoned, and you taste wonderful. All wet and warm and gushy and yummy. It feels like I'm coming home.'

At which point the couple on the next table, the couple who had obviously been together for so long they had run out of conversation and had to rely on people like us at neighbouring tables to provide their entertainment in restaurants, giggled.

I could feel my face flaming up, furious at feeling humiliated over something so lovely. I turned, so angry I was almost spitting, 'You obviously don't have a sex life or you wouldn't be listening in to other people's. Your boyfriend ought to take you home and fuck you stupid, maybe it would spice your boring bloody life up a bit.'

She was shocked. The stupid girl looked like a goldfish, with her mouth just hanging open, and her boyfriend struggled for something to say. My eyes were probably flashing red, and I was lucky I wasn't hit or something, but the bloke was a wimp, and he just looked at his girlfriend and said, 'We're going.'

I turned back to Simon and what was the sod doing? Laughing. He was laughing so hard there were tears streaming down his face and he had to take his glasses off.

'You're amazing, Anastasia,' he finally managed to gasp. 'I've never met a woman like you. Shit, you showed those poor boring bastards. She's probably never even have an orgasm, poor cow. If she'd been any more anal she would have had to order ex-lax, never mind a decaf cappuccino.'

He wiped his eyes and stretched his hand over the table. 'Jesus, woman,' he said with a grin, 'I could fall in love with you.'

I've heard it before and I'll probably hear it a million times again, but there was something in his matter-of-fact manner, that he was smiling as he said it, that he wasn't taking himself seriously, that made me believe in him, that made me believe that wishes do come true after all.

– *Three* –

We may all belong to the sisterhood, my girlfriends and I, but that doesn't mean you don't have to make an effort. Today's Saturday, our day for lunch, and I'm still trying to decide what to wear.

You think it doesn't matter what I wear? Well, we may all think the sun shines out of each other's proverbial asses, but we're a glamourous crowd, and I can't let the side down, can I?

Navy leggings, a caramel jacket with big patch pockets and a belt, and flat caramel loafers. I sit at my dressing table brushing my hair, and pout at my reflection, ever so slightly sucking in my cheeks between my teeth, to give me perfect cheekbones.

Looking at myself now I know I'm attractive, Jesus I'm more than that, I'm stunning, and I don't understand it, I really don't understand why I haven't got a man. But then that's the basic problem with being a woman, isn't it? Doesn't matter how pretty, stunning, or strikingly attractive you are, even when you look in the mirror and *know* you look great, meet a handsome bloke and you're convinced he'll see through the make-up to the fat awkward kid lurking just beneath the surface.

But today's a good hair day, a good make-up day.

That fake tan worked, and I'm a lovely golden brown, not too fake though, just a nice healthy glow. I'm ready to take on the world, as long as there are only women in it.

As usual I'm the first one to arrive. Is this my television training? Why the hell am I always on time, early usually, when everyone else is always twenty minutes late. I should know by now, I should time my arrivals later, but I can't, I get panicky if I think I'm going to be even two minutes late, I've almost got into fights with drivers on the road who are pootling along like goddamned pensioners.

Well of course I suffer from road rage, did you really expect anything less? Wankers, cunts, fuckwits, the words stream from my frothing lips when I'm in a hurry. Every now and then, when I've calmed down, I worry about it, but I always keep the doors locked, ever since someone tried to wrench it open to swing at me. Fuckwit.

Mel's first to arrive. Shit I adore Mel. I met her just before I met Simon, through another friend I don't see anymore, and I have to say I wasn't crazy about her. Mel's not like the rest of us. She drives around in a car affectionately known as the shitmobile – a filthy beaten up Renault 5 that smells like an ashtray on wheels.

Mel doesn't care about clothes, about money, about appearances, and although I respect that, I can't help but think that if she cared a little more she'd look a hell of a lot better.

She's not unattractive, Mel, or at least she wasn't, when we first met, but she's put on masses of weight, and her dark curly hair usually looks like it needs a bloody good brush, with about a gallon of John Frieda's

Frizz Ease serum dumped on it. I thought she wasn't good enough, I was caught up in the superficiality that comes with being successful at an age when you're too young to know any better.

I looked with disdain at Mel's Marks & Spencer clothes, her haphazard life, and I decided she wasn't good enough to be my friend. How stupid could I have been. When I hit rock bottom, when Simon left, Mel spent hours with me, day and night. I used to phone her at three a.m., when I couldn't sleep, when I'd wake up with tear-stained pillows, and she'd come over, she'd leave her boyfriend sleeping and she'd tiptoe out and talk me through.

She's a therapist, Mel, the best person in the world to pour your troubles out to, but naturally Mel's more screwed up than anyone I know. She's brilliant, just brilliant at sorting out other people's lives, but hasn't got a clue when it comes to her own.

As soon as she walks in I can see something's wrong, and my heart sinks. I try to be as giving and understanding as she is with me, but a side of me loses patience. A side of me can't understand why, if she's so unhappy, she doesn't just get out.

'Daniel,' I say with a sigh, and a hint of impatience I can't keep out of my voice. 'What's he done now?'

'He doesn't want to come with me next weekend,' she says, dumping her ethnic tote sac on the floor and collapsing into the chair opposite me. 'He's decided that there's a party he'd rather go to on Saturday night, in London, and he can't be bothered to schlep to a wedding in the country.'

Daniel? You want to know about Daniel? All I can tell you is this is typical of Daniel. A smooth-talking lawyer who's pleasant looking, charming company, and a total shit to Mel. They've been together for five years, but he won't marry her until she's changed. He wants her to lose weight, to wear better clothes. In short, to be more like us.

And shit does he flirt. I've started to dread seeing him, because when Mel's back is turned he'll sidle up and whisper that he's always fancied me, that maybe, when I'm feeling lonely, I should give him a call.

And it's not just me. He's done it to Emma as well. He probably wants to do it to Andy., but I think she scares him. But what can you do? What can you say when your friend's boyfriend is flirting, and since none of us have taken him up on his crappy offer, how do you know whether he's all mouth and no trousers? Think about it, what would you do?

Maybe it doesn't matter, maybe it's the fact that he's saying it at all, but Mel's such a good person, so genuine, and the three of us have agreed not to tell her, we just want her to finish it, to get out, to get on with her life.

Because a woman will always blame the other woman. She never thinks her man could have made the first move, or he's simply a bastard and she should kick him out. A woman will always assume it's the woman, even when that woman happens to be her friend, even when that woman would do nothing, and I mean nothing, to hurt her.

I can see what would happen if we told Mel. She'd be shocked, silent, but then she'd pull herself together and thank us very calmly for telling her. And we'd never hear from her again. If we phoned her she'd be cool but distant, and she wouldn't kick Daniel out, she'd believe his protestations that it was us, that we'd encouraged him, that he was only joking.

And then, eventually, she'd find a new group of

friends, new meat for him to hunt, and so the cycle would continue.

'Why does he keep doing this?' Mel asks, out loud, but you know she's asking herself. 'Five years and I still have to do everything on my own, he never wants to be part of my life.'

'God, he's a bastard. Mel, this keeps on happening. It's not going to stop, he's not going to change. Don't you think it's time you had some space, just to reassess things. You're young, you're attractive, you're wonderful. Daniel doesn't appreciate you but somewhere out there someone else will.' Great words coming from me, aren't they? But you know, as I say them I believe it, I believe that Mel will find someone else to love her, adore her, appreciate her, just as I believe that I will too, that we all will. That there's a lid for every pot, no matter how bent, misshapen, or ugly.

'You're right, you're right. I know you're right,' she says wearily. 'But,' and I know what's coming, what always comes after a row, 'but I know he loves me, and we do have great times. Admittedly not often, but you don't hear about the times he's really sweet to me, the times he cuddles me in bed and tells me he loves me. I know you think he's a shit but sometimes I think it's me. That I make him behave this way.'

'Mel, that's crap. What, so you make him disappear for nights on end without telling you where he is? So you make him tell you you're fat and you should lose weight? So you make him force you to go to everything on your own just so no one should think he was in a relationship?'

'But he says I'm a nag, that if I wasn't so demanding he would want to be with me more.' She's wimping out, as she always does and it's the most frustrating thing in the whole damned world.

'Mel, you're a therapist, for Christ's sake. Why is it you think this is all you deserve? Why are you putting up with second best? Do you not think you deserve someone who adores you? It can happen, look at Freya.'

Freya used to be in the sisterhood, but she committed the unforgiveable sin of getting married. Actually we were all delighted and more than a touch envious. We miss her but she's our role model, she makes us believe, she makes us think we'll find our lids, or our pots. Whatever.

Freya met Paul on holiday. They were friends and then they were lovers. I remember meeting him for the first time, at Freya's flat, just after I split up with Simon and I was dreading it, I was dreading seeing a happy couple, still in that stage where every sentence is punctuated with a touch on their loved one's hands, or shoulders, or leg. Where they can't keep their hands off one another.

But when I met Paul, and saw them together, and saw that he adored her as much, if not more, than she adored him, I felt ridiculously happy and I left their flat smiling, filled with inspiration and hope. It can happen, and I realised that Simon hadn't treated me like that, that it hadn't happened, but that it could. That it would.

'I know. I've got to leave him. But I'm so scared. I'm thirty-three, I want children, I want to get married. I don't want to be on my own.'

'But Mel, isn't it better to be on your own, to be single and happy than to be with a man who treats you badly, who undermines you, who damages you? Look at me, I'm blissfully happy being single.'

Mel looks up and we both laugh at the irony, and I know then that nothing will change, that we will be having this conversation again in a week or a month, the same conversation we have been having for nearly three years.

'Hey,' a big kiss is planted on my cheek by Emma. 'I can't stay all afternoon, Richard's coming back to get me. We've got to choose a new bathroom this afternoon.'

Emma and Richard. Three years and they still haven't got married, but not for want of Emma's trying. I think Richard does genuinely love Emma, he does want to be with her but he keeps saying he's not ready to get married, and as far as I'm concerned when a man says he's not ready to get married what he means is he doesn't want to marry *you*.

You probably don't understand why that's a problem, I admit it took me a while to figure it out. But Emma's thirty-six, and she's already been engaged three times. Each time she's issued an ultimatum, marry me or I'm leaving, and each time they've agreed. For about three months. They've always walked out on her, and she should have learnt, but she hasn't. Ultimatum time is coming around again, I can feel it in my bloody bones.

'New bathroom?' says Mel, smiling mischieviously. 'Does this mean . . .'

The question tails off and Emma sighs. 'I don't know,' she says. 'The latest excuse is that he's waiting for his business to take off, and hopefully by the end of the year he'll be settled and he'll be ready to get married then.'

You see there's always been an excuse. First it was that he had to find a flat, but then they decided to live together so he had to think up another one. Then he left his stockbroking business to set up by himself, so this is his latest, he has to settle. Never mind the fact that he probably earns more than all of us put together, he has to *settle*, whatever the hell that means.

They make a great-looking couple. He's big and brawny, an ex-rugby player, and she's tiny and petite, with perfect features and big brown sad puppy dog eyes, eyes that make men melt, that make them want to take care of her.

On the surface Emma and Richard have everything. Looks, money, friendship, but scratch the surface and you find Emma's lack of confidence, her neediness, her desperation. And Richard? Classic fear of commitment.

The older I get and the more people I meet, the less I think I know. How do you know people? How do you know relationships? How do you know? You only ever know as much as people want you to know, and anyone can pretend to be anything, if it suits them.

I remember a blind date I had last year. I met a woman on the programme, she was being interviewed, and we really hit it off. Six weeks later she phoned and said, 'Can I ask you a personal question? Are you single?' After I'd stopped laughing hysterically, because I'm not just single, I'm famous for it, I told her I was.

'I've got this friend you see. Gary. He's forty-one, tall, good-looking and I think you'd really hit it off. I'd love you to meet him. Can he call you?'

Of course he could call me, you never know how or when the right man will come into your life, so he called, and he came and she was right, he was tall and good-looking, and funny, but there was something about him, maybe it was his over-familiarity, and I decided immediately that we wouldn't make a good couple, but that I'd make the most of the evening anyway.

He took me to l'Altro in Notting Hill and half-way over dinner, half-way through a bottle of wine, I realised that I didn't like him, but Jesus did I fancy him.

He drove me home, walked me to the front door and as I put the key in the lock I turned to face him and this amazing chemistry just locked us together. We were like a pair of bloody teenagers, standing on the doorstep of my flat in this passionate embrace. 'I want to make love to you,' he whispered. 'Not yet,' I whispered back. Not because I didn't want to, you understand, but because I hadn't had my legs waxed in weeks and I was wearing a pair of my oldest knickers, where the lycra had turned blue.

'Can I see you again?' he said, when we finally pulled apart, and we arranged another date, a week later. I went to his flat this time, legs shining like a new-born baby's bottom, and black lace underwear hidden beneath my suede trousers. I knew I was going to sleep with him, and I also knew it would never be anything more. I brought condoms with me, and then he said he was allergic to rubber, that this whole AIDS thing was a myth, that he'd never used one.

You don't have to tell me that I should have got out of there faster than my legs could carry me but I was too far down the line. By that time I didn't even want to sleep with him, but I'd talked myself into a situation, and I felt I needed to see it through.

'We can just play though, and not have sex,' he said, when I told him no glove, no love. So we played, or rather I played with him. The fucker had about an hour of foreplay, complete with a full massage with baby oil that just happened to be on his bedside table. I had about a minute of clumsy fumbling at my crotch.

And then he climbed on top of me, pinned my arms down and started thrusting between my legs.

I twisted and turned, terrified he was going to enter me, and when I looked into his eyes I saw nothing, just an empty space. I don't know how I managed to stop him, but I did, and I cried all the way home. I trusted him because I liked his friend. I thought he was safe and I nearly got raped. How do you know? You only know as much as they want you to know.

And then the last to arrive is Andy, long straight blonde hair hanging down her back, big Jackie O sunglasses, a shining open smile.

However much Andy pisses me off, and she does, frequently, when it's just the girls, I love her. I love her excitement at life, her humour, her willingness to see the funny side in everything. I love the fact that she's single and she genuinely loves it. She sees all men as being adventures, and every fling as being an experience, something she has to learn from, that there's a lesson in everything that happens to us.

'Oh my God, I've met the most amazing man,' are the first words she says, the first words she usually says. 'Go on,' we all sigh in unison, although we're smiling, and Mel adds, 'Who is it this time?'

'He's a client of mine, and we've been flirting on the phone for weeks, and then yesterday he rang and said we ought to go out for a drink, and why didn't we meet later on.' Mel works in advertising sales, and flirts with all her clients on the phone. Even the women.

'I walked in to Kettners in Soho and there was this gorgeous man at the bar. I thought, it couldn't be, but it was, and he was amazing, he looked like a model.'

A ghost of a smile brushes over mine and Mel's faces as we catch one another's eye across the table. All the men Andy meets look like models. Until the rare occasions we meet them, when they look like mechanics.

'I know what you're thinking, that he wasn't that good-looking, but I swear, he was divine. Tall, well maybe 5′10″, black hair and bright green eyes. He looked like Pierce Brosnan. We got on so well, we didn't stop talking all night and he's asked to see me again.'

'Did you shag him?' Sorry for being so crude but I couldn't help myself.

'No!' she says in horror. 'He dropped me off and we kissed in the car. He's the best kisser, I was so tempted but I'd really like something to happen here. I'm going to wait. This feels really different, I can't explain it but this feels good. This could be it.'

Yeah really, Andy, even I'm not that naive. Men aren't as stupid as we give them credit for. They know it doesn't take much to get a woman into bed. I love you may not work as well as it used to, but tell a woman she's beautiful, special or different, that you've been waiting for years to meet her and she's putty in your hands.

'I'm seeing him tomorrow,' says Andy, 'and,' she smiles a Madonna smile, 'and, I've just treated myself to new underwear.'

'Show us, show us,' a clamour of voices, and then we all ooh and aah over the peach and pink lace creation she pulls out of a bag.

'La Perla? You must be crazy. How much was this?' I shout, while Andy looks at me sheepishly. 'Look Tasha, every woman needs at least one item of really good sexy beautiful feminine underwear in her drawer, and white cotton Sloggis, even if they're new, don't count.'

'Go on, how much?'

'£120 for the bra and £70 for the knickers.' She's

wincing as she tells us and all our jaws fall open and practically hit the table.

'You're nuts,' says Mel, but she's smiling. 'I could never spend that money on underwear.' Most of us couldn't, let's face it. Could you?

'But don't you feel more sexy when you know you've got gorgeous underwear underneath?' asks Emma, who's looking so confused you just bloody know her whole underwear drawer is La Perla.

'Yeah, but you can be just as sexy in a black lace thong from a department store,' I offer, slightly jealous that Andy can be so reckless with her money, 'and anyway, it's not exactly on for long, you just need to give them a decent first impression.'

'Exactly,' shouts Andy triumphantly. 'He's gonna get the best first impression he's ever seen.'

The menus come and we order pretty much the same thing we order every week. No lettuce leafs and mineral waters for us. Remember we're the ladettes and not only can we drink men under the table, we can eat them under the floorboards.

Mammoth plates of pan-fried tuna, lamb and mint burgers, aubergine layered with oozing mozarella arrive, garnished with mountains of thin deadly chips and a smidgen of salad for decoration. We wash them down with Bloody Mary's to begin with, before hitting cool white wine.

'Oh my God, oh my God, I've just remembered I've got something to tell you all.' The girls sit around waiting for me to reveal all. 'Yesterday we did a phone-in on betrayal. Simon phoned the show, the shit called in and I was right. The bastard did sleep with her after all.'

– Four –

Those early days with Simon were the happiest days of my whole life. I had done it, I was in a couple and for the first time I felt like a whole person. Don't get me wrong, I don't believe in two halves coming together and all that shit, I do believe one and one make two, but it was so, I don't know, fulfilling.

I ended up staying with Simon practically all the time. He phoned when he said he was going to, he made space for me in his life, he wanted to be with me. All the time.

I'd be in the office, briefing a researcher and being Miss TV Producer, when the phone would ring and I'd hear his voice, 'I'd like to speak to Fantasmagorical Harris please,' or if he was feeling particularly affectionate, 'Fanny'.

Yeah, he stopped calling me Anastasia, shortened it to Fanny because he said it was one of my most redeeming features. And I'd break off my chat, turn away while covering the mouthpiece and say, 'I miss you, Pudding,' because somehow, naff as it was, that became my nickname for him.

So we'd sit and whisper on the phone, testing each other to see who loved the other more.

'I love you this much,' he'd say.

'I love you more.'

'How much more?' his ego would reply, although I was so in love by this stage I didn't care.

'As much as my house.'

'Well I love you as much as my road.'

'Well I love you as much as the whole of Belsize Park.'

And so on and so on, encompassing London, England, the World, the Universe, and finally infinity. Funny how I always won that one, or not so funny, when you look back at what happened.

We became the gruesome twosome. The pair that everyone wanted at parties because we were so entertaining together. Always high on life, on each other.

I used to feel like we were in a film, driving around London together in his lovely old Citroën, hanging out with his friends, who, if I'm honest weren't entirely my cup of Earl Grey, but who cares, I certainly didn't, I was floating through life on a cloud of love.

It was me and Simon and occasionally Adam too, against the rest of the world. Oh I'm sorry, I haven't told you about Adam, have I? Adam was Simon's best friend, his blood brother, his bosom buddy, if men have such things. And Adam was brilliant, I loved Adam almost as much as I loved Simon, but I didn't want to sleep with him. Honestly.

Adam was as different to Simon as chalk and cheese. Where Simon was thin, dark and intense, Adam was big and bear-like, blond and constantly smiling. They were a perfect team, Adam's subtle humour versus Simon's sparkling and often cruel wit. When Simon used to stamp on people's toes, Adam was the one who picked up their feet and rubbed them better. And he was single. Had never, to Simon's knowledge, had a proper girlfriend.

'You know, Ad,' he said one night when we had all kicked off our shoes and were lying around smoking a joint while waiting for a pizza to arrive, 'you could do with a woman like Fanny. She'd look after you, tidy up that shithole of yours you call a flat, cook delicious meals for you. What do you reckon, Fanny?'

'I think Ad's perfectly happy as he is, aren't you, Ad?'

Adam smiled his big warm smile and reached an arm out to stroke my hair. 'If I had a woman like Tasha,' he said affectionately, 'she'd *need* to tidy the flat. I'd never bloody go out, it would be even messier than it is now.'

I laughed and kissed Adam on the cheek, it was that kind of flirtatious friendship. The kind you know will never go any further, where you don't have to worry about platonic kisses on the cheek because you know the teasing is just that, platonic.

Adam used to call me on evenings when Simon was working late, when the magazine was coming up to deadline and he had to stay in the office until the early hours of the morning.

'Just checking in to make sure you haven't run off with some big brawny bloke.'

'If I wanted to do that I wouldn't have to look far, would I, Ad?'

'Oooh, is the lady making me an offer I couldn't refuse?'

'In your dreams, mate.'

'Tash, you'd do a lot more than make me an offer in my dreams. Want to hear about them?'

'I don't think so thank you,' I laughed. 'Not unless you want my baby to come over and kick your head in.'

'What's his is mine and what's mine is mine, Tash, you know that,' he'd say, breaking into roars of laughter.

Sometimes I would think that Adam wasn't joking, that there was a smidgen of truth behind the laughter, that stranger things have happened. But he never made a move, he'd never dare. One look at me and you could see Simon was the man for me.

And then one night Simon phoned at nine and said, 'I'm sorry, my love. I've been trying to get everything done, but one of the features has to be completely rewritten by tomorrow and there's no one else here. It's not my damn job to do it, but if it's not done there'll be serious shit. I'm going to be hours, so don't wait up. Do you mind, have you prepared anything?'

'Don't worry, darling, it's fine. I made some goulash but it's better if it's not eaten for a day or so. I'll leave some in the oven so you can eat when you get back. Don't work too hard, all right, darling? I love you.' I waited for the I-love-you-more scenario but there was a pause and he said, 'Yeah, me too. Bye.'

I put the phone down, puzzled, but hey, he was busy. I suppose *you* would have known instantly that something was up, wouldn't you, but when something extraordinary happens, something out of the ordinary, you don't question it because you don't want to believe that anything could rock your safe, secure world. But you always know. It's a woman's sixth instinct, she can smell infidelity from miles away, but it's only ever afterwards that she'll tell you. When she's phoning you saying he's out all the time you know she knows but she'll never admit it. Put the thought in her mind and she'll dismiss it in fury.

But afterwards, when the tears have been shed and the accusations defended, afterwards she'll tell you that she knew. The minute the thought of infidelity crossed his mind, she knew.

At ten thirty the phone rang again. I leapt on it,

knowing it was Simon saying 'I'm just leaving', but it wasn't. It was another friend of Simon's, wanting to know if he was coming to the football. It could have waited until morning but I wanted to hear Simon's voice so I offered to call Simon and then ring him back.

The phone rang and rang and rang. He's probably gone to the loo, I thought, or popped out to grab a beer. But even as I thought it a little nugget of sickness inched its way into my stomach. I rang again at eleven, and twelve and one and two. Like I need to tell you the rest of the story. Yes I started panicking, and by three I was convinced he'd been run over. Maybe he's at Adam's, yes that's it, he didn't want to wake me so he's gone to stay at Adam's.

Talk about irrational, but you only know what they want you to know. So what did I, the mad woman, do? I put Simon's duffle coat over my men's striped pyjamas and climbed into his lovely blue Citroën that I wasn't supposed to drive, and drove to Adam's in Maida Vale.

I sat outside Adam's flat for ages, because I couldn't see any lights and I tried to calm myself down. He's definitely in there, I told myself, they're probably sitting up talking and getting stoned.

Eventually I was calm, for a mad woman anyway, and I walked up the steps to the front door. This was crazy, it was three thirty in the morning and I was looking for my boyfriend, disturbing his best friend in the middle of the night. I didn't want to take those steps, part of me didn't want to know whether he was there or not. Maybe if I turned round now and drove home, maybe it would all be all right, maybe he would be lying in bed waiting for me, half asleep, exhausted from his work. But I had to go on, didn't I? Had to ring on the doorbell and ring and ring and ring, until finally Adam, poor bastard, opened the door.

The minute the door opened I knew I'd made a mistake, a really big one, and I wished to God I'd never come. 'Oh Christ, I'm so sorry, Ad. I don't know where Simon is. He told me he was working late but he's not in the office and I don't know what's happened to him. I'm so worried, maybe he's been in an accident.' I actually said that! Can you believe it, like something out of a sit-com, isn't it? 'I thought maybe he'd be here with you. Shit. I'm sorry. I'll go. Go back to bed, I'm really sorry.'

'For God's sake, Tash,' Adam said, rubbing his eyes with one hand and reaching out to pull me inside with his other. 'What the hell are you going on about?'

Adam made me a cup of tea, bless him. He had to look in every cupboard to find the teabags, and when he made the tea he smelt the milk before pouring it. Good job because it was about a year out of date. Stunk the place out. But he put sugar in and it was hot and sweet and soothing.

I couldn't keep still. Sitting there trying to sip the scalding tea while tapping one leg furiously against the floor, Adam phoned my home, our home, saying, 'He'll be home by now, I'm sure of it.'

But naturally the bastard wasn't, and Adam pulled his chair up very close to mine and held my hand. 'He loves you,' he said, 'and he wouldn't hurt you. I know what you're thinking but it just isn't Simon. He doesn't look at other women when he's with you. Trust me, he's working. Maybe he had to go out to meet someone, maybe he went round to a journalist's house. Whatever. He isn't doing what you think he's doing.

'Do you want to stay here? You can, but I think

Simon will be home very soon, and he'll want to know where you are.'

I finished my tea, took some deep breaths and stood up feeling much better, trying to ignore those little niggly fears right at the bottom of my stomach. 'Don't tell him I was here. Please. I feel so stupid.' He wouldn't he said, unless of course Simon was already home, in which case he'd want to know where the hell was I.

'Thank you, Adam,' I said as I reached up and hugged him very tightly. The sort of hug that says I'm in way too deep and I'm not sure I'm going to make it. The sort of hug that says please don't let anything happen to me.

Adam hugged me back, and I knew what he was saying. I knew those big warm circles he was making on my back with his hand meant everything's going to be OK. Trust me. Everything's going to be OK.

But of course everything's not going to be OK, is it, you know that as well as I do. When the seeds have been sown, it doesn't take long for them to grow into a big, strong, vibrant affair. All you need is that one tiny seed, and so many of them are blowing around in the wind, you'd have to be bloody holy not to catch one, wouldn't you? At least, if you're a man. Bastards.

I went home then, and as I took off Simon's coat and pulled my trainers off, the front door opened and then Simon was in the doorway.

'I'm so sorry, Fanny. What a nightmare,' he said, as he started unbuttoning his shirt.

I wanted to shout, to scream, to lose control. What I should have said was WHERE THE FUCK HAVE YOU BEEN? WHAT THE FUCK HAVE YOU BEEN DOING? But I didn't. I said, 'You could have called me,

I was worried. I thought something had happened to you.'

It came out sounding like a whine and it was not what I had meant to say at all. I don't know whether this has ever happened to you but when I'm lucky enough to have found what I'm looking for, I'm terrified I'm going to lose it again.

So instead of being Tasha the slasher, Tasha the strong fearsome woman, I'm Tasha the little girl, desperate for approval, frightened to fight, frightened to shout, just in case they don't like me anymore.

So when Simon turned round and said, 'Don't give me a hard time, Anastasia,' – which is naturally what he called me when he was angry. Or guilty – I retreated back into my hole and started apologising.

'I've worked like a demon tonight, but we finished it, thank Christ,' he said, but he wasn't looking at me. He couldn't meet my eyes. 'I'm never commissioning that pillock again. He can't write to save his life.'

I know what I should have said next, I should have asked him straight out, 'Were you in the office?' but I didn't want to trick him, I wanted to give him a chance to escape, to prove me wrong.

'I called you and you didn't pick up the phone. Why not?'

'Jesus Christ, woman, it's four a.m. and you're quizzing me like I'm guilty of something, although heaven knows what. I heard the phone ringing but I didn't pick it up because I was working to deadline. You of all people know what it's like when you're too busy to chat, and I knew it was you and it would just distract me.'

Actually I don't know what it's like, because I've always thought that people make time for things they want to do. When someone says sorry I haven't called,

I've been too busy, it's bollocks. Who hasn't got time to pick up the phone and say a quick hello, a sorry-I-can't-chat-right-now-but-I'm-thinking-of-you kind of call?

Too busy to chat is crap, but I agreed with him, I bloody agreed with him and told him it was OK, but 'Next time you should be a bit more considerate. I *was* worried.'

'Hopefully there won't be a next time,' he said, and he climbed into bed and rolled over, giving me a perfunctory peck on the lips as he did so. I lay awake for hours trying to figure out what he meant.

I cooked for Simon, I cleaned for Simon, I took care of Simon. I took his clothes to the dry cleaner's, and sure enough, you clever readers, that was the beginning of my end.

Everyone checks their boyfriends jacket pockets when they're taking their clothes to the dry cleaners, don't they? Don't *you*? Not even when two weeks before he spent most of the night absent without leave, and has subsequently acted like a moody bastard, putting it down to work worries?

I was just doing my girlfriendly duty, for God's sake, I mean, he might have left money in there, Simon was so scatty. Ah ha, he has left money in here I thought, drawing out three photographs from his inside pocket.

I didn't think anything else after that, I just sat down very quickly, holding the photographs and thinking nothing very much really.

You think you've got it, don't you? Ha! You haven't. You think I was holding pictures of Simon in bed with some bimbo, both of them caught in an erotic embrace, or some such similar damning evidence.

Nothing so obvious, and in some ways I'm still

convinced that what I found was worse. What I found left room for questions. The questions that can never be satisfied by answers, the questions that keep you awake every night, analysing every possibility, trying to rationalise what they mean.

She was a very beautiful blonde girl. Not, like me, strikingly attractive with a hell of a lot of make-up and newly highlighted roots. She was naturally beautiful. Long blonde hair, straight, and it looked natural from what I could see. She was wearing only a tiny bit of make-up, with just a smudge of taupe lipstick. She looked like a model, and she was sitting in Café Rouge in Notting Hill – before you ask I recognised the decor – it was night-time and she was smiling into the camera.

And in the second one she was talking animatedly, as if the photographer had just picked up his lens and shot her in mid-flow, and in the third one she was rubbing the back of her neck with one hand, and looking coyly, flirtatiously, beyond the lens and presumably into the eyes of the photographer. Simon. Who the hell else could it have been?

A man doesn't carry around a photograph, let alone three photographs, of a woman unless she intrigues him, unless she's got under his skin. I didn't know who she was, but I knew instantly she'd wormed her way in, she'd caused his moodiness towards me, and I knew she wasn't going to be going away, at least not without a hell of a fight.

And I didn't want to fight. I didn't think I needed to. I thought Simon loved me, and I thought, oh how stupid I was, I thought love was enough. But do you know the worst thing about looking at the photographs and feeling these feelings? The worst thing was that if I was a bloke I'd feel the same way. If I was a bloke and had to choose between me and her, I'd choose her. No contest.

When Simon came bounding down the hallway I walked out to greet him holding the photographs in front of me, showing him the evidence.

'What's the matter, Fanny? What are those?' He went to put his arms around me and vaguely looked at the pictures.

'Oh yeah. Tanya.'

'What the fuck do you mean, "Oh yeah. Tanya." Who the fuck is she and what the hell are these pictures?'

When a man is innocent, he quite rightly says what the hell were you doing going through my jacket pockets. When a man is guilty he's too busy trying to think up a story to even bother attacking you for looking in the first place. This is how I knew, except I didn't want to know, I didn't want to believe it.

'Darling. She's some model who we're thinking of doing a shoot with. She's no one. What are you worried about?'

'I'm worried that you're carrying around pictures of this girl, and that you were in Café Rouge, and that it was night. I'm worried because you've been strange since you worked late in the office, and I want to know what's going on.'

'I've already told you. Oh Fanny, you don't think . . .' He put his head back and laughed. The bastard actually laughed. 'Oh baby, come here, you're jealous.'

He put his arms around me and I didn't exactly cuddle him back, but I'll admit I did lean into him, but just a little, OK?

'I love it when you get jealous, it proves how much you love me. Fanny, you have nothing to worry about with that girl. Yes, she's OK looking, but believe me, she looks a hell of a lot better on camera than in the flesh. She's got terrible skin which she hides under a gallon of make-up.'

I didn't say anything. I just leant into him a little more, waiting to hear what else he was going to say.

'And God is she thick. She's the thickest girl I've ever met. Believe me, my darling, you have nothing to worry about.'

'So what were you doing with her in Notting Hill? And when were you there?' My voice sounded softer, I wasn't so sure anymore.

'We were with Nick Clark, the photographer, and the three of us had a meeting in Notting Hill. It was ages ago now, about six weeks, I'd completely forgotten about those pictures.'

'But you were there at night. Which night?' As I said it my mind started finally clicking into gear, and I knew there was something I was missing, but I just wasn't sure what it was. I think if I had sat down and thought for long enough that little blurry thought would have shifted into focus, but I didn't want to do that, I wanted to ignore it. I hoped it would go away.

– *Five* –

My mobile rings just as I'm getting in the car to drive to Louise, my therapist. It's Mel, she's in a state.

'I told him I've had enough, I can't carry on anymore. He doesn't want to be my boyfriend and until he does I've kicked him out.'

'What did he say?' I'm cautious, because this isn't the first time this has happened, and in the past I've called him every name under the sun, and within three weeks they're back together again, as blissfully unhappy as they know how to be.

'He didn't say anything. There was a silence and then he said are we still going out to the theatre next week, and would I make sure I picked up his jacket from the dry cleaner's.'

'So once again he's trying to pretend it's not happening?'

'I don't know,' she sighs, 'but I'm serious this time, I've had enough, I don't want him back. I've tried everything, I've tried talking but every time I ask what he has to say he won't bother because I never listen to him anyway.'

I snort with derision. 'Mel, you listen for a goddamned living, if *you* can't listen who the hell can?'

'I know I know. But he confuses me. I start off an

argument being very sure of where I stand, of who's right and who's wrong, and then he throws these accusations at me and I don't know anymore. Maybe he is right. Maybe if I wasn't such a nag things would be different. Maybe it's my fault.'

I say what I always say, and then I have to go because I spy a police car waiting to turn in to the main road and the last thing I need is a fine for using the phone while driving.

I wasn't going to tell you about therapy was I, but now you're here with me you may as well come along for the ride.

I always hated therapy, thought it was for sad people, didn't I? I didn't need therapy, not me, Miss Dynamo. But then again, my childhood wasn't exactly the happiest in the world, and whenever I'm unhappy, or depressed, or simply bored I practically climb in the fridge and eat whatever's there.

You think I'm joking? I wish I was. I've been known to buy a loaf of bread, and while the first two slices are toasting, six more have disappeared into my mouth faster than you can say pass the butter.

So there's food, there's my unhappy childhood, there's my unfaithful father, but I thought I was all right. I mean I know I'm not exactly good at relationships, but after Simon, after it all went horribly wrong, after the bingeing and the quick fucks with faceless strangers, I went.

I liked Louise immediately. She was recommended by Mel, who obviously is too close to me to treat me, and as soon as I walked into the little room she uses as her therapy centre, or whatever the hell you call it, I felt at home.

But I'll admit I wasn't entirely sure about this whole therapy lark at first. Louise looked like a reject from

Woodstock, the movie. Long brown hair hennaed red, a heavy fringe, caught up in a big soft bun at the nape of her neck. The first time we met she was wearing a long ethnic skirt, the kind that should have had tiny little mirrors sewed in to the fabric, except it didn't, it just swirled softly about her ample thighs. On her feet were chinese slippers, the shoes that, if my memory serves me correctly, were the height of fashion in 1981.

'Oh shit,' I remember thinking. 'How in the hell is this woman going to understand my middle-class confusion,' but then I looked in her eyes, and they were so warm and understanding, I knew it was going to be fine. And the minute I started talking, she drew me out so cleverly, so carefully, I knew at once that if there was anyone I wanted to pour my troubles out to, it would be Louise.

There was always the smell of burning aromatic oils, probably lavender, or patchouli, or some such hippy shit to make you feel relaxed, and Louise, even in that first session, forced me to find answers I didn't think I knew, answers I'd pushed to the back of my subconscious because the truth frightened me. Doesn't the truth frighten *you*?

Therapy isn't like talking to friends. When you talk to friends you censor yourself, you tell the truth, or your version of it, but you embellish, you're dishonest, but you've told your stories so often you've come to believe them.

You can't do that in therapy. You talk on a completely different level of honesty, and I think Louise saw the side that no one else saw. She saw that I wasn't hard or tough or sassy. She cut through all that right to the vulnerable, gentle centre. And she didn't care. That was the point. I trusted her immediately, and, I'm being completely honest with you now, I think she's possibly the first person I've ever trusted in my life.

As usual Louise opens the door and without saying anything gestures me inside to her room. Lining the walls are those Ikea shelves, you know, the wooden ones, bending with the strain of all her psychology books. Freud, Jung, every aspect of psychoanalysis you could dream of.

Louise sits down as I sit in the big comfy chair opposite her and she starts as she always starts. 'How *are* you?'

'Fine, I've been fine. I haven't even really thought about Guy, I'm not really that upset which has surprised me, because I came to see you because of men like Guy, men who professed to have fallen in love then disappeared, but maybe things are changing, because even though it's happened again, I'm OK.'

'So you're not seeing him anymore? What happened?'

Here we go again, dear reader. Cast your mind back to when we first met. Do you remember Andy was coming round to hear about the three-monther? Guy was the three-monther.

I met Guy in a queue standing outside a club. I never go clubbing anymore, I have neither the time nor the inclination but it was a Sunday night and I didn't have anything better to do.

And Jesus was this party shit. Everyone was about sixteen, and I felt one hundred. I was there with the gang, and we all hated it, and after about an hour we decided to leave. And as we were walking out, past the huge line that had formed outside the door, praying that they would be amongst the chosen few that the huge black bouncers would let in, I saw Jeremy, an old friend, someone I hadn't seen for years.

He was with 'the boys', and of course they didn't

mind the fact that everyone was sixteen, because men don't care how old their prey is, as long as she's pretty.

And while I was talking to Jeremy, I could feel one of his friends staring at me, couldn't take his eyes off me. I kept glancing towards him and catching his eye and although I liked what I saw, he was obviously very, very young.

He was twenty-seven, which isn't that young, I know, but I'm not into boys, and this guy somehow looked incredibly boyish. He was incredibly pretty, with big brown eyes and a trendy short crop. He looked like he should have been in Take That. But he was, in fact, a solicitor.

Which isn't a bad thing in itself, but I've never been able to see myself with someone who works in law or accountancy. Great jobs, I know, but so boring. Please. I don't even mind if they're bastards from the beginning, but at least make it exciting.

But he *was* very cute, and he obviously liked me, so when Jeremy invited me to join them to go to another party, how could I resist?

'You can come in my car,' offered Guy, as I was about to climb into Jeremy's Golf. I swiftly climbed out and into Guy's Range Rover.

We didn't talk much on the way, but I assessed his choice of music – REM, not the greatest, but compromises are always possible. I assessed his driving – fast and confident, just the kind of driving I like, and I assessed the back of his neck – clean, fresh, waiting to be kissed.

And at the party he leant against the door frame, and he was tall and big, and he towered above me and despite the fact that he was ever so slightly boring, I started to fancy him. Surprise, surprise.

'So you live in Bayswater? Which road?'

I told him grudgingly because the road is a bit of a dump but his face lit up. 'That's amazing, I drive past there every day on my way home from work. I'm going to come for dinner. What day shall I come?'

'Don't come during the week because we'll both have to have early nights. Why don't you come on the weekend?'

'Deal. I'll see you on Friday.' And he dropped me home and outside my flat he didn't try to kiss me, he just said, 'I'll bring the food, you supply the wine.'

I got out the car grinning. And I grinned all through the next day. No one at work could figure out why I was suddenly so happy, but of course you know, don't you, I thought I'd stumbled upon love again.

He turned up for dinner empty-handed, carrying nothing but an aura of confidence, weighed down by good looks and charm. I, trying to be stunning but not trying too hard, greeted him at the door wearing jeans, a sloppy sweatshirt and thick socks. He walked straight past me and into the kitchen to open the bottle of wine I'd bought. He was taking control, taking my breath away. I really had forgotten how cute this guy was.

I carried the wine and glasses into the living room and we sat there and talked, chatting about everything, while I, in my socks and sloppy jumper, pretended to be as cute as cute can be. Gone was the tough Anastasia, here was the gentle, sweet Tasha, the Tasha that could fall in love, the Tasha men could adore.

'I changed my mind,' he said. 'I'm taking you out for dinner.' And so he did, to a smart new restaurant in Hampstead. We feasted on bruschetta, rubbed with garlic, olive oil, and covered with juicy tomatoes and fresh basil. We laughed over fresh pasta, stuffed with ricotta and spinach, and we fed one another spoonfuls of sticky toffee pudding.

'What are you doing for the rest of the weekend?' he asked, and, conveniently forgetting that in the beginning you have to play hard to get, you have to make them work for you a little bit, you have to be slightly unavailable, I said, 'No plans really. Why?'

He took me boating the next day. Luckily, because his first suggestion was rollerblading, and I happen to be allergic to any form of exercise unless it takes place between the sheets. We went to Regents Park and on the way there, in the car, he kissed me. And then, at every traffic light he kissed me again. And he kissed me getting out of the car, walking to the shed to hire a boat, in the boat, on the grass, by the water, and I really thought this could work out.

'I can't believe I met you in that queue,' he said, stroking my hair and kissing the palm of my hand. 'I just can't believe it. I've spent so long looking for someone and then I met you, just like that.'

Reader, bear with me, don't be too judgmental when I tell you we went to bed that night. We spent the whole day together, boating, having a long, lazy lunch, then back at my flat talking by candlelight.

Sex just seemed the most perfect ending to a perfect day. And in the morning he didn't disappear, he stayed with me until lunchtime when he had to go home and do some work, but he wanted to see me that night, and me being me, I said yes.

Playing hard to get is easy when you don't really like someone. When you're testing the theory to see if it works and of course it does, because the victim of your game is an ugly bastard, so when he keeps calling and wanting to see you, you laugh to yourself because your mother was right after all – treat them mean and they really do stay keen.

But then you meet someone who makes your heart stir, and you think, I will try and play hard to get, but what this really means is when they ask can I see you tonight, you say you're busy. But you can see them later, you add hopefully, after the dinner party you had been so looking forward to before you met them. It won't finish late you say, just so they don't think you're changing your arrangements for them.

So you go out for dinner and you sit there quite separate from the conversation around you. Every five minutes you check your watch, and at ten o'clock you excuse yourself and rush back to your new lover. This is how we play hard to get. And then we wonder why they feel threatened, suffocated, why they disappear.

I had an idyllic three months with Guy. Every time I saw him it got better and better, and he really liked me, at least he seemed to. But of course I made a fatal mistake. I started to believe that he meant what he said, and after a couple of months, after I had started to relax, I brought my toothbrush, moisturiser and a sexy nightdress to his flat and accidentally left it there. He didn't say anything which I took to be a good sign. How wrong can you be.

Just before we were about to hit our third-month anniversary he invited me on holiday – a long weekend – with him and another couple, to his parents' house in the South of France.

We flew down there together, me ecstatic with happiness, him kissing me throughout the whole journey. Guy's friends, who I didn't know well, and who were very pleasant, in that pleasant way people have of sizing up their friend's new girlfriend, were arriving the next day.

But Christ were they young. Guy mixed with twenty-five-year-olds, and while there is only a five-year difference, I felt like an old woman. They were sweet, but I knew, after the first night when we made dinner and ate it on the terrace overlooking the swimming pool, I knew that perhaps this wasn't such a good idea after all.

Not that I had any doubts about Guy, I just wished we were here alone.

Guy and I had made dinner, and I want you to know that while I was cooking, Guy couldn't keep his hands off me, spinning me round while I was trying to chop, hands all over me like an octopus, lips desperately searching for mine.

Everything was fine the day we arrived. We were, I thought, in love, even though neither of us had used the dreaded L word, but I could feel it coming. I really could.

And then the next day, Saturday, out of the blue, Guy started to ignore me. Not completely, that would have been too obvious, but every time I spoke this intense look of irritation crossed his face.

So I stopped speaking, unsure of what to do, of what I was doing wrong, of how to make it all right again. I waited until the evening, until we had come back for dinner, where I had done a very passable impression of everything being fine.

We went to bed, and Guy didn't reach out for me as he had done every night we had spent together since we met. He lay in bed and picked up a book.

'OK,' I said, 'what's the matter?'

'Matter?' he said, nose buried deep into his book. 'Nothing's the matter.'

'You're being very distant. Have I done something wrong?'

'No, no,' he said breezily. 'I'm just tired, not really in the mood for sex.' And he put his hand out and ruffled my hair, then gave me a kiss – a highly platonic kiss – on the top of my head.

You know, don't you? I suppose I should have known too. The first sign that a man's going off you is when he finds an excuse not to sleep with you. When someone really fancies you, really likes you, is beginning to fall in love with you, they can't get enough of your body, of you. When the doubts start setting in, they become tired, they don't want to have sex, they don't want to sleep in the same room.

I crawled into bed feeling absolutely miserable, but maybe the kiss meant it was OK. There was certainly affection, if not passion, in that kiss, and maybe he *was* just tired.

And then on Sunday he ignored me again, only speaking to me if he had to, and then it was coolly polite. The four of us went to St Paul de Vence, and I felt like an outsider as the three of them laughed and joked, and bonded, leaving me feeling more and more alone.

On Sunday night I went to bed, and Guy said he wasn't coming to bed yet, he wanted to stay up for a while with the others. I crawled into bed and waited, and eventually Guy came upstairs. He sat on my bed and kissed me – a peck on the lips, and I kissed him back – mouth, tongues, full-on – and waited for more. But he didn't do anything.

I pulled him towards me, on top of me and he pulled back. 'No,' he said. 'This is happening too fast.'

'What is, what do you mean by "this"?' I thought he meant sex in his parents' house in the South of France, but of course the fucker didn't, he meant what I dreaded. He meant 'us'.

'Look, Tasha. I'm sorry but I'm not in love with you. You're not the one so I just can't see the point in carrying on.'

'And you brought me to the South of France, to your parents' house to tell me this? Two days before we fucking go home?'

'I hadn't planned to do this. It just doesn't feel right. I don't feel what I should be feeling towards you. I don't want to sleep with you, it feels like I'm forcing it.'

'Oh, and all those times you dragged me into the kitchen a couple of days ago, when you couldn't keep your hands off me. You were forcing yourself, were you?'

'No, I don't know,' he sighed, looking down at his hands. 'You're just not the one. This isn't right.' This I couldn't believe. I had no way of getting away and all I could think was, I wish I was at home. I wish I was lying in my bed with Stanley and Harvey to cuddle.

'Excuse me, I'll be back in a minute.' I ran to the bathroom and threw up, a combination of too much drink, and too much pain. Not pain because I really loved Guy. Jesus, this was only three months after all, but pain because it was happening again. The pattern I thought I'd broken, the pattern that was the reason I went to see Louise in the first place, and it was still happening.

What can I tell you about that night? That I didn't sleep? That I spent the night wandering along freezing murky black corridors? That at five o'clock in the morning I ran a hot bath just so I could feel comforted? That at six o'clock in the morning I bumped into Sarah, going to the loo, that I didn't let her go back to bed, that I talked her ear off, feeling miserable and lonely, that the most overwhelming feeling of that night was that no one would ever love me?

Monday was a nightmare. We were flying home on Monday evening, and I insisted the others go off for the day, insisted I would be OK by myself. Guy didn't look at me, not once, but Sarah said she'd stay behind. No, I insisted, I needed to be on my own.

I sat in that house, that strange house I didn't know and felt numb. There weren't any tears, not at that point anyway, just a feeling of disbelief. I packed my clothes and sat on the sofa staring into space, watching the clock and willing the hours to pass quickly so I could fly home.

Guy and I, despite sitting next to one another on the flight back, didn't speak. We shared a taxi from the airport, and, still, we didn't speak.

'I'm sorry,' he said as I got out the taxi.

'Forget about it,' I said, swiftly moving my head away as he tried to give me a kiss goodbye on the cheek.

I was fine that afternoon. Really. It was only later that night when Andy forced me to come to a party with her, when I was sitting there watching other couples that I suddenly found myself laughing. Manic laughter which suddenly became short, sharp sobs, and I had to lock myself in a bathroom for half an hour, trying to compose myself.

So here I am now, telling Louise about the grand finale, wondering why it happened again, why I haven't learnt.

'Why do you think it happened, hmm?' asks Louise. 'Why do you think he suddenly got scared?'

Thank God I've learnt something in therapy, because it doesn't take me long to tell her, and even when I was with Guy I was aware that I was falling into old patterns, that I was repeating actions of the past, that the outcome would be the same.

'Moving the toothbrush in wasn't a great idea,' I say, wincing with embarrassment at what was such an obvious mistake. 'I think that was when he started to backtrack.'

'And what about sex? Do you feel good about sleeping with him so soon after meeting him? Why do you think you offered him your body when you didn't really know him, when he hadn't shown you who he was, what he could offer, hmm?'

'You're right, I know. I was doing what I always used to do. I think I slept with him because I thought it would make him want me more, and I rushed in again. I didn't really know him. But I also think I was aware of what I was doing, which I never used to be. I think I'm getting better at recognising the mistakes. Now it's just a question of changing them for good.'

Louise nods. It's a long, slow and often painful process, but finally I think I might be getting there.

– Six –

After I found those pictures of Tanya, or Tanyagate as I called it at the time, Simon turned into the gorgeous, loving, attentive Simon he'd been when we met.

And the crazy woman inside me, the one that drove to his best friend's at four o'clock in the morning seemed to quieten down a little. I knew she hadn't gone away, but she wasn't bothering me. At least, not for the time being.

Simon loved me and I loved Simon and the Tanyas of the world could go screw themselves. It was over and it was nothing, and I truly believed I would be as happy for the rest of my life.

There was one morning when the sun shone brightly through his bedroom windows which were still filthy because there were always too many other things to do than clean the windows, and we decided to drive to the country.

'Come on, Fanny, get up, I'm taking you out for lunch.'

'I want to stay in bed, it's warm. Where are we going?'

'I'm taking you to a pub in the country. Move your arse woman and get dressed. I want to show the country bumpkins the women they're missing out on in London.'

I did get up, I had a bath and while I was sitting at the dressing table, putting on my make-up, making myself look perfect, I suddenly saw Simon watching me in the mirror. There was such an intense look of love in his eyes, I nearly started crying, but I didn't, I just turned round and said, 'What are you looking at?'

'I'm looking at your right eyebrow,' he said, although I know he wasn't, he was looking at the whole picture and he loved me. 'Did you know that your right eyebrow is perfect, but your left eyebrow is ever so slightly crooked?'

I turned back to the mirror in a panic, 'What are you talking about, what do you mean?'

'It means you're not perfect, doesn't it. I'd hate it if you were perfect, but that little imperfection makes you vulnerable.'

'Do you think I'm vulnerable?' But I was pleased. It made me feel like a little girl when he called me that, like he was the big strong father figure looking after me.

'I didn't when I first met you. When you walked in to that party I thought what a hard bitch, not my type at all. But when I took a closer look I thought, nah, she's not hard, she's a softie, you just have to break her.'

'Break me? Bloody cheek. And have you, d'you think, broken me?'

'I've just done a bit of remodelling, just to make you into the perfect wife. Wifey Fanny, my wifey fanny,' and he started nuzzling my neck until I started laughing.

Simon was always talking about marriage, but much as I wanted to believe him, I always felt that it wasn't necessarily me, he was in love with the idea of being in love. He wanted to get married because then he'd have someone to look after him all the time. It just didn't really matter who. Although I only really knew that afterwards, didn't I?

We climbed into the car and on the way, while we were waiting at traffic lights on the A40, Simon turned to me, took my hand and opening my fingers planted a kiss on my palm.

'You know, Fanny, I've never been happier in my life. I never thought I could be this happy. You're everything I ever wanted. I love you so much.' He looked me in the eyes. 'I can't believe sometimes how much I love you.'

There was a silence while I digested the words, the seriousness of them and then I turned to him with a wicked grin, 'I love you to infinity.'

We had a perfect day, too perfect, something was bound to go wrong. And isn't it ironic that just when you think it couldn't get better, just when you start to trust, the bombshell hits and your world explodes in your face.

But how do you know? I didn't know then. I didn't know until later that week, when Simon was back to being a moody bastard, and even then I didn't know.

I was watching television, some early evening interview show, and I was thinking about my own show and who I would get as a fill-in guest, when the phone rang.

'Hi hon, it's me.' It was Mel.

'Hey, how are you?'

'Fine, really well actually. Daniel's being really nice at the moment. I'm a bit worried, I don't know what's come over him.'

'I wouldn't worry, Simon's being amazing too, apart from the last few days but work's tough. Most of the time he's treating me like a bloody queen. Maybe it's something in the air, maybe all the bastards have reformed.'

'As if Simon's ever a bastard! I saw him today actually.'

'Oh?' I was only vaguely curious, Simon's out and about in Soho almost every day, nothing new in that.

'Yeah, he was walking through Soho but I was in a rush so I didn't cross over and say hello. He was with a tall blonde girl.'

Don't ask me how I knew, but at that moment I knew that wherever Tanya had been for the last month, the last month that had been the best of my life, she was back and she'd burrowed her way back under his skin.

I suddenly felt sick to my stomach, and I could feel my voice shaking as I said, 'Tanya.'

'What, that girl in the picture? Oh my God, I'm sorry, Tash. I didn't realise, but I don't know whether it was her, they weren't holding hands or anything.'

'This girl is beautiful, you would know her, Mel. She looks like a bloody model. Did this girl he was with look like a model?'

There was a long pause, and Mel just said, 'I'm sorry, I am so sorry.'

'Maybe I'm wrong, maybe we're both wrong. Look, he'll be home soon, I'll call you back later.' Even as I put the phone down I could hear Mel apologising again.

I stood up and my legs felt like jelly. A drink, that's what I needed, so I poured myself a vodka and soda water – because Simon never had mixers, did he? – and I drank it down as if it were water.

Then Simon phoned from work. 'Fanny darling, I'm

stuck in the office, can we cancel going out for dinner tonight? I don't know what time I'll be home.'

I forced my voice to sound normal as I said, 'That's fine. I'm tired anyway. What have you done today, anything exciting?'

'No, boring day, I've been too busy to get out.'

'Not even for a sandwich?'

My heart had started thumping again, and I was sure he could hear it in my voice but the bastard didn't, he said, 'No, I had to send one of the secretaries out and she got the order wrong and came back with a tuna mix which I hate. I might have to go and grab something this evening.'

'Simon.' The word came out very slowly, and that was when he knew. 'If you didn't go out how come Mel saw you walking down the street in Soho?'

'Well I went out to get some cigarettes. What is this, the fifth fucking degree? What the hell's wrong with me leaving the office?'

'Who were you with?'

'I wasn't with anyone,' but his voice was rising, and it didn't matter what words he was actually saying, all I was hearing was guilt. I'm guilty. Shit.

'Well that's interesting because apparently you were with Tanya.' I didn't even bother giving him a chance to deny it was her, and credit where credit's due, the bastard didn't bother denying it. He didn't do anything. There was just a very long silence.

'I'm coming home. We need to talk.'

'Really,' I snapped nastily, 'I thought you had too much to do.'

'Give me half an hour.' And he went.

You know when you wake up in the morning and everything's great, the sun's shining and life is beautiful, it doesn't seem real how everything can collapse around your ears by the end of the day. And even while it's happening it feels like you're in a film. What would a heroine in a great romantic tragedy do now? She'd pour herself another quadruple vodka and tonic, or soda water. No actually, she'd probably drink it neat. So I did.

I've got to be honest here, I'm not entirely sure what happened that night because by the time Simon came home I was having difficulty focusing. Which is probably not a bad thing because the more drunk I got the angrier I became, and for the first time I didn't give a damn if he saw, I wanted him to feel it.

Simon walked in and hesitated by the front door as he saw me, swaying ominously in the doorway of the kitchen. The bastard hung his head and then came over and put his arms round me. 'I'm sorry,' he whispered. 'I love you and I'm sorry.'

God I'm embarrassed to admit this to you, but do you know what I felt? At that precise moment I didn't feel anger, I felt a little ray of hope, maybe it was all over with Tanya. Maybe we could just carry on as if nothing ever happened.

'What are you sorry about? I don't understand. What's going on?'

'I love you, Tasha. I really love you and I meant what I said last week, I've never loved anyone as much as you, but I don't know whether I'm *in* love with you. You're my best friend, the woman I respect more than any other in the world, but I'm confused, I need some space.'

I pulled away savagely. 'What the fuck do you mean, what are you talking about? This is about that bitch, isn't it? What the fuck is going on with you and her?'

He sighed and said what they always say, 'This has nothing to do with Tanya. This is about you and me.'

'What do you mean this has nothing to do with Tanya? You fucking idiot. Everything was fine before you met her. You're having an affair aren't you? You're fucking that thick bimbo.'

'I'm not sleeping with her, if that's what you mean,' he said. 'We're just friends, but she understands me. I'll admit I was with her today, but we weren't doing anything, we've never done anything, we just went out for lunch. But I talked to her about this, and she agrees I need some space.'

I lost the plot a bit then. 'You tell that fucking bitch to mind her own fucking business.' I was shouting but my voice was breaking up. I couldn't believe this, I couldn't believe this was happening to me, and I slowly collapsed on a chair, sobbing like a little girl, my body shuddering so hard it was physically painful.

It was like someone had ripped out my soul and torn it in two, and to make it worse Simon knelt on the floor next to me, and started crying too. He put his head in my lap and his arms round my waist and we both stayed like that for a very long time, just crying.

'I want to know the truth, Simon,' I said eventually. 'The very least you owe me is the truth. I don't care anymore, I know it's over, but I have to know what happened with Tanya.'

'Nothing, I told you,' but the nothing wasn't as emphatic as last time, and I knew all it would take to get the full story was a little gentle pushing.

'I'm fine now,' I said, wiping my eyes and taking a deep breath. 'But I need to know. I know you've been having an affair, I just need to hear from you when it started.'

'We haven't had an affair. But . . .' he stopped and looked at his hands.

'But what? It's OK, you can tell me,' I said softly, encouragingly.

'I know she's attracted to me, and even though nothing's happened because I didn't want to hurt you, she kissed me. It was just once, ages ago, and nothing's happened since then.'

'What do you mean she just kissed you?' I was still incredibly calm, acting out my role to get as much ammunition as possible.

'That night when I was working late, I was with her and we had been drinking and I ended up back at her flat.'

The bastard should have stopped then. If he'd looked up from the floor he would have seen the pain in my eyes, he would have seen that he was hurting me more than anyone had ever hurt me in my life, but he didn't. He had started his confession and he was going to finish. Or not. We'd see.

'We were sitting on the sofa talking and she kissed me.'

There was a silence. 'What happened then?' I prompted.

'We did go to bed, but we didn't do anything. I didn't sleep with her, I felt terrible. All I could think about was you, which is when I came home.'

'So if you didn't sleep with her what did you do? Did she give you a blow job, did you go down on the cunt? WHAT THE FUCK DID YOU DO?'

'Nothing,' he said wearily. 'We just cuddled.'

'And that's supposed to make me feel better? What were you wearing, were you dressed?'

'No, we were both naked.'

'You fucking bastard,' and I swung at him, but I was frightened by my rage, and just at the last minute, just as my hand was about to shatter his face, I held back and merely clipped his cheek.

'You lay in bed naked with this bimbo, cuddling her, and you think that's OK, you think that doesn't constitute being unfaithful?' A picture of them together flashed into my head, my beloved Simon with his arms round the blonde.

What I did next wasn't very dignified, but Jesus, sometimes you can't help yourself, can you? I ran to the loo and threw up, knowing that he could hear, wanting him to hear what he was doing to me.

When I came back Simon was sitting at the kitchen table with his head in his hands. And I still loved him, oh how I loved him.

'Look, I forgive you,' I said, suddenly panicking that I wouldn't see him again. I wanted to do anything to make things the way they were. 'It doesn't matter, I understand. If you promise never to see her again we can just forget about it, we don't have to ever talk about it again.'

'I can't do that,' he said, looking sadly up at me. 'I love you but I can't stop thinking about her.'

'But we've had the best month ever, I thought we were so happy, I thought *you* were so happy.'

'She went away,' he said slowly. 'To the South of France. She's just got back and I don't know how I feel. I need some time on my own to figure out what I want. I just need some space, I need to be on my own.'

Funny how men always say, I need to be on my own, when what they mean is I need to continue fucking the woman I'm already fucking behind your back, except it's not behind your back anymore because you just found out about it. Actually it's not very funny, it's tragic. Can't they think of anything new to say?

Have you ever been in so much pain that you don't

think you can carry on? I don't think I would wish the pain I went through that night on my darkest enemy. Well, maybe I would, it would definitely hurt them, no two ways about that.

He left me that night. Left me curled up in a big armchair, squeezed in to the very corner, hugging my knees very tight and staring at the wall, with big drippy tears squeezing themselves out my eyes and rolling down my cheeks until everything around me felt like a puddle of salt water.

He left me to go and talk to Adam. 'I can't handle this,' he said as he got his coat. 'I'm going to see Adam, I'll be back later.'

Mel rang but I couldn't talk to her. Every time I tried to say something my chest would start heaving and I couldn't physically get any words out.

'He's left you on your own?' she said in horror, but I didn't want her to come over, I wanted Simon back, and although he wasn't going to be gone for long, or so he said, I knew he'd left as soon as he met Tanya. Or kissed her, or cuddled her naked in bed.

I got up and looked in the bathroom mirror, feeling as if I were in a dream, as if any moment now Simon would walk through the door and take me to bed, as if this couldn't really be happening.

Jesus I looked a state. Red puffy eyes, like Dracula's daughter, and tear-stained cheeks. Simon was coming back but I didn't care, I wanted him to suffer by seeing how much he'd made me suffer. I wanted him to hurt as much as I was hurting.

He did come back and he said he thought it would be best to sleep in the spare room. Remember that first night, when I told you how neither of us slept because we were so happy? I thought about that all night as I lay in his bed, wide awake, crying softly into the pillow. I think I must have fallen asleep at about six, because the birds were singing and light was beginning to filter into the room.

When I woke up, at twenty past eight, I remember thinking, something's wrong, but what the hell is it? And immediately I remembered, and it became real when I realised that Simon wasn't in bed next to me, there was no leg thrown over my body, and no sleepy dry hand gently resting on my stomach.

I didn't cry after I woke up, I think I just felt a bit dead, a bit like life wasn't really worth carrying on with. I went to make a coffee in the kitchen, and while I was standing there Simon came in.

He put his arms around me from behind, and kissed the nape of my neck. I froze. Maybe he had changed his mind, maybe it was a bad dream. But then he whispered, 'I'm sorry,' and I knew it was over.

It wasn't much of a consolation but Simon looked as bad as I did. Before Simon I never understood why you were upset if you were the dumper, you were only supposed to be upset when you were the dumpee, but, Jesus, Simon looked like shit.

'Look, move your stuff out whenever you want, it's no problem, but I think it's best for both of us if you're not here when I get back this evening.'

What could I say? There wasn't anything to say, and I took my coffee back to the bedroom and sat in bed, with the duvet huddled around me for comfort, as I listened to Simon getting ready for work.

He didn't sing that morning. He always sang while he was showering and shaving, snatches of Offenbach and Bizet, mixed with Neil Young and sometimes Oasis if he was feeling trendy, except he never remembered the words, he'd make them up as he went along.

Today will never be the same, is what I have to say to you.

And how, you're gonna somehow find a way to do a great big poo.

It used to make me laugh when he did that. Especially when he sang Bizet, making up great snatches of French, which was a language he never excelled at during O level.

But this morning there was silence. I was almost tempted to break into song myself, *If you leave me now, you'll take away the very heart of me . . .*

I sung the words in my head instead, with the accompaniment of the silent dripping of tears on my pillow. Simon didn't say goodbye, I just heard him shut the front door gently behind him. Maybe he thought I was asleep, but probably he just didn't want to face the music. Good joke, eh? Except it wasn't funny at the time.

You can live with someone, laugh with someone, love someone, and suddenly it's all gone. You want to reach out to them and hold them, but an invisible barrier has sprung up. This is how it was for me and Simon. When we were in the kitchen we were behaving like strangers, bloody strangers, when only the week before we had been whispering how much we loved each other.

That's how it is with relationships, it's part of life, and all the great love songs and poems and films have been written by people who were standing where I was that morning as Simon shut the door. Doesn't make it any easier though.

– *Seven* –

After that phone call from Simon my week went to pieces, are you surprised? David and Annalise threw a joint fit at work when one of my guests, the bloody fill-in guest at that, didn't turn up. We had to extend the item on flower arranging to twenty minutes, and even Annalise – Annalise who lives for dried flowers, country pine kitchens and gingham sofas – looked bored to shit.

The rest of the show went smoothly, but, Jesus, did I get my eyes bawled out by the editor. I walked into his office after the show and said, 'I don't suppose a blow job will make things better?' with a sheepish grin that was more of a grimace trying hard to be a smile.

He wasn't impressed. 'That's not the sort of thing I want to hear when anyone could walk past, Anastasia,' he hissed, 'and, no, for your information the best blow job in the world couldn't make up for the fact that the vast majority of your show today was shite.'

'Oh come on, that's not fair, what else could I have done?'

Oh screw the lot of them. But luckily today's Sunday and I'm going out for lunch. It's Mel and Daniel, Emma and Richard, Adam and a friend of Adam's, some bloke called Andrew.

You're probably wondering about Adam, aren't you? Yes, for your information it is *that* Adam, Simon's best friend. When we first split up, he was my one connection to Simon, I used to meet him to suck information from him like a sponge, but then he became just Adam. Safe, reliable, lovely Adam, and he's one of my closest friends.

Andrew I didn't really know. He and Adam go back years, and I'd met him on and off ever since I was with Simon. I'd been exceedingly polite but I hated him on sight. He is one of those very tall, very good-looking blokes that completely and utterly love themselves. I know what you're thinking, I probably fancied him and you're right, I probably did, but I never thought a bloke like Andrew would look at me twice, so instead of wasting my time fancying him, I decided to hate him.

I wasn't actually rude to him, I was just frostily polite and when he was asking me questions I practically stonewalled him. I wanted to show him that I, unlike all the other women at the party, wasn't taken in by his smarmy charms.

Adam and Andrew arrive to pick me up in Adam's car – a convertible Saab. Nice car I think, as I clamber into the back, trying not to mark my new white trousers, why can't I fall in love with a man like Adam?

Adam jumps out the car to let me in and gives me a quick kiss and a squeeze as his mate Andrew turns round and shoots me an I-love-myself-so-you-probably-love-me-too grin. 'How are you, Tash?' I'm instantly caught off-guard, but secretly slightly flattered that he uses my nickname, that it sounds so intimate rolling off his tongue.

'I could never be as good as you Andrew, but I'm trying.'

'I don't know, you don't seem to be doing too badly,'

and with that he eyes me up from head to toe, and, stupid bitch that I am, I feel myself sucking in my stomach.

We drive to the restaurant in Primrose Hill for lunch. No one needs to talk on the way over because the sun's out, the roof's down and Alanis Morissette is blaring out the four speakers.

I can see Andrew's hair blowing up in the wind and although he looks ridiculous when he turns round to smile at me with his hair all over the shop, I can't help it, my loins stir, this man is so . . . so fuckable.

We get out the car and Andrew says, 'Here, your collar's up,' and he moves his hand to turn it down, and as we walk down the road he leaves his hand resting on the back of my neck, and my stomach doesn't just twist, it does a major somersault.

Adam turns round and sees us walking up the road, with Andrew's hand rubbing the back of my neck and he turns away very quickly. Strange, I think, but I'm enjoying it, I haven't had this sort of attention for ages.

And then we walk in to the Engineer and Mel gives me a huge cuddle. 'I've missed you,' she says, 'I haven't seen you for ages.' It's been a week, but this is how girls are when they love each other and they're there for each other.

'Hi Tash, looking gorgeous as ever,' says Daniel, the slimy bastard, and he stands up to kiss me, aiming for the lips but as usual I turn my head and get a sloppy wet kiss planted on my cheek, with a quick rub on my arse for good measure.

I can't move his hand because Mel might notice, so I just ignore it and move away very quickly.

'Your friend's boyfriend seems to rather, er, like you,' says Andrew, sitting down next to me which I'm very happy about, because now I can flirt with him as much as I want to. Except the problem is I can't, because every time he talks to me I start stammering like an idiot.

Why does this always happen? Why do I always revert back to a shy, chubby sixteen-year-old when a man I really fancy tries to talk to me?

'He's such an idiot. It doesn't mean anything, he does it to everyone. I think he thinks it makes him more attractive.'

'What about if I were to do that to you? Would it make me more attractive?'

You couldn't be more attractive if you tried, I think, but of course I don't say it, I say, 'Looking the way you look right now, anything would make you more attractive.' I laugh, reaching up and combing his hair down.

Shit this man is gorgeous. I'm sorry, I know I keep saying that but I can't remember the last time I really fancied someone, and even though he has DANGER written all over his face, even though he's a heartbreak waiting to happen, I'm not sure whether, when push comes to shove, as I sincerely hope it will, I'm not sure whether I'll be able to resist.

Adam's sitting on my other side, and I feel ever so slightly irritated as he rubs my back while I'm sitting there, the last thing I need is for Andrew to think there's something going on between Adam and I.

But I need to be nice, and I *do* love Adam, I just don't love him right now, but I have to make the effort.

'How's the strange world of shop furnishings?' because this is what Adam does for a living. In fact, you've probably had a cappuccino in one of his restaurants, or possibly admired a staircase he's designed in your favourite designer store in town.

'Strange,' he laughs, 'but not as strange as television. What's the gossip this week?' Adam loves all the gossip from the show. He loves hearing who's sleeping with who, who's in, who's out.

'What?' interrupts Andrew. 'Since when have you been interested in television gossip?'

'It's a whole new world,' says Adam, 'and it's amazing what Tash knows. What was the name of that actor you shagged, you know, the one who wanted you to pee on him?'

I blush a flaming red. 'It wasn't recently, Adam, it was over a year ago and you're not meant to talk about it.'

'Do me a favour. You've been dining out on that one for years.' He's not wrong, and I do talk about it all the time, but not in front of Andrew, not in front of a bloke I fancy.

'Did you?' Andrew's looking at me in horror.

'Did I what?'

'Pee on someone?'

'No I bloody did not. Jesus, Adam, you are unbelievable, you've got such a big mouth.'

'What did I do?' says Adam, feigning innocence.

Andrew laughs and I relax, because he's not shocked, he thinks it's funny, but I still have to stress I didn't do it.

'I would like to clearly state, in company, that I have never, and I repeat, never peed on anything. Other than a toilet, but that's not a person, it's an inanimate object so it doesn't count.'

Emma visibly perks up. 'Sex already? Blimey, didn't take long today.' Because sex, as I've probably already told you, forms a major part of our girls' lunches, but admittedly, we don't usually divulge as much when there are blokes around.

'It *would* take a long time if it were me,' says

Andrew, deliberately picking up on the *double entendre* that Emma didn't mean. 'I believe in giving women pleasure, in making them wait. None of that in, out, shake it all about rubbish for me. If I'm making love to a woman, I expect her to cancel her arrangements for at least two days.'

'Ooh, two days?' I turn to him with a raised eyebrow. 'There's an offer that would be difficult to resist.'

Andrew leans towards me and whispers in my ear, 'But a quickie can be just as fun. How do you fancy a quickie?'

I pull back and look him in the eye. 'Don't tempt me,' and I'm smiling, but Andrew's very serious as he says slowly, 'I'm not joking.' And I only bloody blush, don't I? Don't know where to look or what to say, and as I struggle to change the subject because yes, dear reader, I am embarrassed, Andrew sweeps back my hair and plants a soft kiss on the nape of my neck.

Fuck me, please. Fuck me. Jesus Christ, this man is so sexy, all I want to do is crawl under the table with him and fall into his arms. Pictures fill my head of the two of us together, what we'd do, how he'd slowly unbutton my shirt, kissing my lips, my face, my neck, my breasts.

I can almost feel him unzipping my trousers, move his hand slowly down, inside my Sloggis, except they wouldn't be Sloggis, I'd buy La Perla for this bloke, and feel his thick fingers work their way up inside me.

I'm gazing into space by this time, eyes clouded over with lust, and I'm brought back to earth by a gentle touch on my hand.

'Hello? Tash? Come back to earth.' It's Mel, and she's laughing. She knows.

I'm dying to find out whether Andrew's always like this, but I have to be careful with Adam. It's not that I think he fancies me or anything, but friendship between men and women is a funny thing.

Did you ever see *When Harry Met Sally*? You must have done, everyone did, it's my favourite film of all time. Remember that bit at the beginning, when Harry says men and women can't be friends because the sex part always gets in the way? What do you think, do you think that's true?

When I got really close to Adam, I didn't believe it, but I suppose all the friendships I've had with men have sprung out of an attraction, from either their part, or my part. And since I've never fancied Adam, I suppose, although I've never given it much thought, I suppose he might have been a little bit attracted to me. In the beginning. Not now though. We know each other too well.

So what I've decided is that the sex part doesn't get in the way, but it's always there, in the beginning. I mean let's face it, you don't go out of your way to befriend the ugly bastards do you, not unless you happen to be an ugly bastard yourself.

People gravitate to other people who have a similar level of attractiveness. If you walk into a restaurant and see a very handsome guy with a group of people, you can practically guarantee that all his friends will be beautiful.

And although, perhaps with the exception of Simon who wasn't exactly classically good-looking, although perhaps most of the men I've been out with have been handsome, I don't really think I deserve them. I don't really think I'm good enough for them, which is why I can't believe Andrew fancies me. If he does. He probably doesn't. He's probably just a flirt.

'Is Andrew always like this?' I whisper to Adam when Andrew's deep in conversation with Mel, arguing with her about the benefits of therapy. He, naturally, being a confident, tall, handsome bloke, has never needed therapy in his life. He's so over-confident, so self-assured, you just know that he's always been the golden boy, the apple of his parents' eye, the most popular bloke at school, the heart-breaking shagger at university.

Adam rolls his eyes. 'All the time, Tash. Drives me up the bloody wall. He can't talk to a woman without flirting.'

My heart sinks but I continue pushing, I need to hear that I'm different, that he's not just doing it for a game.

'But what does he do when he really fancies someone? How is he different?' I'm trying to sound as if I'm not really interested, but it obviously doesn't work.

A smile spreads on Adam's face. 'Why, are you interested?'

'God no. You've got to be joking. He's so in love with himself he'd never have time for anyone else. Nah, not my type at all.' Adam almost looks relieved, I suppose he wouldn't want me to get hurt again, not after Simon.

'But he's a nice guy,' I say, wanting to keep talking about Andrew. 'I'm surprised, I didn't think he was this nice.'

'Yeah, he is a nice guy, what did you expect from a friend of mine?' He's smiling.

'What about Simon then?' Adam still sees Simon, not as often as he used to, admittedly, although I don't think that's anything to do with me. I think time has just come between them, and their friendship is not what it was. That's just a guess though, Adam never discusses him with me because Simon has nothing to do with my life any more, and nothing to do with my relationship with Adam.

'Yeah, well, Simon. I know he was a shit to you, but we go back so long, he's been a good friend to me.'

'Yeah, I know. Sorry, I didn't mean that.' I didn't mean to bring Simon into the conversation, I try and forget about Simon, and most of the time I do fine, just fine. But that phone call threw me, it really did.

You gradually get over the pain. It doesn't go away, not for a long time, but it becomes easier to live with. One morning you wake up and he's not the first thing on your mind. And then a few months down the line you realise you've made it through half the day without thinking of him.

Sometimes it takes months, sometimes years, but eventually you reach a point when you only think about them occasionally. You manage to do this because you don't see them, you don't hear about them, you try not to think about them.

And then you bump into them walking down the street, or someone unexpected mentions their name, or the fuckers ring in to your television programme, and the memories come flooding back. But memories also become less painful in time, and I can talk about Simon now without really feeling anything. But I'd rather not. If you know what I mean.

The restaurant suddenly seems to get cold. I shiver, and Andrew looks at me with concern. 'Are you cold, Tash?'

'Freezing,' I say, rubbing my arms to try and warm myself up. Andrew puts his big strong arm around me and rubs my shoulders and my back, and I lean into him, savouring the feeling, wanting to stay there for ever.

'You're very sexy,' he again whispers into my ear. 'I

bet you're great in bed.' Shit, this is ridiculous. I'm in a restaurant with all my friends being chatted up by a bloke who is probably just after a quick fling, and I'm not playing hard to get, I'm playing his game, except I'm not playing it very well because I know what will happen.

You want to know what will happen? OK, I'll tell you, and I know because this won't be the first time this has happened, it's just that I'm not sure whether I want it to happen again. I'm not sure whether I can cope.

One night Andrew will phone me up and he'll say something like, 'What are you doing? Do you want to come over?' And because he lives in Clapham and because I have legs to shave and toenails to paint and I haven't got time and every second is vital, I'll say something like, 'Why don't you come over here instead?'

And he'll say something like, 'Oh? Do you trust me in your flat?' And I'll laugh throatily and sexily and say, 'See you in an hour.'

And then I'll scrabble around the bathroom looking for a razor, and I'll run back down to the bedroom with bits of toilet roll hanging off my legs where I've cut myself, and I'll slap my make-up on and pull on my sexiest underwear.

And in-between I'll be frantically tidying up the living room, lighting the fire, lighting the candles, but not too many, don't want to make it *that* obvious, even though we both know why he's coming.

And when he walks in he'll see me, looking gorgeous and seductive in my faded 501s, a big white shirt and bare feet, and we'll sit on the same sofa, sipping red wine, talking about rubbish.

And then after a while the conversation will move to

sex, as it always does when you both know what's on the menu, and eventually he'll put his glass down and say, 'I'd better not drink anymore, I have to drive home.' And he'll be looking into my eyes as he says this and I'll look into my wine glass for a few seconds, then look back at him and I'll say softly, 'You don't have to go. You could stay.'

And he'll put his wine glass on the table, sit back and take my hands. We'll both look down at his big strong hands stroking mine, and every sense I have will be heightened, and then he'll lift one hand and stroke my cheek, and while the butterflies are fluttering so hard in my stomach I feel almost nauseous, he'll kiss me.

And the kiss will be long and passionate, and then I'll lead him into the bedroom thinking, don't get involved, Tasha. This is just a fuck. Don't believe it will be anything more.

And we'll tear each other's clothes off and he'll be an incredible lover. He'll be, as he is, self-assured, confident, he'll know exactly what he's doing.

And he *will* stay, because he's not that much of a bastard, and in the morning, once I've made him a coffee and walked him to the front door, he'll be friendly, but he won't touch me. The kisses and cuddles he gave me the night before were only for the night before. When he leaves he might give me a kiss on the lips, but he won't open my mouth with his tongue, or lick the inside of my lips whispering, 'I want to make love to you.'

He'll say something like, 'I'll give you a call,' and he may or may not add 'sometime'. I'll get up and go to work, and I'll be too busy to think about him, but when I get home, later that night when I'm cleaning up his debris from the night before, I will think about him.

And I'll think about the way he kissed me, the way he held me, the way he murmured my name as he entered me, and the more I think about it the more I'll want to see him again.

And my telephone will turn into a silent black monster, sitting menacingly in the corner of my living room, accusing me of not being good enough, not being pretty enough, not being thin enough, because he doesn't call.

If I'm very lucky he might phone again in a couple of weeks, when he's bored, or horny, and if we do make love again it won't be making love, it will be fucking, and I'll want him more. And more. And more. I'll savour every sign of encouragement the bastard unwittingly gives me, and eventually, when he stops phoning and he's found someone else, someone who he wants to be with, to take out for dinner, to spend days with, I'll cry for a few hours, or maybe a couple of days, and then I'll be fine.

This is why I don't want to respond to Andrew. Because I deserve better than a cheap fuck. Because I deserve to be the one they want to take out for breakfast. But I can't bloody help myself can I. Could *you*?

– *Eight* –

Jesus, do you know how long it's been since I last had a fuck?

– *Nine* –

Sometimes you can tell when people have had happy childhoods, people like Andrew, and sometimes you get it completely wrong. I know for a fact people assume I have always been successful, popular, one of those people born with a silver spoon in their mouths.

But let me tell you how wrong they are. How wrong you might be. This painted veneer hides a hell of a lot of pain. You think it will get better as you grow older. You think you'll be able to sweep it under your Habitat rugs, but every time you have a relationship, those problems come back, and screw you up all over again.

'When we're adults we spend our lives trying to recreate our childhood homes, hmm? For some that means happiness, security, warmth. For others, like you, it means unhappiness, infidelity, insecurity, hmm?' I was lying back in what I've come to call my shrink's couch, although it's not a couch, it's a chair, and if you push the arms forward the back shoots backwards and this shelf thing appears under your legs.

This was sometime last year, and Louise was looking at me very intently as she said this, as she tried to explain why I attracted men who couldn't commit, or weren't faithful, or didn't want me enough.

'There was no consistency in your childhood,' she said, 'and no trust.'

'You're right,' I nodded. 'I don't actually think I know how to trust,' I said slowly, thinking about each word as it came out my mouth. 'I don't think I've ever trusted anyone in my life.' Louise was nodding as I said this, gently encouraging me to dig a bit deeper and find the answers myself.

I never thought of myself as being unhappy as a child, you see. I remember there being a lot of love at home, with few arguments. I remember telling Louise that and her seeming surprised. I think she expected there to be alcoholism, arguments, at the very least a few broken plates.

But that isn't my memory, honestly, although after I'd been seeing Louise for a while, I started to realise that the insignificant things were the things that mattered. It's a bit like receiving compliments as an adult. If you're anything like me, you can receive ten compliments and one insult. You immediately forget the compliments, while the insult plays on your mind for hours, days, sometimes years.

'Let's go back to what happened when you were eleven, hmm?' prodded Louise, gently but firmly. 'When you first became aware of your father having affairs.'

'I think the first time I became aware that there was something wrong was in the summer. I remember it being hot and sticky. I remember playing with my friends in the park down the road from the house.'

'What were you playing?'

'Rounders? I don't know, something like that.'

'Were you a good team player?'

'I loved playing games even though I was never

particularly sporty. I used to look at the girls and boys in my class and wish I could be like them. I was always good at art, occasionally English but I was always the last to be picked for any team. But I was quite good at rounders. I had good, what do you call it, hand–eye co-ordination, so even though I couldn't run very fast, I was quite good at hitting the ball.

'I came home and went to get something to eat, as I usually did. I used to walk in and pray my mother was upstairs, or out, so I could go to the fridge and make huge sandwiches, pre-dinner snacks, although I didn't have a name for them then.

'I always seemed to be hungry as a child, hence my rather rotund stomach and little chubby thighs. I didn't understand emotional hunger then of course, I just thought I must have been a pig. My parents obviously thought so too, because even then, even at ten years old my mother was putting me on diets.

' "*Well* done," she'd say, if I managed to lose a few pounds off my chubby little frame. "*That's* better." And I'd feel so proud, that I'd been able to do it, to please my mother. But of course it wouldn't last. I'd go to school with a lunchbox filled with Ryvita, cottage cheese, fruit and a yoghurt as a special treat.

'And I'd sit in the playground at lunchtime surrounded by schoolfriends whose mothers had packed white bread sandwiches filled with processed cheese and thinly-sliced ham. They had Coca Cola, Wagon Wheels, Club biscuits. I'd sit there and wait for them to finish, because they never did finish, and I'd be ready and waiting with little open mouth to hoover up the leftovers.'

'Do you know what emotion you were trying to suppress with food?'

'I suppose I never felt good enough. My parents had

it all, or so it must have seemed to anybody peering through the windows of our comfortable, mock-Tudor, middle-class home.

'My father, Robert, was a successful lawyer. Tall, handsome, and the apple of my eye. I was a complete Daddy's girl and in turn he adored me. Whenever I fell, hurt myself, needed a cuddle I'd go running to Daddy who would scoop me up in his arms and smother me with love.

'My mother, Elaine was a housewife. Tiny, petite, immaculately dressed all the time in designer clothes. The first woman in the street to try every new fashion, and the only woman to really look good in it. I loved my mother, at least I tried, but there was always a barrier. I could see her, even at the age of eleven, look me up and down disapprovingly.

' "Why can't you be more like Helen?" she'd say. "Look at her lovely slim ankles, why haven't you got ankles like that?" And she'd grab my ankles before laughing, while I took the insult, couched in affection, and carried it with me for the rest of my life.

' "You'd be so pretty if you lost a bit of weight," she'd say, dishing out biscuits to my friends and withholding the jar from me. She never actually said, "You're not good enough. You're not the daughter I wanted," but I could see it in her eyes, in those silent glances she used to give me, those looks that said I wish I'd had a different daughter. I wish I'd had a daughter like Helen.

'Helen was my best friend. She was slim, pretty, well-spoken. She had shiny blonde hair hanging in a perfect veil down her back. Every morning her mother used to plait her hair with different coloured ribbons. She was so popular, and I was so grateful she was my best friend.

'I was never hers you understand, she used to split her time between various people, and she used to tell me I was lucky she was my friend, because I wasn't that pretty, but she liked me anyway, she liked my craziness when the adults weren't watching.

'I think even at eleven I was mature, aware that I was slightly different, the cat that walks by herself. I wasn't happy, but there was no real reason for it, until that summer's day when I knew something was wrong.

'Anyway, where was I? Oh yes, I had been playing rounders, and I came in to the kitchen to find my father sitting at the table with my mother standing at the other end of the room, glaring at him. I don't think they heard me, I don't think they knew I was there, and I crept back on tiptoes, thinking that my father looked guilty, although I'm not even sure I knew what it was then. I just knew he looked the way I looked when my mother was accusing me of eating a cake, and I had done it, but I was telling her I hadn't.

'I crept back and stood just beside the door frame, just out of sight, and I stood and listened to their conversation while my heart was pounding because I knew this was a grown-ups conversation, this wasn't meant for my ears.

' "How could you?" my mother was shouting, a rhetorical question, but of course I didn't understand the meaning of the word then. "What about me, what about Tasha? Didn't you think about us?"

'My father didn't reply, so I peeked around the door frame and saw that his elbows were on the table and his head was in his hands. I suddenly became very frightened, when didn't he think of me, what was he doing?

' "You really want to throw away your marriage for a lousy affair with some cheap tart? This isn't real. You selfish bastard. I don't even want to talk to you, I want you to leave. I want you out of here tonight."

'I ran upstairs with my hands covering my ears. I didn't want to hear anymore. I'd heard too much already. I threw myself on my bed and instantly started crying, big baby heaving sobs. My parents were going to divorce. Friends at school had divorced parents. It meant they got extra presents on their birthdays and at Christmas. It meant that when they saw their fathers on the weekends they did extra special things like go to the zoo, or funfairs, or picnics in the park.

'But I didn't want that. I loved my father and I wanted my parents to stay together. My parents getting divorced was the worst thing that could ever happen to me, and they must be getting divorced. Why else would my mother tell my father to leave?

'He didn't leave that night. I came downstairs a bit later on, terrified at what I would find, which turned out to be a frosty silence, an atmosphere you could have cut with the smooth round ankle of my Barbie doll.

'My father couldn't look at me, and my mother tried to pretend that everything was normal, but I, of course, knew that it wasn't. Knew that perhaps things would never be normal again.

'I cried again later that night, and this time my mother happened to be passing my bedroom door. She came in and sat on the bed putting her arms around me and stroking my hair. I think she started crying too, but after a while she said, "Did you hear Daddy and I having a fight?"

'I nodded sadly while hiccuping, and looked up at her with tear-stained cheeks. "It's nothing to worry about," she said, "everything's going to be fine."

'"But you told him to leave." She looked shocked, she didn't think I'd heard that bit.

'"He's not going to leave, darling. It's nothing important, just a little fight. Grown-ups sometimes argue about things but they get better, it will all be fine. Sometimes you get angry with Helen, don't you?"

'I nodded. "And sometimes you have a little argument with Helen, and you don't talk to each other for a little while and then it's fine and you forget all about it and you're friends again. That's what it's like for me and Daddy too. It's just a little argument, I'm not very happy with Daddy at the moment."

'"But you're going to get divorced," the hiccups became sobs again, as I considered the prospect of a fatherless family.

'"No we're not, darling. I promise you, we're not going to get divorced."

'But I told Helen they were going to get divorced. I didn't tell her because I was proud, I told her because there wasn't anyone else to tell.

'"An affair means he doesn't love your mum anymore, he loves somebody else," she stated firmly. "And then they'll divorce and you won't see your father except every other weekend, and when you do he'll be with his new girlfriend."'

'How did Helen know about affairs and divorce?' asks Louise.

'Because her parents were divorced, and naturally, her father was now living with the object of the affair.'

When you're eleven years old, there are very few terrible things that can happen. When your happiness, security and stability are dependent on there being two parents, together, who can give you what you need, the most terrible thing you can envisage is those parents splitting up.

As an adult it may still be difficult if your parents divorce but you can cope because you are surrounded by a network of friends who have experience, wisdom and your best interests at heart. As an eleven-year-old, you have no one, other than a best friend who is merely projecting her own pain and confusion onto you. And you wonder why I'm screwed up?

I carry on talking, almost wincing with the pain this still causes me, even as a thirty-year-old.

'They didn't divorce, but from my perspective it was touch and go for a few weeks. It was touch and go while there were still frosty silences, while my parents didn't touch, while I felt guilty, because perhaps this was something to do with me.

'Perhaps if I was more perfect, if I tidied my room, helped my mother in the kitchen, tried not to eat as much, perhaps that would make everything OK.

'The funny thing is that everything was OK for a while. It was OK until I was seventeen, until I discovered my father having an affair myself.

'I was with a group of friends, sitting in a café in Covent Garden, talking about boys and sex, which none of us knew much about, and smoking myself stupid, as we all tended to do in those days.

'We were having what we thought was a deep and meaningful conversation, when I happened to glance up and out of the window. There, walking along the pavement opposite me was my father. My face lit up as I got ready to run out the restaurant and greet him, what a lovely surprise.

'But then I noticed that the woman at his side was holding his hand, and of course she wasn't my mother, she was a friend of my parents, a woman who had never been married, a woman who, I suppose, used to have affairs with married men.

'I stopped in confusion. Why were they holding hands, but inexperienced as I may have been at seventeen, even I wasn't that naive. And then, as I watched through the window feeling like an eleven-year-old girl whose world is about to shatter into pieces, my father turned to this woman and kissed her. Not a hello, goodbye kiss. A kiss of passion, a kiss of longing.

'Perhaps I should have run towards them, I wanted to tear her face off, to slap her until she screamed, to pull her hair until tears ran down her cheeks.

'But I didn't. I sat back down again very quickly, and tried to act normal, tried to pretend there was nothing wrong. I was so angry, so upset, that I couldn't talk to my father, I couldn't tell him. I was terrified I was right, and I was terrified I was wrong. Maybe it was just a kiss, maybe it didn't mean anything. I had kissed boys who I hated, it was just a snog. But of course I knew, I just didn't want to know.

'Other things started fitting into place after that. The times my mother had been on holiday alone, and the phone had rung late at night and I'd heard my father murmuring into the telephone.

' "It's Anthony," he'd say, his partner. "He sends his love." And I'd back out the room because I knew that men don't murmur to other men, they murmur to other women. Women who aren't their wives.

'And the times he'd go out saying, "I'm with Joe if you need me. Won't be back late." And I'd phone Joe, needing to ask my father something, needing to be reassured that he wasn't going to leave, that everything was fine and Joe would say, "Oh, he's just popped out to get some cigarettes, I'll get him to call you when he's back."

And five minutes later my father would call and I'd

want to trap him, I'd want to ring Joe's house immediately, knowing of course he wouldn't be there, but I never did. I knew, but I didn't want to know.

'Or he'd come home in the early hours, while I was lying in my bed pretending to be asleep, but listening for the sound of the front door and watching the hours tick by on the clock. And the next morning I'd say, "What time were you home?" and he'd roll his eyes and say, "Not late. Around eleven I think."

'But of course he wasn't. I accused him one day. When I picked up the telephone extension to hear the tail end of a woman's sentence, and then my father shouting, "Put the phone down, Anastasia."

'For the first time in my life I got angry with my father, and wasn't afraid to show him. "How dare you?" I hissed at him. "You're having an affair. I know."

'He put his arms around me and said, "Tasha, I would never do anything to hurt you or Mummy. You need to know that. Never." But of course that's not a denial is it? That's justification.

'Imagine being a seventeen-year-old who loves both her parents, and doesn't want to hurt them, doesn't want them to hurt each other. Imagine carrying the burden of your father's infidelities around for your whole life. You can't talk to your friends because they don't understand why it matters so much. You can't talk to your mother because you don't want to cause her unneccessary pain.

'So you carry this betrayal, this lack of trust around with you, and slowly it colours every relationship you have. You start off trying to choose men who aren't like your father, and in the early days of your relationships you say things like, "The worst thing you could do to me would be to have an affair. That would be unforgivable." And they nod and say they'd never hurt you, but of course inevitably they do, because you're expecting it, you almost want it to happen.'

'Why do you think you want it to happen?' I'd almost forgotten about Louise, lost in my own thoughts, and I'd almost forgotten about you too. I'm sorry, this is heavy shit, I know.

'I think subconsciously it's what I think I deserve. It's what I know, family equals betrayal. My father betrayed me and my mother, so I wait for my boyfriends to do the same thing. If they're not betraying me by being unfaithful, I'll find another reason.'

'And as a child you felt that you weren't good enough to hold your father, hmm?'

'Yes. And as an adult I feel I'm not good enough to hold a man. Even the times when I have had relationships with men who are faithful, who do appear to love me, I can't trust it. I introduce them to my friends who are, I think, prettier than me, and I sit back and watch, watch them chatting, being friendly, and in my head I convince myself they're flirting.'

'And how does that make you feel?'

'It makes me feel sick. I literally feel like throwing up, pure panic. I am absolutely terrified of them walking out. Of being alone. Which is so ironic, because the times when I am single, when there aren't any men around, I am so together, so happy. But the minute I start a relationship, I go to pieces.'

'We have to look at why, as a child, divorce was the worst thing that could have happened,' says Louise, in the tone of voice that means she's about to start a roll, she's going to tell me something I don't want to know, something I already know but I've been too frightened to admit.

'You have never broken away from your father. There's an incestuous psychological relationship going on, you've never broken that attachment so even as an adult, when you know your parents are adults too and their lives have nothing to do with yours, you can't let go.

'And there's a huge well of resentment there. You are furious. You are furious that you have these parents, that your father was unfaithful, that you were made to feel you weren't good enough.

'And now you have to take responsibility, you have to become accountable. Until you start to tell yourself that you are in control, that your parents aren't to blame, nothing will change.

'But when you say, OK, this happened, it moulded me into the person I am today, and yes I do have anger, I do have resentment, I am pissed off, you will start to grow. You will start to break away, and to live your life as an emancipated woman.'

'But how do I do that? Is that just a process I have to work through with you?'

'Yes. And it will take a long time. It happens differently for different people, but it *will* happen. You *will* get there.'

– *Ten* –

I leave Louise's and just as I'm putting the key in the door I can hear the phone ring. The one thing I hate more than anything else in the world is when people phone and I don't reach it in time, the machine picks up and by the time I get there they've hung up.

Thank God for 1471, the four digits that have changed my life, but even then, even though you are supposed to be able to trace most of your calls, if someone's calling from work, or a mobile phone, or they've barred their number, you're up shit creek, and you haven't got a clue.

When they first introduced 1471 I spent my whole life ringing back numbers I didn't recognise and telling some stranger that someone in their household had phoned me. Most of the time I found them, but now I don't really bother. It's only important when you're waiting for a man to call, and I'm not. Not really anyway.

I run to the phone and pick it up breathing heavily because fitness is not, er, one of my strong points, and even a short dash down the hallway, round the corner and into the living room has rendered me slightly breathless.

'Tasha? It's Andrew.' A smile spreads across my face,

I didn't give him my number, he must have got it from Adam.

There's a silence while he waits for my reaction, which is the bog standard, 'Hi, how are you?'

'I'm well. Actually I'm not that well, I could be better.'

'Oh, why's that?'

'Do you know it's been ages since I last had a shag.'

I can't quite believe he's started already, this early on in the conversation, but he's tempting me again.

'I can't believe that, why not?'

'Maybe I haven't met the right woman. Or maybe I have, maybe it just hasn't happened yet . . .'

'You don't strike me as the relationship type.'

'Who said anything about relationships? What I need is some nice uncomplicated sex with no strings attached.'

A pause while I digest what he's saying. Does he mean with me? Is this an offer I wouldn't refuse? I can't take him up on his offer, because I'm not sure what he means, so instead I say suggestively, 'Don't we all, darling?'

'So what are you up to?'

Well I'm hardly going to tell him I just got back from my therapist am I, so I quickly say, 'Just polishing up a script for the show.'

'Does that mean you're going to be working all night? I wanted to know whether you'd like to go out and play.' My heart skips a beat, and damn, I'm seeing Adam tonight.

'Well I won't be working all night, I'm going to grab a bite to eat with Adam later on. Why don't you join us?'

'I won't be intruding then?'

Hardly. But of course I can't say that, I say, 'No, the more the merrier.'

'Well I'm coming straight from work so why don't I meet you at the restaurant?' I tell him to be at The Red Pepper in Formosa Street at eight thirty, and I put the phone down and can't wipe the smile off my face.

I hadn't thought about what I was going to wear; after all, it was only going to be Adam and I was going to go straight out in my jeans and boots, with make-up that hadn't been freshened up since this morning.

But now, now I have to plan. Now I have to decide whether this is a good hair day or a bad hair day. I have to pull everything out of my wardrobe, try everything on and decide which outfit is flattering, sexy, sophisticated.

I have to spend at least half an hour applying the same make-up that normally takes me ten minutes, and I have to stay calm. I have to make the bed, tidy the clothes up and shove them back into the bottom of the wardrobe. I have to leave a bottle of white wine chilling in the fridge just in case.

I have to frantically sprinkle that disgusting Shake 'n' Vac stuff on the carpet, and quickly polish my wooden furniture with lavender-scented beeswax, and light a small oil burner with a few drops of Ylang Ylang to make the flat smell sensual, inviting, delicious.

I have to do all these things because even though I want to resist Andrew, even though I know he's bad for me, tonight could be the night, you never know.

Because enlightened as I may be, enlightened as you may be, wouldn't you agree that deep down every woman goes for the Andrews because she hopes she'll be the one to change him? Oh come on, you must.

She goes in with eyes wide open, fully aware of what he is and why it won't work out, and even though he's told her it's just a fling, he's not ready for a relationship, she'll hang on and hang on because she prays that one morning he'll wake up, see her sleeping beside him in her lovely silk Janet Reger special, and he'll be hit by a *coup de foudre*, a flash of lightning. My God, he'll think, I'm in love with her.

God, we are so pathetic. We know this, we talk about this with our girlfriends and if a friend happens to be in the same situation we'll advise her to get out because we know he won't fall in love with her, we know she'll end up with tears on her cheeks and cracks in her heart.

Here's my theory on men and women. When a man meets a woman he decides within around thirty seconds whether or not he finds her attractive. If he doesn't, they become friends. If he does, they might become friends, but the potential for them to become lovers never quite goes away.

When a woman meets a man she decides within around thirty seconds whether or not she finds him attractive. Even if she doesn't, they become friends, but at any given point in their relationship, she could fall in love with him. She could fall in love with him because he's kind, sensitive and he makes her laugh. Because she grows up and realises that sexual attraction is not the be all and end all to life. Because she finally realises she deserves a nice guy. That nice guys aren't all boring. That sometimes they do wonders for your ego, that sometimes they're just what you need.

Men are far more visually stimulated than women who want to go deeper, want to find out what makes a person tick. And you wonder why all my close friends are women? Jesus, makes you wonder why you bother with men at all sometimes.

And I know that Andrew won't change. I know he's

attracted to me, and I know I won't make him fall in love with me, but I still make that extra bit of effort. Just in case.

Finally, when my flat is perfect and I am happy with my reflection and my hair, and my choice of clothes – a black silk clinging cardigan with my best underwear underneath, black lace just visible if I lean forward, which of course I don't plan to do, much, and black lycra trousers with a little flare at the bottom – I'm ready.

I drive up to the restaurant and Adam is already waiting. Adam is so reliable, he's always on time, never moans if I'm not, and he's always happy to see me.

'Wow. You look gorgeous,' he says, as he gives me a big hug. 'You look so well, how are you?'

I do look gorgeous because my eyes are lit up, and I'm glowing inside because Andrew will be coming, a man I fancy, a man I've been daydreaming about.

'I'm really well. Did Andrew call you?'

'No. Why?'

'Oh, he just phoned me earlier and he's bored so he's joining us. That's OK, isn't it?'

'Of course,' and I could be wrong but I'm sure I saw a faint shadow of a cloud pass over Adam's face.

'Let me go and tell them it's now a table of three. I'll be back in a sec.' I watch Adam's big burly frame as he walks through the restaurant, feeling a pang of affection.

It's funny, isn't it, how your true family are not your flesh and blood? They are the people you meet throughout your life who prove themselves to you. The people who you grow to love, who love you equally in return, who are always there for you.

Mel is my family, Emma and Andy are my family.

And now Adam is my family. And it's becoming increasingly difficult to remember what my life was like before I met them.

So I'm standing there, watching Adam and thinking about how much I adore him, when I'm clasped round the waist and a big smacker of a kiss lands on my neck.

This is evidently becoming Andrew's trademark greeting, the equivalent of a kiss on the cheek, and as I stand there I hope and pray that I'm the only one he does this to. That I am special. That his kiss on my neck means infinitely more than hello.

If I thought Andrew was gorgeous before, seeing him now, in his dark blue single-breasted Armani suit positively takes my breath away, and I can't help myself, I have to say something, to feed his already over-enlarged ego.

'You look good in a suit,' I offer lamely. 'It suits you.' He smiles and raises one eyebrow because of course he knows he looks good in a suit, he'd look fantastic in a bin bag, for Christ's sake.

'Thank you, Tasha. And I have to say, you look incredibly edible yourself.'

I laugh, and as I do so I lean forward, ever so slightly, just enough to give him what I hope is a tantalising glimpse of the black lacy bra.

Adam comes back and they shake hands then hug. They actually hug, although Adam seems slightly reticent, but Andrew's so tactile you can't resist him. At least, I can't, and sorry for being selfish but that's all I really care about right now.

We go to the table to sit down and I'm so proud walking through this restaurant because every single woman in the place turns to look at the two tall handsome men I'm with, and I can feel their eyes piercing into my back thinking, what has she got that I haven't, and I don't care, because they're with me.

It's a complete treat going out for dinner with two handsome men. Especially when both are flirting with you and you can sit and bask in your reflected glory, which is what I do, aware that people are watching me with envy, and enjoying every second of it.

'I bumped into Kay last night,' says Adam to Andrew. I know Kay, not well, and I'm not too sure I like her. She's always pleasant, always friendly, but I can't put my finger on it, she's just not someone I feel completely comfortable with.

'She still doesn't talk to me,' says Andrew, sighing. 'You would have thought after all this time it wouldn't matter, but apparently I'm still the biggest bastard she's ever met.'

'You went out with Kay?' I lean forward, interrupting Andrew and he ignores me. 'Andrew, did you go out with Kay?' He's still talking but this is urgent, I need to know his type, I need to know whether he went out with plain Kay, Kay who's not that attractive, Kay who's not that dynamic.

'Tasha, don't interrupt, just wait until I finish talking.' I sit back in my chair, embarrassed, I've been put in my place, and as I sit there I feel a grudging respect for Andrew. No one, no man, no woman, no boss, no one has ever managed to put me in my place.

This is a man I could love, I think. This is the first man I've ever met who hasn't been intimidated by me. Stop it, Tasha, I think, he doesn't want you. If he wanted you he'd ring and say he wanted to take you out for dinner. If he wanted you he'd want to be with you. He wouldn't ring and say he wanted to go out and play. He wouldn't turn around and say what he needs is some nice uncomplicated sex with no strings attached.

Finally he turns to me and says, 'Now I'll answer your question. Yes, I did go out with Kay.'

And I'm flummoxed, I don't know what to say, whether he realises why it's so important to me. 'I'm surprised, that's all,' I say. 'I couldn't see the two of you together.'

'Neither could he,' laughs Adam, 'that was the problem.'

We sit and we talk and I cannot take my eyes off Andrew. I hardly look at Adam, just occasionally glance his way as I'm talking, just so he doesn't feel too excluded.

And Adam grows more and more quiet, allowing Andrew to take centre stage, as he so obviously needs to do, but I can't help but feel there's something more. Andrew gets up to go to the toilet, and I look at Adam who's looking down at the table.

'Are you all right? You're very quiet tonight,' I ask gently.

'I'm fine,' he says, a bit too abruptly.

'Are you sure? There's nothing wrong is there?' Adam doesn't say anything, he just sighs and then looks up at me. Just as he's about to say something, something that I feel will be important, our food arrives, huge pizzas, flowing over the edges of the plates, and bowls of salad, and then Andrew's back, and whatever Adam was going to say, has gone. The moment has passed, and for a second I wonder what it is, but then Andrew is holding a slice of his pizza to my mouth saying, 'Try this, it's wonderful,' and I concentrate on eating his pizza, on accepting this gesture of intimacy in as sensual a way as I know how.

Andrew doesn't ask about me, I spend the evening

listening to him talk, occasionally adding my own comments, but for once, I am not the centre of attention, I am not the one who is entertaining, and although it is strange, I quite enjoy it.

So many of my old friends are married, or in long relationships and they invite me over for dinner and sit there hanging on to my every word. 'We live our lives vicariously through you,' they all say, each and every one thinking they are the only ones who say it.

The grass is always greener, isn't it? When you're single you ache to roll over in bed in the mornings next to someone you love. You gaze wistfully at couples kissing in the park, and you spend hours daydreaming elaborate fantasies about what you will do when you're in a couple.

But when you are part of a couple, when you have grown accustomed to waking up next to your lover in the morning, when you know that weekends aren't filled with wandering down canals and sharing intimate breakfasts, they are filled instead with small rows because He never wants to do anything, He's playing rugby with the boys, He wants to watch the match on television, you long for the excitement that comes with being single.

And, oh, how they look forward to their glamourous single friends, women like me, coming over to fill their life with second-hand excitement. They'd never change their life, they say, but they can't help a small regret that it will never be like this for them again.

But their excitement at my life fuels me. It makes me embellish, exaggerate, and of course, they only ever hear the good bits. They hear about the flirtatious conversations, the first kisses, the first time you have sex . . . if you know them well enough.

They don't hear about the nights you sit at parties

and watch other couples, wondering what is wrong with you that this never seems to happen to you. They don't hear about the times you sit on your sofa feeling sorry for yourself, when you put on a compilation of love songs and cry softly for three hours.

They don't feel your pain when yet another man, another potential soulmate turns around and says he doesn't want you anymore. When he echoes your mother telling you you're not good enough.

Once Freya turned around to me, Freya, my oldest friend who is so perceptive and so wise and so married, and she said, 'You always make it sound wonderful. But sometimes I think it must be so awful for you. That you do a great job of hiding the pain, that sometimes you must feel so lonely.'

I didn't know what to say. I couldn't in fact say anything, because my throat closed up and I thought I was going to cry. Because of course I do a great job of hiding the inner turmoil, and people only see the cool, tough, exciting life of a single woman. They see what they want to see, and very few people will bother to look deeper.

When our meal is finished Andrew reaches into the inner pocket of his jacket and draws out a cigar. A big, fat, Havana cigar, and slowly, sensually, he rolls it in his fingers before cutting off the end and lighting it.

I love watching men smoke cigars, and Andrew looks up to find me watching him in rapture.

'Do you smoke?' he says.

'Not cigars, but I'd like to.'

'You have to learn, you have to be taught by a connoisseur,' he says. 'Look, I'll show you.' And he offers me his index finger across the table.

'Show me how you'd do it.' And as I guide his finger to my mouth Adam, the restaurant, the past and the present recede, and it is just me and Andrew, here and now. I slowly take his finger into my mouth, and I'm not imagining it's a cigar, I'm imagining it's his cock, and I'm looking into his eyes as I take his finger deep within my mouth.

'*Very* good,' he says, looking into my eyes, 'but not quite. Give me your hand, I'll show you.' And he takes my finger and does the same to me and my hands being as erogenous as they are, I sit there feeling so turned on I think I'm going to faint.

And then he hands me his cigar and watches me through narrowed eyes as I suck slowly on it, knowing how phallic it is, knowing what he's thinking, knowing what Adam's thinking and not giving a damn.

'My God you do that well,' he says. 'I love watching women smoke big fat cigars. Do you have any idea how sexy you look?' Of course I do, otherwise I wouldn't be doing it. Cigars make me feel ever so slightly sick, but this is the best flirtation I have had in years, and I am relishing every bitter taste, every smoke-filled mouthful.

'No wonder you're so successful with men, it's a great technique,' he says, and I wonder what he's talking about.

'What do you mean? I'm not successful with men, I'm single for God's sake,' I laugh.

'Yes, but you're not short of admirers. Or sex, I would imagine. When was the last time you had sex?'

'What are you trying to say? Do you think I'm easy?' I'm absolutely horrified, the last thing in the world I want Andrew to think is that I'm a slut.

'No, I don't think you're easy. I think, if you want me to be perfectly honest, I think that you're the sort of woman who knows what she wants and isn't afraid to pursue it. I think that if you met a man who you were attracted to, you would enjoy him just for the sake of enjoyment.

'Don't get me wrong, it's a huge compliment, I wish there were more women like you.'

And of course I take the compliment and cherish it, because he sees me as a sexual, sexually mature woman, but there is an insult hidden in there too, he has just said the words I had dreaded hearing. He has said that I am the kind of woman you shag, not the kind of woman you fall in love with.

God how I wish it were different, how I wish I were different. How, at times like these, I wish I were like Mel, or Emma, or anyone, my friends who have long relationships, my friends who might know the pain of being in a relationship that isn't going where they want it to go, but who have no idea what the pain of being single is like.

We finish and Adam and Andrew insist on paying for me. Adam gives me a big hug goodbye and says he'll call me tomorrow, and Andrew and I walk together up the road to our cars.

But the funny thing is he's different now. I'm walking up the road thinking, this is it, now he'll kiss me, now it will happen, and he's distanced himself. Like so many men, at the crucial moment he's backing off.

We reach the car and I turn to him, face raised expectantly, and he puts his hand to my cheek, leans down and gives me a long, soft, kiss on the lips. My eyes are closed waiting for more, until he says, 'Take care, I'll see you soon,' and the look of disappointment is so obvious he stops, takes another step closer to me and puts his hand back to my chin, pulling it towards him.

His mouth meets mine again, and this time he

kisses me properly, and I'm so nervous that my legs practically buckle. We stand there, tongues intertwined, and he pulls away and says, 'Jesus, you are unbelievable. I can't believe you just did that.'

'Are you serious? It wasn't me. You kissed me!'

'I couldn't help it, your lips looked so kissable. You live near here don't you?' I nod, not trusting myself to speak.

'Shall I come back for a coffee?' And he's smiling, and all of a sudden I'm not sure. I'm not sure.

I'm not sure because I have seriously fallen for him and I'm not sure whether I can deal with the consequences.

'I don't know. What do you think?' I'm praying he'll say he can't stop thinking about me, that this will be the beginning of something big, that perhaps we could start slowly and see where it goes.

But of course this isn't a film, this is real life and he says, 'I think I'd like to take you to bed, I'd like to make love to you.'

'That's all though, we wouldn't be having a relationship.' I make it sound like a statement, but in fact it's a question, and Andrew knows this.

'No, we wouldn't be having a relationship, but that doesn't have to stop us enjoying each other just for tonight.'

There it is, in black and white, dear reader, and you know what? I can't do this. I can't deal with tomorrow morning, if he's kind enough to stay the night, that is.

'No.' I shake my head firmly, almost in disbelief at the word that just came out of my mouth. 'It's better if you go.'

I must be bloody crazy, but a part of me whispers that perhaps if I play a bit hard to get, even though I know it would just be a fling, perhaps I might make him fall for me after all.

So I kiss him one more time on the lips, and walk off to my car. But you might be proud of me because I didn't turn around to look at him. Not once.

– *Eleven* –

What can I tell you about my life after Simon left? That I woke up each morning with tear-stained cheeks, when I was lucky enough to sleep at all, that is.

That most nights I drifted off to sleep like a baby, and dreamt about Simon, yes, actually dreamt about him, until I woke up crying at three o'clock in the morning and then spent the rest of the night wandering aimlessly around my flat, reliving every minute of our relationship.

That if it hadn't been for Mel, and then Adam, I don't think I would have made it. That up until that point I had never ever understood what it was like to lose someone you really loved. That up until that night Simon left, I never really understood what pain was like.

The day after he left I tried to go into work and I got the bus. I walked up to the bus stop, climbed on to the bus and leant my head against the window as huge sobs took over, and I didn't care. I knew that everyone on the bus was staring at me, but I couldn't stop.

A middle-aged woman came and sat down next to me and took my hand. 'What's the matter?' she demanded. 'Why are you crying?'

In between the sobs, and the huge deep breaths that seemed to take all my strength I told her. 'I've split . . . my . . . boyfriend.'

'Bastards. They're all bastards,' she said. 'Was it another woman? It's always another woman.' I nodded as a fresh wave of sobbing took over. The other passengers had stopped looking at me but, Christ, were they listening. It was probably the most exciting bus journey most of them had ever had.

'My husband left me for another woman. Slung him out, I did, you're much better off without them.' She was talking so loudly, so passionately, it was almost funny.

'Came home one day and caught him in bed with some tart from the shops down the road, and now it's just me and the kids and we're all happier without the sod.'

I couldn't help myself, I smiled through my tears. She kept talking at me, all the way to work, and in the end, just as I was getting off the bus, she squeezed my hand. 'You'll be all right, love, you'll see. Pretty girl like you? Won't be long before you find another one. Like bloody buses they are.'

But I don't want another one I remember thinking as I stepped off. I want Simon, and boom, another fresh round of tears.

Three weeks later I slept with Jeff. He was a friend of Simon's who had always had a crush on me, although he never said as much. I bumped into him in my lunchbreak. Tall, good-looking but absolutely not my type, he took me for lunch.

Jeff had always fancied me, had always gone along with the flirt, but his smooth, suave good looks, his penchant for the theatre and the ballet were a world apart from mine, and I knew quite categorically that we would never make a good team.

'How *are* you?' he said, which is what everyone said in those early days. 'Have you spoken to Simon?'

'No. Have you?'

'I saw him last weekend, we were at the same party. Adam was there too.'

'Who was Simon with?' I couldn't help myself, I had to know.

'Some blonde. Pretty but thick. Not a patch on you.'

I felt physically sick. It was Tanya, and that was when I made up my mind. Forcing a flirtatious smile when it really was the last thing on my mind I said, 'Do you mean that? What have I got that she hasn't?'

'Well for starters you're stunning. Plus you've got a brain, and you're good fun. What more could a bloke ask for?' I remembered going out in a group when Jeff was there, when I was enjoying the attention and being the life and soul of the party.

When I didn't care whether or not blokes fancied me because I loved Simon and Simon loved me, and I could flirt because it didn't mean anything. That was what Jeff meant by good fun. He meant a good flirt.

'You wouldn't go out with someone like me though, would you?'

Jeff smiled. 'Tasha, I spent nine months feeling jealous as hell that Simon had got you.'

'So what about now then?'

Jeff stopped smiling. 'What about now?'

'Would you go out with me now?' Talk about self-destruct but I didn't care, and Jeff was as close as I was going to get to Simon. I could hurt Simon through Jeff. Even if he never found out it wouldn't matter because I would know, and in my own way I would be getting my own back.

Jeff's eyes were wide. 'Are you serious? Would you seriously go out with me?'

Now it was my turn to smile. 'Maybe it's a bit early to tell. Maybe we should just have an affair.'

Jesus Christ. Anyone would have thought someone had told Jeff it was Christmas every day for the rest of his life. 'When?' he said slowly.

'Why don't you come over tonight?'

'I'm going to the theatre, but it won't finish late. Why don't I come over afterwards?'

'OK.' Even as I said it it didn't feel real. It felt as if this was happening to someone else so I didn't think about it for the rest of the day, I just carried on as if everything were normal.

And I got home and sat there watching the clock, not really thinking about anything, my mind a complete blank.

At ten o'clock I got up and poured myself a very large vodka. I didn't fancy Jeff, I never had, but this was something I had to do. I phoned Mel.

'Mel, I know you're going to think I'm a complete slut but I think I'm going to have an affair with Jeff.'

'Oh Tasha, that's not the answer. You're just trying to hurt Simon more. Just let it go and get on with your life.'

'I can't. He's on his way and I'm going to do it. I have to.'

'Why, so Simon can feel better about Tanya because you're sleeping with his friends?'

'No, because I need to feel someone other than Simon. Because I need to know that Simon isn't the only man in the world. Because I've been feeling like shit and I know Jeff fancies me and I need to still feel that there are other possibilities.'

Mel sighed deeply. 'I know you're going to do it,

Tash, but be careful. This really isn't what you need right now.'

I put the phone down and poured another drink. Dutch courage, and at ten fifteen I put on a silk dressing gown and that was all. At ten thirty, on the dot, just at the time Jeff said he'd arrive, the doorbell went.

'Hi,' he said, 'I didn't think I'd make it on . . .' and he stopped, because I had already wrapped my arms and legs around him like an octopus and I started to kiss him passionately, forcing his mouth open with my tongue, stopping him from saying anything else.

I wish I could tell you the kiss was worth it, but it wasn't, it was pure performance on my part. I felt nothing. Absolutely nothing, but I had to go through with it, had to prove something to myself and to Simon. *In absentia.*

'Wow,' Jeff said eventually, hooking his arms round my waist, 'you are hot stuff.' I didn't want to hear his voice, didn't even want to look at him so I just pulled him by the hand and led him to the bedroom.

Talk about aggressive. I pushed him back on the bed and he lay there, arms behind his head grinning at me as I undid the belt on my dressing gown and let it slip to the floor.

'Jesus you are beautiful,' he said, reaching up to stroke my breasts, and then he didn't say any more because I climbed on top of him and furiously unbuttoned his shirt, unzipped his trousers, pulled his clothes off.

'Slow down,' he whispered, 'there's no hurry.' I moved down his body, down to where his cock stood erect and I knew I had to take him in my mouth. As I closed my mouth over his straining cock, I heard him gasp, and I knelt there, crouched over his body, head bobbing up and down as I swirled my tongue round the tip and took him all the way to the back of my throat.

I felt nothing. He moved his hand between my legs and started stroking me, and I felt nothing. I lay back and he climbed on top of me, gently pushing my legs apart and I expertly rolled a condom on and guided him inside me. He was kissing me all the time, kissing my eyes, my lips, my cheeks, my neck. 'Do you know how long I've dreamt about this,' he whispered. And I felt nothing. Numb, numb, numb.

And then, as he was moving inside me, faster and faster, getting closer and closer, I felt a huge wave move up from my stomach, up through the tightness in my chest and I started sobbing. Like a fucking child. There I was, lying underneath this man who was practically a stranger and I was crying like a baby. Talk about passion-killer. *Coitus interruptus* by tears. All I kept thinking was it's not Simon. I want Simon.

But Jeff, and I have to say I was surprised, Jeff was absolutely amazing. He moved out of me, lay beside me and put his arms around me. I kept on sobbing and he didn't say anything, he just cradled me in his arms, gently rubbing my back, and I carried on crying for the best part of an hour.

Eventually, when I had finished crying, and just lay there sniffing, Jeff got up, went to the bathroom and came back with a tissue. He held it under my nose like a child and said, 'OK, blow.' And I blew and I smiled because although the sex was a complete waste of time, something in me had shifted. I can't tell you everything was OK after that night, but everything started to get a little bit better.

You make slow progress when you come out of a relationship with a man you love. Every day is another step, and in the beginning there are so many setbacks you feel as if you won't make it. But slowly you realise that every step backwards is preceded by three steps forward, and one day they're not just steps, you're making huge bounds.

My first setback, not counting Jeff, was when Adam called me a week later.

'Hi, baby. I wanted to check you're OK.'

I sighed. 'I'm OK, Ad. Not much better than that though. Have you spoken to Simon?'

'I spoke to him last night, he's in a terrible state.'

My heart turned over, maybe it's true what they say, give them some space and they realise what they're missing, they realise they've made a huge mistake.

'Why, how?'

'Well, I shouldn't tell you this, Tash, but he does miss you. He said he keeps wondering if he's made a terrible mistake.'

'So he's not with Tanya then?'

There was a silence. 'Yes,' he said finally. 'He is with Tanya but I think he's confused. Tanya has somehow got under his skin, and he can't let her go, but he also realises what he's lost in you. To tell you the truth, Tash, I don't think he's ever going to find another woman like you.' I wanted to put down the phone, grab my coat and go running into Simon's arms. To put my arms around him and say it's OK, I'm here now, everything's going to be OK.

But of course I couldn't do that because everything was not going to be OK because right at that moment, while I was talking to Adam, Simon was probably sitting there with Tanya's arms around him, and she was probably telling him that everything was going to be OK.

'Tash? Are you there, Tash? I'm sorry, have I made a mistake in telling you, I didn't mean to upset you.'

'No, it's OK, Ad. I'm fine, it just hurts to hear he's hurting. Bastard.' I smile and I hear Adam laugh down the phone.

'That's more like it, there's the Tash we all know and love.'

'*Do* you love me, Ad?'

'Of course I do, Tash. You've become one of my closest friends, and I hate to hear you in such pain. I shouldn't say this because Simon's such a good friend, but you know you really do deserve better, and you will find it.'

'I know,' I say, even though I don't know at all, but it sounds better than thank you.

Jeff was my first step back to life after Simon, but he wasn't the last, not by a long shot. It was almost as if I had to prove I was still loveable, still sexual, still human by sleeping with everyone who asked me.

I'm not proud of that time, although while I was going through it I stuck a big smile on my face and kept everyone amused with my latest stories.

There was Jamie, who was so good-looking and so crap in bed. Who wouldn't stop until I faked five orgasms, and even then, even when I told him he had to stop because I was exhausted, even then asked, 'Do you want to go to sleep or do you want some more cock?'

There was Tony who I met at a party, who phoned and who I seduced, just for the hell of it. Yes I fancied him, in as much as I could fancy anyone who wasn't Simon, but the sex was rubbish. Not just with him, the sex was always crap because I didn't care about them and they didn't care about me.

Sure I made all the right noises, I pretended to be this wild, abandoned woman while feeling completely dead inside. But I knew that eventually I would stop, when I started to come back to life I would stop.

No one ever judged me, although I never heard what they said when I wasn't around, but Mel used to try and talk me through it, try and explain that sex wasn't love, and I didn't have to do this, and that was when she recommended me going to see Louise.

The last time it happened was just after I started seeing Louise. I went to a party with Adam, Adam who knew all about it, Adam who didn't judge, merely laughed with me as I regaled him with my ridiculous tales.

Adam who occasionally glimpsed through the pain, who would put his arms around me and give me a great big hug, while I buried my head in his shoulder and tried hard not to cry.

Adam saw me come back to life again, and he was there the night I said no. The night I realised that a stranger's arms held nothing for me any longer.

The party was at a house in Fulham. A friend of a friend of a friend, and it was like the parties of my youth. A student party in a professional's house, one of those terraced houses with a double reception room, a kitchen at the back and french doors opening onto the garden.

It was a french bread and pâté party, a cheap wine and dustbin filled with ice and beer kind of party. As soon as we walked in it became clear that it was full of old friends Adam hadn't seen in years.

'Ad,' shrieked pretty much everyone there, rushing up to slap him on the back and wrap their arms around him. 'This is Tasha,' he tried to say, but they weren't interested in me, only in their old friend.

Except for one bloke in the corner, just my type. Tall, short brown hair and big green eyes. He was wearing faded jeans and a T-shirt and he was watching everyone greet Adam with a look of intense amusement in his eyes. Finally he sauntered over. 'Jesus,' said Adam, 'I thought you were living in America.'

'I was,' said Jesus, who turned out to be called Sam, 'but I came back a couple of months ago.' His accent had a slight American drawl, and as he turned to look at me I knew that he was the only man at that party worth bothering with, and I knew from that first look we'd be going home together.

'You must be Adam's girlfriend,' he said, shaking my hand.

'No,' laughed Adam, 'Tasha's my friend who happens to be a girl. Unfortunately.'

'Are you anyone's girlfriend?' asked Sam, and I mutely shook my head, wondering what he'd look like without his T-shirt, how his skin would feel, whether he'd groan with pleasure.

'I'm single, definitely single.' I raised an eyebrow.

'And searching?' His turn to raise an eyebrow.

'I'm always searching.'

'For your other half?'

'Wrong.' I laughed. 'About as far away from the truth as you can get. No, just searching for fun, looking to enjoy myself.'

'Permanently or temporarily.'

'Permanently having fun, it's just the people who are temporary.'

'Men I presume.'

'Women aren't my style'

'So where do you meet these men?'

'Where do you think?'

'Parties like this?'

I smiled knowingly and looked into my beer before

looking up again, looking him deep in the eyes and repeating slowly, 'Parties like this.'

'I thought you and Adam were together. Are you really just friends?'

I frowned, 'Why would you think we were together, just because we arrived together?'

'No, there seemed to be some chemistry between you.'

'Very perceptive,' I smiled. 'But very wrong. I went out with one of Adam's friends once, that was how we met, and we've become friends ever since.'

'Good. I'm glad that happened or we wouldn't have met.'

'Good.'

Adam walked back up to us and put his big arms round my waist. 'I hope you're not chatting up my friend,' he said to Sam, who just smiled. 'Careful of him,' he said to me, 'the biggest heartbreaker at school, not to mention university.'

'You've known each other that long?' I looked at Adam in amazement, and he nodded with a grin.

'Yup, we used to beat each other up on the rugby field.'

'Oh God,' groaned Sam. 'Don't remind me. He was a complete rugger bugger. Thank God that's changed.'

'Careful,' said Adam, 'it doesn't take much to get on my bad side, and rugby tackling is still my speciality.' We all laugh.

'So what was Adam like at school?' I say to Sam.

'Well,' he smiles at Adam. 'No, I can't lie. The teachers dreaded teaching him but you could always tell they had a real soft spot for him.'

'Why did they dread teaching him?'

Adam groans. 'Oh please, not the old school stories.'

'No no,' says Sam. 'I've started so I'll finish. He was

always clever, but he didn't, what was that phrase, he didn't apply himself. He used to sit at the back of the class and drop stinkbombs. I remember one time he got hold of a can of mace and squirted it during a maths lesson.'

'Jesus, I'd forgotten that.'

'Mrs Jenkins didn't. The whole class had to be evacuated and they had a huge investigation but they never found out who it was. That was one of his better tricks, although in terms of popularity it worked, he was infamous for years afterwards. Now, what else can I tell you about Adam?'

'Stop it now,' warns Adam, but this is all new to me, I'm dying to hear about Adam's schooldays.

'What about that time you sneaked that girl into the dorm and she had to hide under the bed when Matron came in.'

'I'd hoped you had forgotten that,' says Adam, but he's smiling.

'This poor girl had to dive under the bed while we all stood in front to hide her.'

'Did she get caught?' I'm fascinated.

'Luckily no,' laughs Adam. 'She was really nice,' he says dreamily, obviously thinking back to memories he hadn't thought about in years.

'But what were you planning to do with her in a crowded dorm, Ad?'

'I don't think even *I* knew that,' he laughs. 'I just wanted to get her up there to give the boys something to talk about. Anyway, Sam was the real heartbreaker, especially at university.'

'I've changed,' said Sam. 'University was a long time ago.'

'Do people really change?' I said. 'I don't think they do, not that much, leopards not changing their spots and all that. I suspect you probably are still a heartbreaker, and I suspect you probably enjoy it.'

'What about Adam then?' says Sam with a wicked grin. 'Is he still dropping stinkbombs and sneaking girls into his bedroom.'

'I haven't dropped a stinkbomb in at least ten days,' says Adam, laughing, 'and as for the girls, I rarely get to sneak them anywhere these days. Unfortunately.'

'Oh Ad,' I reach up and give him a friendly squeeze. If only he could find a woman, but right at this moment in time I'm more concerned with me finding a man. Or to be more precise, Sam, who is once again holding my gaze so steadily I have to look away.

Adam was aware of the chemistry, how could he have missed it as it hung heavy in the air between the three of us as we stood there not saying anything. 'Right, I'm off to get another beer,' said Adam moving away. 'Anyone want anything?' and we both shook our heads as he walked off.

Sam looked at me and asked, 'What were we talking about?'

'You. Being a heartbreaker.'

'Oh yes. And you're so different? I don't think so. Why do you think we're talking, you're the female version of me.'

'What the hell do you mean by that?'

'Don't take offence, please, we've only just met, but I could tell as soon as I saw you. You're a hedonist, taking pleasure wherever you find it and there's nothing wrong with that, believe me. Nothing wrong at all.'

'I'm glad you think that there's nothing wrong with it. I wouldn't want you to get the wrong impression about me.'

'Oh, wouldn't you? What kind of impression would you want me to have of you?'

'What kind of impression would you want?'

It was that kind of meaningless, ridiculous conversation that is endlessly going round and round in flirtatious circles, and can only end up in one place . . . the bedroom.

'How about the kind of impression that lingers in the sheets?' It was his turn for the questioning look.

'How about it?' said I, Tasha on self-destruct, Tasha who didn't care.

'Can you leave Adam?'

'I can leave anyone.'

'Let's go. I'll get my coat.'

Sam walked upstairs to get his jacket, and suddenly I knew this was wrong. I didn't want another stranger, I didn't need to spend the night in a bed I didn't know, with a man I didn't want to know. I wanted to go to sleep in my bed, in my house, alone.

'Adam, we have to go, quickly. I'm sorry.' Adam didn't question me, he heard the urgency in my voice and he just pushed me out the front door before Sam had even reappeared downstairs.

We got in the car and as we drove off I started laughing. Adam looked at me strangely, carried on driving, and then eventually, while I was wiping the tears of laughter from my cheeks, said, 'What the hell is going on?'

'Oh Adam, I'm sorry, I'm sorry to drag you away, but I had to go. Sam was about to whisk me home and I couldn't go, I can't do this any more. Adam, I'm happy. I'm really, really fine. I'm fine without Simon and I'm fine on my own. This feels amazing.'

Adam should have been royally pissed off with me, for pulling him away from friends he hadn't seen for years, but I knew he'd do this for me, and he stopped the car and gave me a big hug. 'I knew you'd make it, Tash,' he said, and I could hear he was smiling deep in my hair.

Then he sat back and said, 'Let's go and find somewhere to drink champagne. We need to celebrate and it's on me.'

– *Twelve* –

'So what did Adam do?' Andy's leaning forward, trying to get every last bit of the anecdote out of me. We're all here at lunch again, our Saturday ritual, and I'm telling them all about Andrew.

'I don't know, he seems a bit funny about it, and I can't really talk to him about it, I just don't feel comfortable but I don't know why.'

'Tash, have you ever thought that maybe Adam has a soft spot for you?' asks Mel.

'I've always thought that,' says Andy, as Emma adds, 'Yeah, me too.'

'Are you all serious?' I look around the scrubbed pine table and see that they are. And don't you start too. Adam and me? No way.

'Why not?' says Mel. 'He's your best male friend. He's a good man, he's honourable, he's decent and he's good-looking, what more could a girl ask for?'

'Yeah but he's *Adam*,' I say, 'and there isn't anything between us, you're all wrong, I know he feels the same way as me, that we're just friends.'

'I think you're wrong,' says Emma. 'I don't know him well but when I have seen you two together he does seem to adore you.'

'Of course he does, in the same way that I adore him, the platonic way.'

They all smile knowingly but they don't know, I know and they're wrong.

'But anyway, we're not here to talk about Adam, we're talking about Andrew, what do you think?'

'You know what we think,' says Mel. 'He's gorgeous but he's a total shit, and he'll hurt you, no two ways about it.'

'I know,' I sigh, 'but I don't know what to do, I'm not sure whether I can stop myself.'

'Of course you can,' says Andy, the woman who wouldn't know how to stop if all the red lights in the world were flashing, 'you just say no. Anyway, there are plenty more where he came from.'

A silence falls on the table as we all contemplate her last statement. We've all said it, but none of us really believes it. How easy is it to find a man, I think. A good, kind, decent man who has the required amounts of good looks, charisma and chemistry?

It's not easy, not easy at all. Yes there are always men around, but how often do we get it right? How often do we feel the same way as they feel about us.

Emma sits there thinking she has to hang on to Richard, she has to marry him because she won't find anyone else. Mel is thinking, I do deserve better than Daniel, and maybe I have got the strength to end it all for good, and Andy is thinking, another day another man.

'Have you invited him to my barbeque?' asks Andy eventually. It is her party tomorrow, the party which will doubtless be a huge success because Andy has spent weeks creating the food, the drink, the ambience, the guest list, the numbers of available men.

'Can I?' A grin as I contemplate a whole evening

with him, an evening where perhaps, if I look as good as I've ever looked, perhaps he might change his mind. Perhaps he might decide that he wants more than a fling, perhaps he might look at me and think I am the kind of woman he could love after all.

'Then we can all meet him!' says Andy excitedly.

'Hands off,' I say, suddenly serious because I know that Andrew will be just her type, in fact, if I think about it they would make a great couple. Andrew and Andy, the perfect match, except they are so similar, they would both be constantly fighting for centre stage.

'As if I would,' she says, noticing that I am not joking. 'I won't go near him but what *will* you do if he chats someone else up?'

'What *can* I do?' I shrug. 'If he makes a beeline for someone else, there's nothing I can do, but if any of you lot make a beeline for him, I'll shoot you.'

'Don't worry,' says Andy, 'I wouldn't be interested anyway, I've had enough of men for the moment.' And then she adds ominously, 'After last night.'

'Uh oh. What happened last night?'

'Remember Tim?' How could we forget? Tim was the man Andy picked up at yet another party, and he's been phoning her every night for the last two weeks.

'Of course we remember Tim,' offers Mel. 'You saw him last night?'

'Yes,' Andy says with a grimace, 'I saw *all* of him last night.'

'You mean he shagged you senseless and now you've gone off him?' I don't mean to sound this harsh, but please. This has happened so many times before.

'No, we never actually got to the shagging stage, it was awful.'

We're all alert now, all desperate to hear what

happened, a touch of *schadenfreude* never did anyone any harm. Did it?

'We went out for dinner and then he came in.'

'For coffee?' says Emma, and we all laugh, knowing that none of us ever invites a man in just for coffee.

'For coffee, and then as we were standing in the doorway he kissed me, which was fine.'

'Fine?' I say. 'That doesn't sound encouraging.'

'Well, the kissing was OK, but then he started doing this really peculiar thing, he started banging his groin against mine really quickly.'

'What do you mean. Grinding?'

'Well not exactly, because that can be quite sexy, but he was banging away and I was standing there thinking what *is* he doing? Does he think this is turning me on?'

We still haven't quite grasped it so she stand up to demonstrate, oblivious to the curious stares from other diners in the restaurant. She stands there, in her slim-fitting beige trousers, and effectively simulates sex standing up, sex right at the end, just before orgasm, when the pounding becomes fast and furious, and it looks so ridiculous we all open our mouths in amazement.

'So then what did you do?' Emma's looking horrified.

'Well I decided to give him the benefit of the doubt. I mean after all, this guy's thirty-nine, I assumed he had to know what he was doing so we went to bed. But he didn't, he didn't have a clue.'

'What do you mean? You think he's a virgin?'

'I really think he might be.' Her voice lowers as she prepares to confide the intimate details. 'I got undressed, and he lay on the bed and he started kneading my breasts as if they were lumps of dough.'

'No nipple rolling then?' Yup, me again.

'No, far from it, he ignored the nipples completely. He just kept kneading away and I was lying there getting more and more bored. Then,' she pauses for dramatic effect, 'then he moved down my body and I thought, this is better, at least I'll get some oral sex out of it, but he didn't seem to know what he was doing.'

'So you did have oral sex?' Emma, despite being the most prudish of all of us on the surface, is not so different underneath.

'No, he sort of knelt between my legs and fumbled at my crotch, but he didn't actually seem to do anything, he didn't seem to know where anything was.'

'Didn't you show him?'

'I thought about it, but I decided it was too much hard work, and I should just lie there and let him get it over and done with.'

'So then what happened?'

'Well this is the worst part. He knelt there fumbling for ages, and I just lay there with my eyes closed, feeling as if I was having a medical examination, and eventually, after about five minutes he whispered, "Andy?" And I whispered back, "Yes?" And he said, "Are you asleep?" '

We all screamed with laughter, at the notion of Andy, Andy who is normally so rapacious, being so inert with boredom her partner thought she had fallen asleep in the middle of foreplay.

'That's how bloody bored I was, can you believe it?'

We start a fresh round of sex stories. Each of us has the worst experience of our life to share with the others, and then, when we have all spoken, we start a fresh round, more memories, more laughter. We stay there, heads huddled together round the table, speaking softly, then moving apart to wipe the tears of laughter from our eyes, for a very long time.

*

I leave a message on Andrew's machine. A message that sounds professional, friendly and cool. 'If you're not doing anything tomorrow, my friend Andy is having a barbeque and I thought you might like to come. It starts at around three, and her address is bottom bell, 15 Queens Gardens. Hopefully see you there.'

I love Sundays. I love the feeling of waking up in the morning and knowing that there's nothing to get up for. I don't even mind being alone on a Sunday, not being able to reach out and stroke the man you love.

My typical Sunday? I wake up early, always, and call Harvey and Stanley over for a big cuddle. Harvey's a big softie, happy for me to tickle his tummy while purring big deep grumbles of love. Stanley's a bit more independent. Stanley likes to be near me, hates missing out on any of the action, but try and pick him up and he'll run for cover.

So after our group love-in, or rather my love-in with Harvey while Stanley plays voyeur, I stumble out of bed in my nightdress, sling a coat on top and walk down the road to buy the Sunday papers.

Every time I do this I thank God I'm not famous. Jesus, if I was Annalise, the tabloids would be falling over themselves to capture me like this. BLONDE BOMBSHELL BECOMES BAG LADY I suspect the caption would run. Looking the way I look right now I'd have to opt for homeless.

The papers I buy are always the same – *The Sunday Times* and the *News of the World*. Occasionally, if there's a story I've been following for the show, I'll buy all of them and frantically skim-read the relevant bits. But usually it's just the two, and, walking back along the road to my flat, I hug them to my chest to stop my bra-less breasts getting too excited.

And back to bed with toast and occasionally a boiled egg. I eat in bed while reading, first *Sunday* magazine, then the *News of the World*, then the Style section, then the magazine – Zoe Heller, my heroine – and then the News Review.

Today I can't concentrate though, today's the day I'm going to see Andrew so I give the rest of the paper a quick glance, even though I can't really be bothered, and then the clock tells me it's time to get ready. It's 1.24 and I promised Andy I'd help her with the food. Yesterday afternoon I made a huge salad with roasted peppers and asparagus, and now, pulling it out the fridge, I add the finishing touches with some fresh parmesan. Next to it is a bowl of potato salad, mixed with *crème fraîche*, mayonnaise and sprinkled with parsley and chives, and I stop at the deli on the way over and pick up some fresh, hot baguettes.

I battle up the path to Andy's, trying to balance the bread on the bowl on the other bowl, and just as I'm thinking shit, the whole thing's going to go flying, Andy opens the front door and comes whizzing out to help me. She's already high as a kite on the excitement of a party, albeit a barbeque during the day, and she flits around her tiny kitchen putting the finishing touches on the food and crisply snapping clingfilm on before taking the bowls into the garden.

'You're not wearing that, are you?' I say, looking at her uncharacteristic tracksuit bottoms and greying T-shirt.

'God no!' she laughs. 'Are you mad? I've got the perfect little number upstairs that I bought yesterday, I just didn't want to get it dirty. I'll go up and change in a minute.'

'What about a quick drink before you do?' I look slyly at her, knowing that however much time it will take her to expertly apply her 'face', she'll never turn down the offer of a drink.

I proffer a bottle of white wine but she shakes her head before whirling around the kitchen opening cupboard doors, looking for something.

'Pimms, Pimms, we need a Pimms,' she says, finally locating the bottle she bought earlier that week.

We sit there and toast one another. 'Here's to summer,' she says. 'To summer. And to handsome men.' We sit there each thinking of the next one. 'To true love,' I say. 'To true love,' she echoes. 'To passion,' I say, and she laughs and nods her head, echoing loudly and firmly, 'To passion!' and we both take big long swigs.

The food is on the table, every available chair has been dragged out into the garden and Andy has proved to be a dab hand with a barbeque which has just caught light, the flames leaping high above the grills. From the stereo perched on the window sill the Gypsy Kings fill the air, and summer has finally arrived.

'So will he come?' asks Andy.

'Who?'

'Andrew, who else?'

'I don't know,' I try to shrug nonchalantly. 'I left a message so if he comes, he comes.'

'So what do you think, will you go for it?'

'I don't know, Andy. In the beginning it would have been fine, it would have been, you know, just a fuck, but now I like him.'

'Yeah but if he comes on to you again, surely you won't say no.'

'Probably not. God knows, willpower has never been my strong point. Heartbreak, here I come again.'

Within an hour the garden has filled up with friends from the different walks of Andy's life, not to mention mine. There are her work colleagues, her old schoolfriends, her friends from her courses, and us. Adam can't make it, he has to drive to the country for a family do, but the rest of my inner circle is here.

Emma and Richard are standing together, Emma looking stunning in a long white floaty number, with one hand protectively around Richard's waist as they talk to Andy.

Andy is doing her Hollywood hostess film star bit, big tortoiseshell sunglasses, a tight lime green shirt with an A-line mini skirt and high, high strappy heels that are slowly sinking into the grass as I watch.

Pathetic, I think, eyeing my own flat black mules, pathetic that on a sunny summer's day Andy still has to go over the top, but perhaps I'm a little envious of the looks she's attracting . . .

The doorbell keeps ringing and people keep striding out of the kitchen with cans of beer, plates of meat, marinaded chicken breasts, lamb skewered onto metal sticks. I'm talking to Mel, trying to ignore Daniel dick-for-brains eyeing me up and down lasciviously, but one corner of my eye is constantly on the kitchen doorway, checking to see when he'll arrive. Whether he'll arrive.

'You're not with us, are you?' says Mel as Daniel wanders off. She follows my quick look at a nondescript couple of men who have just walked in.

'Sorry, Mel, I just can't believe how nervous I am.'

'What, because of Andrew?'

'Well yeah. I know it's stupid but I haven't had a crush on someone for ages, and I know that's what it is, a crush, but I can't help it. I'm going to be so bloody pissed off if he doesn't turn up.'

A crush. The very word brings up memories of

teenage years. Of going to parties praying for the object of your crush to be there. Of treasuring his every sentence, every look, every touch. Of lying awake at night daydreaming about what the two of you could do together.

But crushes rarely come off do they, at least not in my experience. The relationships that you have creep up on you, take you unawares. The relationships you have are not with men who provide fodder for your dreams. They are the men who pursue you, and you, through a process of flattery, insecurity and need, grow to love them in return.

The crushes never amount to anything other than a few weeks of dizzy excitement, followed by the pain of disappointment.

'I don't know, Tash, I still think he's dangerous.'

'But since when was danger not allowed?' I smile.

We both turn as we notice a male presence hovering, and Mel beams her sunshine smile and introduces herself.

'I'm Martin.' An average-looking bloke with a shy smile shakes both our hands, only shooting me a cursory glance before fixing his attention on Mel. 'I hear you're a therapist too?'

'Too? You're a therapist as well? God, how amazing, I never seem to meet other therapists at my friends' parties.' Mel, being Mel, is as bright and friendly to this stranger as she is to everyone. I watch him instantly relax, and soon the two of them are chattering away together, and Mel is making him throw his head back with laughter.

This is good for Mel I think, as I look around to see where Daniel is and spot him through the kitchen window, leering animatedly at Annie, a slim, exotic beauty who, at this very moment, is smiling blankly and answering Daniel's inquisition with monosyllables, obviously desperate to get away.

'Excuse me,' I say to Mel and Martin – now there's a good couple in the making – as I back off, leaving the two of them to get on with their conversation, and I honestly don't think either of them notice, they're so taken with each other.

'Who's Martin?' I whisper in Andy's ear as she's standing next to the barbeque turning the sausages.

'Who?' she says, a hint of excitment at there being an available man at her party who she doesn't know.

'Martin. The guy talking to Mel.'

'I don't know,' she says, looking at him, her face falling with lack of interest as she quickly assesses the fact that he is not her type. 'He came with Tom.' She turns to me in horror. 'You can't be interested in him, surely? He's the sort of man who eats quiche for breakfast, lunch and dinner every day. Not *your* type at all.'

So what, you're probably asking yourself, but I can see her point. I mean whoever coined the phrase that real men don't eat quiche was definitely onto something, and this guy, pleasant though he seemed, wasn't nearly enough of a bastard for me.

Yes, I'd like a nice guy, wouldn't we all, but put me in a room with ninety-nine quiche-eaters and one rare steak kind of a guy and who do you think I'll choose? Exactly.

'Andy, just because I ask who someone is doesn't mean I want to rip their trousers off, for Christ's sake. He seems to be getting on with Mel, that's all, and he seems like a nice guy.'

'Hmm. I think they're ready, do you want a sausage? SAUSAGE ANYONE?' she shouts out, holding a charred black sausage on the end of a fork.

Funny how drink seems to affect you more during the day. By six there are some seriously shit-faced people at the barbeque. The music's been turned up, and as the sun starts losing its lustre you can see it's going to be a long night.

It would also be a bloody good one if Andrew was here, but, and don't tell me you're not surprised, but the bastard hasn't turned up.

I've avoided drinking too much all day because I know what I'm like with a bit too much alcohol. My mascara will run, my eyes will be bloodshot and I'll turn a rather unattractive shade of flushed red. But Jesus, if the only man I fancy isn't coming, I may as well drown those sorrows somehow.

Andy's running around flapping that there isn't enough food, Emma's entwined with Richard at one end of the garden and Mel, well, Mel isn't anywhere to be seen. Neither is Martin.

Daniel's worked his way through all the women at the party, and, deciding there are no conquests to be made, he's talking football with some of the other guys. I watch them for a while, contemplating whether or not to join them because one of them is rather nice, but just as I'm about to walk over I see that Andy has the same idea.

There she is, shaking their hands, throwing her head back with laughter, flirting outrageously with the man I had my eye on. If I wasn't waiting for Andrew I might have been pissed off, but she's welcome to him. Tonight.

I grab the Pimms, pour myself what would surely constitute a triple in any decent bar, and head for the bathroom to check my hair and make-up. Just in case. The strangest thing happens as I'm coming out the bathroom, I hear Mel's familiar peal of laughter coming from a bedroom with a closed door.

Jesus, she wouldn't. Would she? No. Can't be. I hover for a few minutes outside the door, debating whether or not to knock but actually I'm listening for some heavy breathing or groans. I don't hear anything other than soft voices, two, Mel and, presumably, Martin, so eventually I knock. The voices stop abrubtly, and then footsteps.

The door is wrenched open and a guilty-looking Mel breathes a huge sigh of relief as she sees me. 'Oh God, I thought it was Daniel.'

'What are you two up to?' I ask with a sly sideways look at Mel, as I jump on the bed and lean back against the pillows.

'As if,' says Mel with a grin. 'You have such a one-track mind.'

Oh excuse me, reader, but wouldn't you have jumped to the same conclusion? I thought so.

'Well?' I push. 'Shooting the breeze or shooting something else?'

Martin looks embarrassed but Mel just laughs. 'Ignore her,' she says, giving me a shove. 'We're just talking. It turns out we both studied at the same place.'

'No!' I exclaim in surprise, which unfortunately comes out sounding ever so slightly sarcastic. I rectify matters by asking politely, 'Did you know each other?'

'I was there a few years before actually,' says Martin.

'Which would make you, hmm? Let's see, thirty-six?'

'Stop it,' warns Mel, laughing.

'Stop what? So, Martin, are you married?'

'Nope.'

'When was your last relationship?'

'A year ago.'

'Why did you break up?'

'We just grew apart.'

'So you don't have a fear of commitment, then, Martin?'

'Are you sure you're not a therapist too?'

'Evasion. Answer the question.'

We're all laughing as he shakes his head, 'No, I don't have a fear of commitment.'

'Children?'

'Not that I know of.'

'Where do you live?'

'Hampstead-ish.'

' –ish?'

'South End Green.'

'Hampstead-ish. Yes, you pass the test, Martin whatever-your-surname is, welcome to our lives.'

Martin's grinning broadly and he leans over and gives me a huge kiss on the cheek. 'That was the most unusual welcome I've ever had.'

'Sorry,' says Mel, 'but we love her anyway. God, Tash, I'm surprised you didn't ask Martin his annual income.'

'Damn.' I slap my leg. 'I knew I'd forgotten something.'

Martin stands up and says he's going to get a drink. I'm fine with my Pimms, and Mel asks for a mineral water.

'So, tell me, tell me, tell me.'

'Tell you what, Tasha? That I've been having a very interesting chat with a very nice guy?'

'Yeah, but that's not all it is, I can tell, I've known you long enough.'

'Tasha, Martin's lovely, but I'm already in a relationship. When are you going to stop pairing me up with people. I'm very happy.'

But there's doubt in her eyes and I can't stop myself mumbling, 'With Daniel the asshole? I think not.'

'So where's the hunk then? Has he turned up?'

'No he bloody hasn't.' But then I think, shit, he might be here, he might have arrived while I was up here and someone else, someone in a lime green shirt and A-line skirt might have her claws in him already.

But just then the door opens and Andy runs in. 'God, I've met the most amazing man,' she says, as Mel and I start to laugh. 'Did you see him, Tash? The one talking to Daniel?' I nod. 'Isn't he gorgeous?' I nod again, smiling, relieved that just this once, she's not competition.

'He said he'd stay later if I wanted and help me clear up. Wish me luck!' she says with a wink, and she's gone.

Mel and I stand up and I turn to her with a quizzical look. 'Aren't you going to stay here and wait for the lovely Martin?'

Mel smooths down the front of her tunic-dress thing. 'No, I'll come with, I've been up here ages, Daniel will be wondering where I am.'

At two o'clock in the morning my doorbell goes. Fast asleep, a bell seems to be ringing in my dreams, and finally, after the third time I wake up. What the fuck is going on?

Stumbling into a dressing gown, my head still groggy with alcohol I shout out, 'Hello? Who is it?'

Nothing. I put the chain on the door and open it to see Mel, hair all over the place, red-rimmed eyes and cardigan done up with all the buttons in the wrong buttonholes, looking, in other words, bloody terrible.

'Mel? What's the matter?' I undo the chain and put my arms around her just as her face starts to collapse and tears start pouring from her eyes.

'He, he he . . .' She can't talk, her sobs are growing stronger and she's fighting to talk. 'He's left me. What am I going to do? What am I going to do?'

Fear of abandonment is a phrase bandied about by everyone I know who's ever been in therapy, or into pop psychology. We sit there and discuss the reasons behind it for hours, with very serious looks on our faces as we each try to outdo one another with the pain of our abandonment.

But the odd thing is that even when we're terrified of being left, when we decide we've had enough of the fuckers, when we decide we want to go it alone we can handle it. We can cope with the pain because it's our decision, and in a strange way we take strength from that.

But heaven forbid it should be their decision. No matter how unhappy we are, how low our self-esteem has sunk, when they turn around, out of the blue and tell us they're leaving, they've had enough, we collapse, turning into heartbroken children all over again.

So I lead Mel into the living room and sit her down on the sofa, not removing my arm from around her shoulders, and I let her lean her head against my body and cry until she manages to compose herself.

'What am I going to do?' she keeps repeating. 'What am I going to do?'

Eventually the story comes out. Daniel ignored her for the rest of the party, and on the way home started his usual litany of how she could improve herself.

'He told me I was ridiculous, that I was flirting with

Martin who would never be interested in me because I was such a state. He told me I'd put on weight, that I looked dowdy, frumpy and ugly. He said he was only with me out of habit, and it was a good job because if he wasn't I'd never find another man.'

I'm so horrified I can't think of what to say and she continues. 'I was so upset I told him that actually Martin did fancy me and he wanted my phone number but I didn't give it to him, I told him I was already in a relationship.

'He said that quite frankly he'd had enough of taking me out and being embarrassed and maybe I should be with someone like Martin instead, who he seems to think is infinitely inferior to him.'

'Oh God, Mel, then what?'

'Then we got home and he started packing my clothes in a suitcase. He told me I should get out and go to Martin, that he didn't want me around anymore, that he should have done this years ago.' And with this comes a fresh round of sobs.

What do you say when your friend splits up with a bastard and comes round to cry on your shoulder? All the usual epithets come out – you deserve better; you'll find someone else; he's never treated you well – but you know that nothing will make them feel better.

So I just listen thinking why do we bother, why do any of us bother, and eventually, when Mel's cried out, I put her to bed and sit in my kitchen with a cup of tea and a hundred cigarettes, and I wonder where we've all gone wrong.

– Thirteen –

It's been three weeks and Daniel the asshole hasn't bothered to call Mel. Oh no, I am the one who has to phone him to arrange a convenient time – eight o'clock on a bloody Monday morning – to pick up her stuff.

And what does the bastard do as soon as I walk in? Lunges at me, telling me he's always fancied me and now he is a free agent too, why don't we get it together. I can't believe his audacity, I am so damned shocked I can't even speak.

It is only when he moves towards me and presses against me until I am backed up against a wall that I finally find my voice.

'What the fuck do you think you're doing?' Ice-cold and hard as steel.

'Come on, Tasha, you know you want to.'

'Jesus you're disgusting. I'm amazed that Mel stayed with you as long as she did, and, incidentally, even if I were to take you up on your offer I know I'd be disappointed.'

His expression suddenly changes, the leer replaced by uncertainty. 'What do you mean?'

'Well, not that Mel is indiscreet, but let's just say that my four-year-old cousin is better hung than you.'

That gets him. He moves away immediately and

doesn't say another word, while I push past him and run round the flat trying to find everything on the list Mel had hurriedly scribbled last night.

Aromatherapy oils in basket in bathroom (leave the patchouli, – it's disgusting!)

Scarf Emma gave me for my birthday (purple with silver mirrors – in left-hand cupboard).

Birkenstock sandals under the bed.

Contents of drawer in left bedside table.

Papier mache jewellery box on dressing table and all contents within.

Wok in kitchen. (Not Habitat one – one from China in bottom cupboard)

Grey box files on top bookshelf in living room.

I keep passing Daniel as I run downstairs with my arms full of boxes; he is sitting at the kitchen table pretending to read the *Daily Telegraph*, refusing to look up as I clatter about.

Eventually it is just the wok, and I march purposefully into the kitchen, looking in horror at the state it's in. Piles of filthy washing-up overflowing out of the sink. Three filthy pots encrusted with food on the stove and a few flies buzzing round hoping to be fed.

'Oh, new pets?' I ask sarcastically.

'What are you talking about?'

'The flies. I'm assuming they're pedigree. Must have cost a fortune.'

'Haven't you finished here yet?' he says, looking more and more pissed off.

'Yup,' I say breezily, pulling the wok out the cupboard. 'I'm off, and do give us a call if you want the name of a good cleaner,' I shout as I disappear down the hallway, slamming the front door before he even has a chance to reply.

It's my show today, and I leave Mel's stuff in the car as I run around like a panicked bride checking that everything's OK.

The guests have all arrived and there have been no last-minute changes, and David and Annalise are in the studio going through their daily half-hour haphazard rehearsal.

'I don't like this,' whines Annalise. 'Teen Chic sounds a bit old-hat. Can't we call it anything else?'

'It is teenage fashion,' says David, trying to placate her. 'I think it's fine.'

'What would you suggest, Annie?' I say into my microphone that travels down to her earpiece.

'Well, what about Teenage Trendsetters?'

'Fine,' I sigh. Once again Annie is trying to make changes just for the sake of being difficult. Any minute now she'll start spouting off about how she's a journalist so she should know better.

'I *am* a journalist,' she smiles graciously at the camera knowing I'm watching, 'and headlines *were* my business.'

Actually headlines weren't her damned business, and if she'd have ever worked for a newspaper she would have known that an editor or a sub writes the headlines, not a bloody journalist. But no, Annalise joined the company as a cub reporter straight out of college doing ridiculous features at the end of the local news on any wacky events that happened to be going on in Hertfordshire, or wherever the hell her television company was based.

And because these soft items happened to be shown at the end of the news, Annalise decided she was a journalist. She wouldn't know a news story if Bob Monkhouse planted a bomb in her Mazda MX5.

'Five minutes to go,' I hear the floor manager say, and, shit, I have to phone Mel before the show starts.

Mel's still staying with me and I have to admit I quite like it. Not that I'm into flat-sharing as a rule, but it makes such a change to have company. We've been acting like a couple of teenagers, jumping on one another's beds and giggling long into the night.

And you know, even though she's still going through pain, I think this has brought us even closer together, if that's possible. I've learnt so much stuff about Mel since she's been staying. I've learnt her stories.

We all have stories, God knows you're probably sick to death of hearing mine, but unless you've got a huge mouth like me, it's rare to hear them. You might hear a few, over the years, but you never hear enough to have the full picture. You form a person in your mind from the stories they tell you but on the rare occasions you have enough time to spend with someone to bond with them, that person in your mind changes, and your friendship enters a whole new level.

Three years into my friendship with Mel I thought she was wonderful. Slightly scatty, full of love, and someone who was very comfortable with who she is.

But these last three weeks I've learnt that Mel doesn't really like herself. That she sees herself through Daniel's eyes and that her relationship with him has gradually worn her down. That she too thinks she is dowdy, frumpy and unattractive, and that she does want to be more like me. And Andy, and Emma.

I've learnt about her childhood, and we've gazed at one another in amazement as we realised how similar they were. That her mother also told her she wasn't good enough, and that Daniel was her mother, in masculine guise.

We've buoyed one another up these last three weeks, and we've shared more than some friends share in a lifetime together.

And I've also learnt that she has an incredible strength. That despite missing Daniel every second of every day, she is willing to get on with her life, to give life a go.

But that doesn't mean she should miss today's phone-in. I catch her before she leaves to go to her clinic.

'Hi darling, it's me. You have to watch the show today, at quarter to twelve you have to be watching the television set.'

'I can't,' she says. 'My patient won't be too happy if I say excuse me if I watch a bit of TV in the middle of our session.'

'Damn. OK, set the video then and we'll both watch it when you come home. You know how to set a video, don't you?'

'Of course, I'm not stone age woman, you know.' I don't bother adding that I haven't got a bloody clue how to set my own video, and on the rare occasions I video something I have to make sure I'm there at the beginning to press the play and record buttons together.

'OK. I'll see you later.'

'Have a good one. Big kiss.' Mel blows me a kiss and then we're on air.

At 11.38 Annalise and David introduce our special celebrity guest. Molly Turner is one of these women who is famous for being famous. No one is exactly sure what she does, except she seems to have made a damn good career from shagging famous men.

Every time one of her new affairs start they pose happily in *Hello!* and she announces that this time it's true love. This time they're going to get married. The woman must have had ten engagement rings, each of them big fuck-off solitaire sparklers.

Her age is indeterminate, but she'll admit to being thirty-eight. I suspect she's more like forty-eight, but she looks damn good. She ought to, the amount of times the surgeon's attacked her with his knife.

And now she's on to talk about her latest affair that just went wrong. Richard Beer is one of the world's wealthiest men, and their engagement party made it into every tabloid – three hundred of their closest friends, most of whom they'd never seen before in their life.

Molly thinks she's here to plug her latest facial exercise book, but after a minute of talking about the book, David launches in.

'So Molly,' he says before she's finished telling us fascinated viewers how much her book is selling for, 'our phone-in today is When Love Goes Sour. This is presumably something you can relate to. Is it true that it's all over between you and Richard Beer?'

Molly smiles graciously and runs a perfectly-manicured hand through her russet red bob. True professional limelight-hogger that she is, she doesn't give a stuff if she talks about her personal life instead of plugging her book. Hell, she's on television, isn't she, still glamourous, still famous.

'Well David,' she purrs in her mid-Atlantic accent, although rumour has it she was born on a council estate in Birmingham. 'I'm in love with love, and every time it comes along I get swept off my feet.'

'How many times have you been engaged now?' says Annie, who quite obviously can't stand the woman, plus she's trying to be a journalist. You know she's a journalist, don't you? Yes, we all bloody know she's a journalist.

'Darling, when you've been engaged as many times as I have you lose count.'

'So tell us what happened with Richard Beer?' says David, who seems to be losing himself in the green of Molly's eyes.

'I was really in love with Richard, and Richard was really in love with me. It was perhaps the most passionate affair of my life, but sometimes things don't work out the way you plan.'

'The papers, although they're probably wrong (David covering himself as usual), reported that he left you for a young model. How did you feel?'

'Delighted for him. Naturally I was upset when he told me, it was via e-mail as well, and of course I have no idea how to work the computer at home so I didn't find out for a week, but if he wants to leave me for someone else, some model, that's his choice, and now I will move on to the next.'

'But hadn't the model – Cora Cherry wasn't it? – hadn't she been a guest at your home in the South of France? That must have been terrible, knowing it was going on under your roof.'

'Richard's a wonderful man who loves beautiful

things. Cora is not only beautiful, she's also very sweet, so in some ways it was almost inevitable.'

Annie laughs in disbelief. 'I'm amazed you're being so magnanimous.' Ooh, we all shout in the gallery, good word, Annie.

'I've been through this too many times to be upset,' says Molly, looking remarkably happy about it. 'I wish Cora good luck. Maybe she'll be better equipped to deal with his more . . .' she pauses. 'More . . . unusual habits.'

Annalise perks up. 'Unusual habits? What sort of unusual habits?'

'Well, Richard is a collector of beautiful things, of paintings, rare Lalique glass, vintage Ferraris and women. If he wants something he will generally buy it, and money is no object, particularly when it comes to women.'

Annalise is looking confused and I'm holding my breath in the gallery. Is she saying what I think she's saying?

'Do you mean he buys women?' David's now looking uncertain, and I'm praying that the lawyers will help me out should this turn out to be a massive case of slander.

'That's a very polite way of putting it.' Molly smiles.

'Did he buy you?' Annalise is looking horrified.

'No darling, he didn't have to, I'm not a call-girl. There are a few men scattered around the world who are incredibly wealthy. Where these men go there will always be women who are after their money. The girls tend to be very young and very beautiful. They would never describe themselves as prostitutes because they don't pick up their clients on a street corner. They are introduced to their clients, and payment generally comes in the form of gifts.

'Occasionally the gifts are cash, and we're talking thousands of dollars – these girls are the very best – but generally it's a gold Rolex, or a diamond bracelet, or a sable coat.'

'So you're saying that Richard Beer uses prostitutes?'

'Richard is a man with a huge sexual appetite and a huge amount of money. That's all I'm saying.'

'Molly, that's all we have time for I'm afraid but thank you for coming in.' Annalise looks at her with total distaste before looking into the camera again. 'Join us after the break for our phone-in, When Love Goes Sour.'

I'm walking into the Green Room – the hospitality area for guests and presenters – after the show when David walks out of his dressing room. 'Oh Annalise,' he says, 'could I have a quick word?' and he holds open the door of his dressing room for me to walk in.

'Sit down,' he smiles and gestures to his make-up chair, and I sit as he stands and leans back against the table in front of me. Because the room is so small we are perhaps a foot apart, and David is asserting himself as the dominant man, towering above me and leaning over ever so slightly.

'Well, Tasha,' he says. 'I think the show today was excellent. Truly, truly excellent.'

I'm so shocked my mouth just drops open. Never in the history of my television career has a presenter ever given such lavish praise.

'We've worked together a while now,' he says, 'and I want you to know that you're an invaluable member of the team. You've come a long way, and I truly believe you have an incredible future ahead of you.'

'David, um, thank you. Christ, I don't really know what to say.'

'Sometimes in television people forget to give credit where it's deserved. It's a fast industry and most of the time we're too busy running around to thank people, so I just wanted you to know how much you mean to this programme.'

This is unheard of and I smile broadly, can't, in fact, wipe the smile off my face.

'I'm off to the café down the road for a spot of lunch before we go into the meeting, would you, er, like to join me perhaps?'

Ah-ha. Now we're getting to the crux of this little chat. Yes, David Miller is interested in me, and assumes that flattery will get him everywhere. Except in this case it won't, because attractive as he is, he's also married, and as I think about how to respond to his invitation, my eye catches the photos stuck into the frame of the mirror behind him. Two cherubic blonde girls and a plump but still pretty wife.

'I'd love to, David,' I say, looking him in the eye and watching his expression change, the nerves replaced by a smug smile, 'but I can't. I promised Jilly I'd help her with some editing which has to be done today. Another time perhaps?'

'Oh yes,' he blusters, 'of course. What time is it?' He looks at his watch. 'Goodness, better be getting along.'

Mel brings in a half-full bottle of wine and plonks a couple of glasses on the coffee table. We settle back, I point the remote control at the video and I'm about to press play when the phone rings. Mel rolls her eyes and I pick up the phone.

'It's me.' Me, in this instance, is Andy, although sometimes I don't know, sometimes I get it wrong because every single one of my friends calls me and says, 'It's me.'

'Hi Andy. How are you?'

'Oh Tash, he hasn't called,' she whines.

'Who hasn't called?'

'Rick, that bloke from the party.' Ah yes. The one who gave her a lift home, came in for coffee and stayed until the next morning. The one that Andy has not stopped talking about ever since. The one who left her house without her phone number, so she had to quickly scribble it on a piece of paper and run out the door after him shouting that he had forgotten something.

'I'm sorry, Andy, but these things happen. Just put it behind you, you're bound to meet someone else.'

'But I really like him.'

'I know you do.' She always does. 'But if he hasn't called just leave it.'

'But what if I phoned him and said I had tickets to something, something that he wanted to see, then I'm sure he'd say yes. I'm sure he does want to see me again, he's probably busy.'

I sigh loudly. Does this woman not recognise a losing battle when she sees one?

'Tickets to what?'

'Well that's what I wanted to ask you. Have you got any film premières or anything coming up?' I look at Mel and it's my turn to roll my eyes. As part of my job I am regularly sent invitations to launches, premières, press parties, events that sound so glamourous but are, in fact, so boring, I have stopped going.

They were great in the beginning. I'd go along, play spot the celebrity and if I was lucky I'd even get to talk to them. Once or twice I even managed to snog a couple, but now I avoid them. I think I've outgrown them but Andy obviously hasn't.

'I'm sure I've got tickets to something but they're in the office. Why don't you give me a call tomorrow at work?'

'Fantastic! Thanks, Tash.'

'But, Andy, I still don't think you should call.'

'Why not? We're in the nineties now, women are equals.'

I say goodbye without telling her my theory on men and phones. That when a man doesn't call it's not because he's too busy or he lost your number. It's because he doesn't want to call.

I repeat the conversation to Mel who shakes her head. 'When will she learn?' and then we both settle back to watch the phone-in. I press play and . . . Cricket. Yes, a bloody cricket match.

'Oh Mel! You recorded the wrong bloody channel.'

'No, I'm sure I didn't. Press fast forward, this must be what you recorded before.'

'Yeah really, Mel, God forbid I should miss England vs the West Indies or whoever the hell they are. Why would I ever have recorded cricket?'

'Oh sorry,' she groans, 'but forward anyway just in case.'

'Oh well,' I shrug, 'you just missed some interesting calls, I thought it might help put things in perspective.'

'Sweetie, that's really kind of you but I'm OK. Of course I miss Daniel, all the time, but in some ways I feel relief. I'd forgotten what the old me was like, and I think I'm starting to find her again.'

'So what about that guy from Andy's party? Martin.'

'What about him?'

'I just think you should go out with him, it's only a drink, and it would do you good. We're not talking

about walking down the aisle with him or whipping your knickers off, it's just a friendly drink.'

'I don't know, Tash. I'm just not ready to even entertain the thought of another man, even though he was nice, really nice.'

'Are you hungry?' I've just thought of a superb diversion tactic.

'Starving, what can we eat?'

'Well, I haven't got any food, but I could go out and get something.' I check my watch. 'The deli's still open, we can gorge on taramasalata and tzatsiki and olives. I'll go.'

And Mel says, as I knew she would because staying with me she's trying to do everything to thank me, 'No, I'll go. You stay here while I pop out.'

For once I don't argue and as soon as she's out the door I pick up the phone and ring Tom to get Martin's number.

Martin's machine picks up. 'Hello Martin? I don't know whether you remember me but this is Anastasia, Tasha, and we met at Andy's barbeque a few weeks ago. You were talking to my friend Mel and she's staying with me at the moment. I know you wanted her number and she wouldn't give it to you because she was in a relationship but um, they've actually split up and I think she'd really like to hear from . . .' The phone is picked up by a breathless voice.

'Tasha?'

'Martin?'

'Hi!' I can hear his grin down the phone.

'Did you hear my message?'

'YES! I'd love to speak to her. Is she there?'

'No, she's popped out but she'd kill me if she knew I'd done this. Take my number then call in about an

hour's time and say that you tracked her down via Andy.'

'That's just smashing. Thanks, Tasha, I'll call in an hour.'

Smashing? Who the hell says smashing any more? Thank Christ Mel and I have such different tastes.

Mel comes back laden down with food and we eat on the floor in front of the television. When the phone rings, exactly one hour after I called him, I pick it up with a bored, 'Hello?'

'Oh hi . . . Martin, how are you?' I look at Mel, widening my eyes in fake disbelief. Mel widens her eyes in genuine disbelief and puts down her plate.

'Yes it was a good party, wasn't it? Sure, she's just here, hang on.' I cover the mouthpiece as I hand the phone to Mel, and whisper, 'Jesus, talk about coincidence.'

'I know,' she whispers back as she takes the phone. 'That's amazing.'

I collect the plates as quietly as I can and take them into the kitchen to wash up. I can hear Mel laughing as I clatter around, and just as I'm finishing she comes into the kitchen.

'Well I can't believe that,' she says, and she can't stop smiling.

'Me neither.' I add, 'So what did he say?'

'I am going out for that drink with him, tomorrow night in fact, but it's just a drink, I'm not ready for a relationship at all, but he is nice. He's really nice.'

'What are you going to wear?' I'm asking out of habit, knowing that Mel doesn't give a stuff about what she wears.

'Oh nothing special, it's just a friendly drink.'

'If you say so.'

'What are you doing tomorrow night? Why don't you join us?'

'MEL! Are you nuts? I really enjoy playing gooseberry . . . I don't think. I can't anyway, I'm going out with Adam.'

I'm not going out with Adam. I'm not doing anything, but now I have to call Adam and I do this while I'm lying in bed, feeling hugely sorry for myself.

Yes I love Mel, and yes I want her to be happy, but when will it be my turn? When will I meet someone who will take care of me? I sigh wearily and dial Adam's number.

I tell him about Mel and Martin and he is over the moon for Mel. I also tell him about me, and about how even though I am happy for her, how I can't understand why it never happens to me.

Adam says all the right things and when I tell him he has to take me out tomorrow night he says he hasn't seen me on my own for ages and it is just what the doctor ordered.

He tells me that one day, and probably not too far away, one day I will meet a man who will adore me because I'm special and beautiful and any guy would be lucky to have me.

But even as I put the phone down I still feel miserable. Why me? I think as I'm drifting into a dreamless sleep. Or rather, why not me?

– Fourteen –

Mel's been bubbling away ever since I got home. She even – and believe me, this is seriously unusual for her – she even went to The Body Shop and bought a herbal face mask.

Can you believe it? Mel, in a face mask? She *is* excited, but I think she feels she shouldn't be, that she needs to grieve for her bastard boyfriend. Sorry, bastard ex-boyfriend.

I press-gang her into allowing me to do her hair for her, and when I've finished she looks wonderful – soft dark curls falling about her face instead of her usual frizz.

'Good Lord, it looks nothing like me,' she says, admiring herself in the mirror, but she can't keep the pleasure out of her voice.

'Make-up time now,' I say, diving for my MAC make-up bag filled with goodies of every different shade.

'I *can't* wear make-up,' she says. 'He'll think I'm a tart. Not that you're a tart at all,' she's horrified at what she's just implied, 'you're so glamourous and sophisticated it suits you, but I couldn't.'

'Just a tiny bit,' I plead. 'I promise I'll make you look as if you're not wearing any.'

'No foundation?'

'No foundation.'

'No eyeshadow?'

'Just a tiny bit but I swear you won't see it.'

'No red lipstick?'

'What the hell do you think I'd do to you, make you look like a clown? No red lipstick.'

'OK,' she says grudgingly, 'but if I feel really uncomfortable do you mind if I wash it off?'

She looks gorgeous, and she's happy, more than happy, delighted with the subtle difference, but there is still a shadow of uncertainty, and I'm not surprised when she turns to face me and says, 'Do you really think I should be going out for a drink with him?'

'You know the answer to that, Mel. Of course I do.'

'I know,' she sighs, 'and I am looking forward to it but I haven't been out with a man in years, I don't know what to say, how to act.'

'It's just first date nerves, Mel, it happens to everyone. Jesus, I've had more first date nerves than you've had hot dinners, but you get over it.'

'Yes but what if we run out of things to talk about?'

'Did you run out of things at Andy's party?'

'No, but that was different, that wasn't a date. Oh God,' she suddenly groans, 'what do I do if he tries to kiss me?'

'Mel, I don't think Martin's the type of guy who would do that, I really don't think you need to worry about it.'

'You're probably right,' she says looking relieved. 'He probably just wants to be friends anyway. He's so nice though, he'd be a good friend. He's really nice,' she says again, to herself this time and I can't help but smile.

When the doorbell rings I watch as she floats to the door on a cloud of self-esteem, and she and Martin just stand there grinning at one another.

'Have a good time with Adam. I won't be late,' she says, giving me a quick hug and a kiss on the cheek before she follows him out of the door, and I go to the mirror and wipe away the faint pale pink lipstick mark she's left on my cheek.

So tonight I want to feel good, I want to make an effort, I'm hoping that if I look fantastic on the outside I'll start feeling fantastic on the inside. Even though I know life doesn't really work like that.

I know it's only Adam, but sometimes you're not doing it for a man, you're doing it for yourself, and I'm hoping against hope that this wave of self-pity will recede as quickly as it appeared.

What to wear? My bedroom cupboard doors are flung open, and the bed is piled high with a confectionery of clothes, but no bright colours, what on earth do you think of me.

I wouldn't be caught dead in anything patterned, floral or bright. My wardrobe blends subtly together – black, white, the occasional navy and every shade of camel and cream you can imagine. This is what you must wear if you are single, sophisticated and searching.

Tonight I'm in a dress mood. A short, flippy navy halterneck which brushes my thighs as I walk and makes me feel unutterably feminine. Navy and white strappy sandals, with my vampish toenails peeping out the ends, daring you to take a closer look.

My hair is gleaming, the streaks of blonde catching the light of the last rays of the day, and the finishing touch is a dab of MAC taupe lipstick. I do look good, and what a pity only Adam will see it.

'You never wear dresses,' is the first thing he says.

'I know, a bit too feminine for me. But do I look OK, does it suit me?'

'You look beautiful,' says Adam, as he always does but because he means it I start to feel a tiny bit better. Just a tiny bit though, I'm not that insecure.

We get in his car, the roof is down and as we drive through London I stare at other male drivers on the road and note their approving glances. Not that it means much, but every little bit of admiration to feed my depressed ego helps.

It's like walking past a building site. There's only one thing worse than a host of builders whistling and shouting out, 'Cor, wouldn't mind a piece of that,' and that's walking past a building site and being ignored.

You steel yourself, body tense as you approach the onslaught, praying they won't say anything, and then you're past and the bastards haven't said a word and your first thought is, well why the hell not, what's wrong with me?

Or perhaps you don't do that, perhaps it is just me. But tonight I catch the sideways glances, the odd smile of regret that I am with another man in a nicer car, and I hug the glances to myself and start to feel better.

We pull up outside a little Greek restaurant in Camden Town, and the waiter – a tall, handsome Greek man with the obligatory thick brush moustache, greets us effusively before leading us inside, upstairs, and back outside to the tiny little terrace.

Small candles flicker on the two tiny tables squeezed together outside and Adam pulls the waiter aside and speaks to him softly before another waiter removes the table, giving us evil glances for making him work so hard.

So it's just us, and I breathe in the clematis climbing up the railings and the heavy night air, which, even in

Camden, smells deliciously fresh, and I sit back and smile at Adam, at my old, familiar friend who has been so good to me.

'This is a bit romantic, isn't it?' I say finally, grinning at the irony, at the fact that, to a casual observer, we look like a perfect couple.

'Don't you like it?' Adam looks alarmed.

'Of course I like it. I love it, it's gorgeous. Thank you for bringing me here and I'm sorry I was on such a downer last night.'

'I understand, Tash, it happens to all of us, even me.'

'You never get depressed, Ad.'

'You'd be surprised.'

I never think that men feel sorry for themselves, that they have bouts of loneliness and insecurity, but perhaps that's because they keep it so well hidden. I have the girls, and most women have a support structure, a network of friends who help them pick up the pieces when things go wrong.

But men keep it inside. When they go out with their friends they talk of football, of 'birds', of anything other than emotions, which is why when men hurt, they hurt harder and longer.

Adam looks away and all of a sudden I notice he's fidgeting, which is most unlike him. He's picking up the knife and examining it closely, before putting it down and playing with the table mat.

'Ad, what's the matter, are you depressed now?'

'I'm fine, I just want everything to be perfect.'

'I'm starving,' I say, looking at the menu because I don't know what he's talking about, except something in the back of my head tells me I do know, and perhaps I don't want to know. Perhaps not. We shall find out.

'The *meze* here is their speciality,' he says, sounding relieved at being on familiar ground, so we order their

meze for two and sit there chatting about life, work, us, until the food arrives.

A dozen small plates laden with taramasalata, houmus sprinkled with paprika and puddles of olive oil, aubergine, gleaming dolmades, tabouleh, spicy sausages and a basket of pitta bread arrive.

We tuck in, and because it's Adam I can scoop up dollopfuls of taramasalata with pitta bread and not worry about being a pig. Because it's Adam I can eat to my heart's content and not worry about what he thinks of me.

'If this was a date,' I say, mouth filled with rice and vine leaves, 'I would never pig out like this. I'd sit here and push a lettuce leaf around my plate and say that I never eat very much.'

Adam laughs before saying, 'Isn't this a date though?'

'Nah. Ad, this is us,' I laugh, shovelling another stuffed vine leaf into my mouth.

Adam puts down his fork and starts playing with it again.

'Actually, Tash, there's something I've been wanting to talk about.'

'OK, here we go again. Hang on while I put my agony aunt hat on. Let me guess, you're in love with someone and she doesn't love you back.' I'm joking of course, but the terrace suddenly becomes very silent, almost as if the passing cars have stopped, the people all around have become quiet.

'Ad?' I say quietly, not feeling so bloody cocky anymore. 'What is it, Ad?'

Because Adam is sitting opposite me and I swear if I didn't know better, I would say his face had turned white, with just a hint of green. The sort of colour that

would look gorgeous on your living room wall, but right now, on Adam's face, looks bloody frightening.

'Tasha, I don't quite know how to say this . . .' He stops mid-sentence and all of a sudden I know exactly what he's going to say, and I'm not sure I want to hear it.

'Adam, maybe if you don't know how to say it, maybe it's better that you don't.' My voice is gentle, but Adam shakes his head.

'I have to and I'm sorry if it comes between us as friends, but you have to know, I've waited too long.'

My knife and fork are sitting patiently on my plate, and my appetite has completely disappeared. I suspect, but of course I can't know this for sure, but I suspect that my face is a very similar shade to Adam's.

'Tasha. Jesus. I don't know how to say this.'

There really isn't anything at all for me to say, but I cross my arms, as if to protect myself from the words I've been dreading, the words that will change everything, that will undoubtedly spoil our wonderful friendship.

'Tasha, I love you. I'm sorry, but I do. I love you and I'm in love with you and I want to be with you and I know you probably don't feel the same way and it really doesn't matter but I needed you to know.'

Adam fidgets with the fork as he says this in one breath, and when he's finished he exhales loudly and runs his hand through his hair. I feel a burst of affection for him, followed swiftly by a canyon of disappointment.

These are the words I've longed to hear. For years I've dreamt of being in this situation, of sitting on a terrace, lit by candlelight, facing a man who I love, who tells me he loves me too.

But this is Adam. Yes he is a man I love, but a man

for whom I feel no attraction whatsoever. I love Adam, but I don't want to feel his arms around me. I love Adam but I don't want his tongue in my mouth, his hand on my breast, his body in my bed.

I love Adam but I am not in love with Adam, and I, I who am never lost for words, I am rendered completely fucking speechless.

Adam reaches over to take my hand, and I watch it for a moment, resting in his, and then I slowly pull it away.

'God I'm sorry, Tasha. I've ruined everything. But say something, anything. Please.'

The silence gets thicker and thicker and I look up and say, 'I don't know what you want me to say.'

'It's not what I want you to say. It's what you want to say.'

'I don't know, Adam. In all the years I've known you I never expected this. I mean, I'm hugely flattered and everything, but . . .'

'For Christ's sake don't say that, Tasha, say anything but that.'

'OK, I'm sorry. Adam, you know how I feel about you, you know I love you more than anyone else in the world, but I've never thought about it as anything more.'

'God, if you knew the times I had.'

Curiosity gets the better of me and I can't help but ask when, when he decided, when he knew.

'When you were with Simon, that night you came to me in a state and wanted to know whether Simon was with me. You were wearing pyjamas with a big coat, and you looked so vulnerable. I think I knew then, but you were Simon's girlfriend and I would never have done anything.

'You're so different to how you were then. You were

so tough and cynical, but you're much softer now, and I've kept these feelings in for so many years, I had to tell you.'

'Adam. There is nothing in the world I want more than to be able to tell you that I feel the same way, but I'm not sure I can. It wouldn't be fair.'

'But Tash,' he says urgently. 'I'm not expecting you to say that you love me too, I know that right now you don't feel the same way. But maybe you could. I mean, we would be so good together. I know you better than anyone and I love you for who you are, not this tough person you pretend to be. Time isn't a problem for me, I can wait, I can wait for you to change your mind.

'All I'm asking is that you think about it. That you think about us. You know how you're always banging on about *When Harry Met Sally* and how that's your dream situation? Well that's what we would be. We could be them.'

I can't help myself. Despite the seriousness I laugh. 'What? When Adam met Tasha?'

He blushes, bless him, and says defensively, 'Why not? Jesus, why the hell not?'

I don't know what to say, so we sit there not saying anything. My appetite disappears and I search my mind, desperate to change the subject, to fill the silence which is becoming increasingly uncomfortable.

'I just don't know,' I say eventually. 'If you want me to think about it I will, but I can't promise anything. This is such a shock, I never expected this, never dreamt you felt like this. I need some time.'

'That's fine,' he says. 'I just needed you to know.'

Silence descends once again, and I look at the tablecloth, at the half-eaten meal, at the traffic rumbling past the restaurant and eventually Adam breaks the silence by asking for the bill.

We drive home in silence and as we pull up outside my front door I say, 'You'll understand if I don't invite you in for coffee,' and I grin falsely which comes out like a grimace.

Adam smiles faintly, then puts both hands on my cheeks and moves his head towards mine. I freeze, terrified of the physical contact from the one man I've been able to trust, but he doesn't kiss me on the lips. He plants a soft kiss on my forehead and then looks me in the eye and says, 'Call me when you're ready.'

Walking into my flat, I'm in a daze. I can't think about it, even walking in and sitting on my sofa, staring into space I can't think about what happened tonight, it's too momentous, too much to take in.

Mel's not home yet, so I wait for a while, needing to sort out my own thoughts, getting them in order to share with her when she walks in the door.

But the minutes tick by as I sit and think about nothing, an unwitting form of meditation, and finally I sigh and get up to go to bed. Why is my life always so fucking complicated?

– *Fifteen* –

I wake bleary-eyed at 10 a.m. and stumble into the kitchen to make some coffee. I woke briefly last night, just in time to hear Mel softly shutting the front door, and I fell back into a deep sleep, too tired to even get up and ask how her date went.

I feel like shit. I should be elated, someone is in love with me, the most wonderful man in the world desires me, but I feel like hell, and I have never needed to talk to anyone more than I need to talk to Mel now.

I make two cups of instant coffee, stirring two heaped teaspoons of sugar into Mel's, and walk up to her room, putting the cups down to knock softly on the door.

No reply. 'Mel?' I say softly as I push the door open. 'Mel, I've brought some coffee, wake up.' But she has woken up and she's not there. Her bed is already made and the curtains are drawn, and there's a note lying on the bed.

Darling Tash,

Had the most amazing time last night – walked and talked for hours on Primrose Hill. Sorry I was so late – didn't have a clue what time it was until I got home!!! Don't worry, didn't misbehave at all, he's just so nice!!

Meeting him this morning to help him buy a sofa. I'll be at lunch, though, so see you there. Hope you had a good time with Adam,

Big huge kiss,
M xxxxxxxx

Oh God. Please don't tell me I'm about to lose my best friend to love. I've never had to worry about it in the past because when Mel was with Daniel she always put me first. But now she's met someone new will she disappear?

Not literally, but I know so many women who forget their lives, their friends, themselves the minute they meet a man they could love. You suddenly realise you haven't heard from them for a while, and when you phone it takes them two weeks to return your call.

They'll never agree to see you at night because that's when they're with their new man, so occasionally if you're lucky you snatch a quick cup of coffee together. And you sit there and look at this friend who used to

be so entertaining, so full of life, and all she wants to talk about is her man.

Every sentence is punctuated with the dreaded word 'we', and you leave with a mix of envy and regret while she promises to invite you over for dinner to meet Him, except you know you'll never receive the invitation because she only mixes with other couples now.

And eventually, when it's all over she'll be back on the phone as if she never left. And you, being the understanding soul that you are, welcome her back and make her promise she won't abandon her friends the next time. She promises, and she keeps her promise. Until the next time.

And don't be fooled into thinking it's only women who do this. Once upon a time I had a friend called Jamie. Pre-Adam, Pre-Mel, Jamie was my best friend. We met when we were children, and we grew up together, fading in and out of each other's lives until we were seventeen, by which time we were firm friends, and swore we'd never lose touch again.

And we didn't until Jamie got his first girlfriend at twenty-one. He lived with her for two years, and although he still called me all the time, I hardly ever saw him. When I did he'd bring Kathy along which always made me feel slightly awkward and uncomfortable.

But after Kathy, when he was single again he said I was more important to him than any women, and I relaxed, I trusted he meant it. Then he met Mags, and I never saw him. I still invited them both to every party I had, every dinner I organised, but three years on I realised I'd never been invited out with them. That I hadn't even met a single friend of theirs. That I'd never seen the inside of the flat they shared.

I forgave him again, grudgingly this time, but by the

time Sarah came along I had had enough. I abandoned our friendship, and when, after six months of not speaking, I received an invitation to his thirtieth birthday party I ignored it. Large impersonal thirtieth birthday parties are for everyone, small intimate dinner parties are for friends, and I had never been invited to one.

I missed Jamie desperately until Simon, when I was too busy becoming the sort of woman who does things in couples and abandons her friends herself. But Mel I've never had to think about, and I pray she doesn't do this. I need her. We all need her.

And I need her now. I need to ask what I should do, whether I could make myself fall in love with Adam. Because I want to, you see, I really want to feel passion for him, but I'm not sure I ever could. I'm not sure friendship is enough.

It's a pain in the ass getting dressed today. All I can think about is the conversation last night, and as I'm pulling on clothes and putting on make-up, I talk out loud into the mirror, replaying what happened, what I should have said, what he should have said.

But of course the conversation doesn't make sense because I haven't got a clue *what* I should have said, or how I should have said it.

I check my watch before I leave. One twenty-five, five minutes before we're due to meet and I'm determined not to be the first to arrive this time. It takes me ten minutes to get there and as I walk in I spot Mel, sipping a cappuccino and smiling to herself as she gazes into space, her chin resting on her hand.

Her eyes light up when she sees me, and, despite feeling like a miserable fucker, I can't help but smile at her excitement. Particularly when I see she's wearing

make-up, except she hasn't quite got the hang of it and her cheeks look like Aunt Jemimas – round red blotches of colour.

'I'm sorry I wasn't at home this morning,' she says in a rush. 'Did you get my note? I had such a great time last night, Tash, he's so nice.'

I laugh, 'I know he's so nice, Mel, that's all you keep saying. So where did he take you until the early hours of this morning hmmm?'

'We went to this pub in Primrose Hill and we just talked all night. When the pub closed neither one of us wanted to go home, there was still so much more to say, so we went to sit on Primrose Hill and finally he walked me home.'

'From Primrose Hill?'

'Yes, it was miles but I hardly even noticed, I just had such fun!'

'And did he try and kiss you?'

Mel blushes. 'Yes, and we did and it was really nice.'

'Jesus Mel, I'm going to have to teach you some more adjectives. What do you mean it was nice?'

'It was weird, kissing someone else when I've only kissed Daniel for years,' her face only clouds slightly at the mention of his name, 'but it was, I don't know, it was exciting, and comfortable at the same time.' She sighs happily. 'We feel like we've known each other for years. It's just so easy being with him and he was so nice to me. He told me I had beautiful eyes!'

'You do have beautiful eyes, Mel.'

She looks flustered, so unused to compliments. 'But no one's ever told me that before, and even though the kiss made me think of Daniel, the conversation made me think that this is what I've missed. I loved it when he complimented me, I loved it that he made me feel special and in some way it's helped, because Daniel

never made me feel like that, not even at the beginning.'

'I've always said you deserve better. Maybe now you've found it . . .' I smile.

'I don't know,' she shakes her head. 'I have to take things slowly, I'm really *not* ready for a relationship, but I had fun, both last night and this morning, we didn't stop laughing in the furniture shop.'

'I'm so happy for you.' I am, I really am, but Mel doesn't miss the tone in my voice that says all is not completely well. All is, in fact, completely fucking skewiff.

Mel takes my hand and looks me in the eyes, 'Something's the matter isn't it?'

'Oh shit, Mel,' I say, 'it's all gone bloody wrong.'

'What has?'

'Adam. He told me last night he was in love with me and I don't know what to do.' Mel's expression is one of total shock, but before she has a chance to say anything Andy breezes in and kisses us hello, while Mel never takes her eyes off my face.

'Good Lord. Oh sweetie, what *are* you going to do?'

Andy pushes the hair off her face with her sunglasses and reaches into her bag for the omnipresent pack of Silk Cut Ultra Low. 'What are you going to do about what?'

'About Adam. He told me last night he was in love with me.'

'You're joking.' Now both Mel and Andy are sitting there in shock.

'Yes I'm joking,' I say, 'I wish. I wish I'd woken up this morning and found it was all a bad dream, but unfortunately it really happened.'

'I knew it,' says Andy, slapping her thigh to reinforce

the point. 'I always knew he was interested. What did you say?'

'What the hell could I say? I mean, it's *Adam*, I'm not in love with Adam, I've never even thought about it.'

'But how do you feel?' Mel's skills as a therapist are coming into play.

'Confused. And angry.' I stop to think. 'And betrayed. And flattered. And confused.'

'Why betrayed?' Andy doesn't understand.

'I don't know whether betrayed is the right word, it's probably too strong, but I feel as if our friendship's been a sham. I mean I know it hasn't, but I just think of all those times I've talked to Adam about everything, and all the time he had an ulterior motive.'

'Don't you think that's being a bit harsh?' Mel asks gently.

'But it's true, and also I'm embarrassed, I mean I've told him so much about me and about how I feel and it must have been killing him, hearing me talk about these other men.'

'So you feel his pain as well?' Mel.

'Yes,' I shrug and look at her, 'I suppose I do.'

Emma arrives and we all kiss hello as Andy determines to be the first to explain: 'Adam told Tasha he was in love with her last night and she doesn't know what to do.'

'Thank you, Andy,' I say through gritted teeth, 'but I can talk for myself.'

'Sorry,' she grumbles, 'I'm just concerned.'

'I know, I'm sorry. What am I going to do?'

'You do love him, don't you?' asks Emma.

'Well of course I do, but I'm not in love with him.'

'But those feelings of lust don't last,' Emma says earnestly, 'and friendship is the most important thing. That's what keeps a relationship going, that's what I

have with Richard.' She stops while the waitress comes to take our order and we all studiously scan the menus and tell her what we're having for lunch.

'When I met Richard I thought he was one of the best-looking men I'd ever met, really, he swept me off my feet. Now I look at him and I see Richard. I don't see him as good-looking, he's just Richard, but because we still have so much to talk about, we still have so much in common, we're together.'

'No I disagree,' says Andy. 'I think passion is vital. If you don't have passion from the very beginning, you're far more likely to look for it later on.'

'I'm not sure whether that's really true,' interjects Mel, looking doubtful.

'It is true, I'm telling you. I have so many friends at work who are having affairs and how do you think it starts? It starts because they got married to the first men that asked them. They weren't passionate about these men but they'd reached an age or a time in their life when they wanted to get married, and they married men who would be good husbands and good fathers.

'And what happens? A few years down the line they start to look elsewhere for that excitement, that lust, that old stomach-churning feeling that I would rather die than live without. At least if the passion is there in the beginning you always have the memory which is enough to keep you faithful.'

'Sorry, Andy, but I don't think passion is that important,' says Mel. 'I tend to agree with Emma. Look at couples whose children have grown up and left home. The passion, if there ever was any, has long since disappeared and the people that divorce are the ones who find they don't have anything in common anymore.

'For years they talked about the children, they went on family holidays together, the children were the one thing they had in common, so when the children go the marriage breaks up. But the ones who stay together after the children have gone are the ones who were friends in the first place. They love each other's company because they have become each other's best friends. They like doing the same things, going to the same places and they end up with the strongest marriages.'

We all sit in silence for a while, thinking about what Mel has just said, and each of us wishing that we had that sort of marriage.

'I'm not saying friendship isn't important,' says Andy finally, and slightly defensively, 'but you need passion as well. They're equal.'

'Oh God knows,' says Emma. 'Who the hell knows what love is anyway?'

'Well,' I venture, 'I read an article once, an interview with William Wharton and, if I remember correctly, just before his daughter got married she rang him and asked him whether he knew what love was.

'He said as far as he could see love was passion, admiration and respect. If you have two of those it's enough. If you have all three you don't have to die before you go to heaven.'

'But which two?' asks Andy.

'I know,' I sigh. 'That's what I've been trying to figure out for years.'

'I think admiration and respect would be enough,' says Mel. 'There are thousands of women who have fallen in love, with their bosses, for example, because they are men in positions of power. Because these women admire and respect them.'

'No way,' says Andy. 'Passion and respect. You can't

live without passion. I tried it once, Tasha, believe me it's bloody impossible.' She looks around the table. 'Did I ever tell you about Stephen?' We all shake our heads while I silently smile at the fact that even now, even though it's my problem we're discussing, Andy still has to be the centre of attention.

'I met Stephen when I was twenty-six. He was thirty-two, not that good-looking, certainly not my type but a really lovely guy and very rich. He fell madly in love with me and kept pestering me to give him a chance.

'I wasn't into him physically, but I liked him as a person and we got on really well, so eventually I said yes, I'd go on one date with him but that was it. He came to collect me in his black Porsche convertible, and when I got in the car there was a huge bunch of lillies on the seat for me. I'd told him they were my favourite flowers.'

We are all listening intently, because Andy, despite her faults, is a hell of a good storyteller.

'He drove up the A40 and refused to let me know where we were going, and eventually we left the motorway and pulled in to Le Manoir aux Quat' Saisons.'

'Le what?' says Mel.

'Oh,' sighs Emma, 'Le Manoir aux Quat' Saisons. It's my favourite restaurant, it's Raymond Blanc's restaurant in Oxfordshire, a beautiful country house and the food is exquisite.'

'Your favourite restaurant?' I can't help but ask with a grin. 'How many times have you been there?'

Emma blushes. 'Just once actually. But I loved it and I'm trying to get Richard to take me for my birthday but it's hugely expensive.'

If Emma thinks it's hugely expensive then it must be

a fortune, because Emma doesn't settle for less than the very best. Slumming it at this brasserie for our Saturday lunches is about as low as she'll go.

'Exactly,' said Andy, desperate to get on with her story. 'It *is* amazing, and it is hugely expensive, but money was no object. We had a perfect evening, and all night I was thinking, shit, if only I fancied him.'

'And then what?' Mel looks like a little girl who's being told a fairy story, which in a way I suppose it is, because that world is so alien to her sensible middle-class upbringing.

'He was a perfect gentleman, he drove me home and dropped me off, which was a relief because I didn't want to ask him in, I couldn't stand the thought of kissing his thick, fleshy lips.' She says these last three words slowly and with relish, knowing that we'll all cringe with disgust, which is exactly what we do.

'The next day he sent another bouquet of flowers with a note saying thank you for a wonderful time and would I be free to go to the opera with him. Of course I went, and he had his own box and we sat and drank champagne all night, and afterwards he took me to The Ivy for dinner.'

'What did he do?' God I'm so superficial.

'I'm not entirely sure, something in entertainment, but I think most of his money had been inherited. Anyway, he knew loads of people at The Ivy, all these celebrities were coming up and saying hello to him, and I started to really enjoy this lifestyle.

'The only problem was him. Every time I looked at him, and believe me, he wasn't a pretty sight, I just gagged.'

'Describe him,' says Mel, wanting every detail.

'He was about 5′6″, and large. I mean really large.'

'You mean fat,' I laugh, because none of us ever want

to use the f-word, even if we're talking about someone we despise.

'I suppose so. And he was balding, and he had these disgusting lips. He dressed beautifully, or as beautifully as you can when you're a fat bastard, but I really loved him as a person, we got on so well, and I wanted to fancy him, I was trying to fancy him. Eventually, after he'd taken me out for about three weeks he invited himself in for coffee and I couldn't say no. He came up behind me in the kitchen, put his arms round my waist and kissed the back of my neck. I froze.

'I had to kiss him didn't I, and it was horrible.'

'So you never saw him again?'

'No, that was the thing. I kept on hoping that it would grow, that one day I'd wake up and fancy him but it just got worse and worse. I adored him but every time we went out I'd know that towards the end of the evening I'd have to kiss him and I would be dreading it.'

'What did you do?'

'In the end I told him I'd got back with my ex-boyfriend, and that I was really sorry but I had to give this relationship a go. I was just so bloody relieved I'd never have to kiss him again.'

'What happened to him.'

'I never heard from him again, and then a year later I was flicking through *Hello!* and there he was, getting married to this stunning blonde model before flying off on their honeymoon on his private jet.'

'You're kidding,' we all gasp.

'Bloody wish I was, but she was obviously a woman who didn't give a monkey's about passion, and I'd put money on her being unfaithful. I mean, what sort of a marriage could it be?'

'Probably a good one,' says Mel. 'OK, perhaps it's a

business venture, she'll supply him with a son and heir etcetera in return for a wonderful lifestyle, but perhaps she met a man she liked, a man she could be happy with, and you never know, maybe she found herself falling in love with him.'

'With those lips. Yeuch.' Andy makes gagging noises and we all laugh.

'But Adam doesn't have thick fleshy lips,' Mel says, when Andy's stopped retching. 'Adam's eminently fanciable.'

'But Tasha doesn't fancy him, and that's the key issue.' Andy's refusing to let it drop and I've got to be honest with you, I'm more confused that when we started.

'I don't know,' I say shaking my head. 'I just don't know.'

– Sixteen –

Great. I really need to bump into a practical stranger first thing in the morning when I look like shit and I'm half asleep.

I get up this morning to go to the bathroom and who should I walk slap bang into as I'm opening the bathroom door? Well who else. Bloody Martin. I mean I don't mind that he's stayed, I think he's a really nice guy but this is my flat for Christ's sake, not a bloody hotel.

But what do I do? Despite being half-asleep I stand there on the landing and make small talk with him before offering him a cup of tea.

'That would be lovely,' he says with a smile. 'I'll wake Mel.'

So I grouch downstairs and slap three mugs on the surface while I'm waiting for the kettle to boil.

'I'll just leave them here,' I say, putting two mugs on the floor outside Mel's bedroom door, but then Mel shouts, 'Don't be silly, come in.'

So I walk in to Mel's bedroom, which also happens to be *my* spare room in *my* flat, and there they are, cosy as anything, snuggled up together in bed. Martin has quite a nice body, which surprises me it has to be said,

and Mel's looking disgustingly sexy for first thing in the morning.

Yes, Mel has succumbed to the thrills of a new relationship. Not only has she had a new hair-cut, she's also had a make-up lesson and she's growing in confidence by the day. Plus, what she's eating would hardly sustain a rabbit, and the pounds have dropped off her.

She looks fantastic. She looks like she belongs, and although I'm ever so slightly jealous of this new Mel, ever so slightly missing my old scatty Mel with the frizzy mass of hair and no make-up, I'm also thrilled. Thrilled to see her become the woman she's always wanted to be. A woman like the rest of us.

I loved Mel as she was. I knew she was good enough, better in fact, than the rest of us, but Mel didn't think so and that was the problem. Her new-found confidence is shining out, and that's what I'm thrilled about.

Mel pats the bed. 'Come and talk to us.' Us. Already. Two weeks and it's 'us', but of course I sit and when she opens her arms to give me a hug I readily succumb, eager to somehow belong to this 'us', which Mel seems to sense.

'Martin thinks you should call Adam.'

It's been three weeks since I talked to Adam. Three weeks of confusion. Sometimes I wake up and think, yes, I'm going to go for it, I'll give it a whirl and see if passion grows, and other times I wake up and think, no, I can't sleep with Adam, it would be tantamount to incest.

I even did a phone-in on the show to try and solve my dilemma. Outside input is what I need, I decided; stories about other women, women who I don't know, I need to know whether passion can grow.

So we did it. Passion Junkies we called it, which went down a treat with David and Annalise, neither of whom had heard the expression before.

'Are you a Passion Junkie?' asked Annalise, grinning inanely into the camera. 'Do you go from one passionate relationship to the next, and wonder why none of them are Mr Right?' added David by her side.

'Can we live without passion, and more importantly, should we?' said Annalise while David looked at her and ad-libbed, 'How about you Annalise, are you a passion junkie?'

'Oooh David, I'd never say no to a bit of impromptu passion.'

'That's what I thought,' he said with a chuckle, doubtless fuelling more ridiculous rumours of an off-screen affair. In case you're wondering whether the rumours are true, there's about as much chance of David and Annalise sleeping together as me getting married within the month. Exactly.

'If you're addicted to passion, perhaps you've managed to break that addiction. Tell us how. Ring us here on *Breakfast Break*, you know the number, 01393 939393.'

The calls came in thick and fast. There were women who fell head over heels in love at first sight, and were still blissfully happily married twenty years later.

There were women who married their best male friends, who didn't have passion, but who were still blissfully happily married twenty years later.

And there were some people, both women and men, who didn't have passion but started the relationship anyway, who just fell into a situation without realising what was happening, and who gradually fell in love. Who gradually felt passion.

Did it help? Did it hell. There I was thinking some

wise woman living in the depths of Somerset would phone up and say, 'Tasha, passion can grow, give him a chance.'

But after the programme there was a phone call that caught my eye, except she didn't even get put through because we ran out of time. I went up to the phone-in room after the show and was scanning the calls we'd got and there was something about this woman, maybe the fact that she was thirty, she lived in London, and her husband's name was Adam, that made me think she might have the answer.

I called her. I know there was no reason for the call but I rang anyway to apologise for not putting her on air.

'That's OK,' said Jennifer Mason, in a voice that immediately gave her away as someone who came from a similar background to mine. Someone perhaps much like me.

'I was quite relieved actually. I wanted to share my story because I thought it might help anyone who wasn't sure, but as I was waiting on the line I suddenly thought that I might not want to tell people because Adam doesn't know. To this day he doesn't know how I felt at the beginning.'

'I know you might think this odd, but I'd really like to hear your story. Can you tell me what happened?'

She laughed and said, 'I thought there was an ulterior motive behind this call. Sure I'll tell you, just don't tell anyone else.' We both laughed and she started to tell me.

'I had rented an office in the East End, in one of those buildings where they rent out serviced units, and Adam had the unit below me. I bumped into him in the café down the road, and he recognised me. We had a

chat, and that was that, I never gave him a second thought.

'Adam wasn't my type at all, you see. I'd always gone out with these good-looking, successful men, and Adam was none of these things. He was forty-five then, completely grey, with a large paunch. I never gave it a second thought.

'He started to pop in to my office regularly. I suppose I knew he liked me but I never encouraged anything other than friendship. We were both single, and soon we became friends, seeing each other on the weekends, and popping out for a meal after work.

'I started to like him more and more, only as a friend though, and he was becoming a very important part of my life. One night I invited him over to dinner, and he told me he felt more for me. I remember sitting there thinking, well, he's not my type, but he was so lovely to me, he had always treated me so well I just thought, why not?

'I slept with him that night, the end of a long period of celibacy for me, and I remember waking up in the morning and feeling really proud of myself. Not that it was anything earth-shattering, but it was nice. Comfortable.

'As soon as we embarked upon a physical relationship my feelings for Adam started to change. It took time, but after a few months I realised I was in love with him, but not the sort of passionate rollercoaster of emotions that I'd experienced in the past.

'In the past you see I had lived my life through extremes. When the man of the moment phoned I would be as high as a kite, and if he didn't, I would spend the night in tears.

'Yet here was Adam, a man I felt truly comfortable with, who I knew adored me, and who I never had to

worry about. It wasn't extreme, it was normal, I think that was how I knew, and I felt, what's the word? Content. I felt content for the first time in my life.

'And now we've been married for two years and can I tell you something? I look at Adam, at this forty-seven-year-old man with grey hair and a paunch, and I think he's a Greek God. I think he's the best-looking, most wonderful man in the whole world, and I've never been happier.

'So you see I was a passion junkie. I still am a passion junkie, but the passion grew through love, and it's the most reassuring kind of passion in the world.' She stops and there's a silence before she asks gently, 'Does that help?'

'More than you'll ever know. Thank you.' I smile as I put down the phone.

I thought about Jennifer Mason all day. I'm still thinking about her now, so when Mel tells me Martin thinks I should call Adam, I think he's right.

It's eight o'clock and I feel like a teenager about to embark on her first ever date. Mel's staying at Martin's flat tonight, and I'm so nervous I have to sit down and take deep breaths, to try and quell the butterflies fluttering around my stomach.

And Christ, did it take me *for ever* to choose what to wear. I tried on everything in my wardrobe, threw it off and tried again. Finally when I was happy with my navy jersey shirt and long flowing layered skirt, I had to shove all the clothes away, make the bed, make it immaculate.

What the hell am I doing I thought, even as I pushed the clothes under the bed and out of sight. I'm getting the bedroom ready just in case, said a little voice. Don't be ridiculous, I'm not going to sleep with Adam, and then I started to feel sick with nerves all over again.

But all the time I was getting ready, all the time I was tidying the flat, Jennifer Mason's voice echoed in my head, only this time it applies to me, to my Adam, to my future. 'Here is Adam, a man I feel truly comfortable with, who I know adores me, and who I never have to worry about. It isn't extreme, it's normal.'

But could I ever look at Adam and see a Greek God? Shit, I don't think I'll think about that one just at the moment, I think I'll just pour myself another glass of wine and wait for the doorbell.

When it eventually rings I walk very slowly to the front door, and after I open it I see it isn't this terrible thing on the doorstep, it's Adam, my old, reliable Adam.

Who was it said there's nothing to fear but fear itself? How true, I think, as I stand there and wonder how we will greet each other. Normally I get a bear hug, but we're both awkward, and Adam bends to kiss my left cheek, as I stretch to kiss his, and our noses clash because we had been heading straight for one another's mouths, and we both laugh at the sheer awkwardness of this meaningless kiss hello.

He gives me a hug, and suddenly he feels different. It's not just Adam anymore, it's a man, a man I could be having a relationship with, and I move my hand slightly on his back, just checking, just feeling what there is underneath, what his body might feel like.

'Can I get you a drink?' I feel ridiculous, like a hostess inviting a stranger into her home, and yet the easy intimacy we've always shared seems to have disappeared, and Adam feels much like a stranger.

By telling me he was in love with me Adam changed. Superficially of course he's still the same Adam, but inside have I ever really known him? Have I ever

really known what he was thinking or feeling? Quite obviously no, which accounts for my watching his every moment, trying to find some familiarity.

I pour him a glass of wine and we both sit on opposite sofas, facing each other, while I draw my legs up underneath me, an upstanding foetal position, a position of comfort.

'So how have you been?' he says.

'Fine,' I shrug, 'really fine. You know, same old life, lunch with the girls, wankers at work, Mel being here which I love.'

'And how's it going with that guy she went on a date with?'

'Martin. It's going fantastically, they're seeing each other all the time and she's really happy. You wouldn't recognise her.' I tell him about the changes in Mel and we both start to relax. We're talking about something other than 'us' – the 'us' that is so comfortable for Mel, the same 'us' that is so difficult for Adam and I.

'That's great,' he says. 'That's just great.' And he looks down at his glass and then back at me. 'I've missed you.'

'I know. I've missed you too.' I have. Desperately. All the times those stupid little things, or funny little things have happened at work, I've picked up the phone to call Adam, to make him laugh, and just as I've picked up the receiver I've remembered, and it's been awful.

The silence between us stretches out, and I sit there trying desperately to think of something to say except I can't think of anything. I can't bloody think of a way to form the words I want to say, which is that I love him, but I'm not in love with him, but I'd like to try. I'd like to see what could happen. I'd like to be another Jennifer Mason.

'Why am I here, Tash?' He's not looking at me as he says this and my heart goes out to him. He looks like a little boy, scared, unsure and I just want to put my arms around him and cuddle his fears away. But do I want to make love with him? Let's not think about that just yet.

'This has been the most impossible three weeks of my life, Ad. Jesus, this was harder than the run up to my bloody degree, so firstly I want to say thank you for causing all this misery.'

He smiles, and I think he senses that it's all going to be OK.

'I love you, Ad, you know that. I'm not in love with you, but maybe it could work. I don't know, but I suppose there's only one way to find out, so I guess,' I pause, not quite knowing how to say it, 'I guess the answer to your question is yes.'

'What was the question?' He's smiling broadly now, all the nervousness disappeared.

'I don't know, but yes, I'd like to give it a go.'

'Give what a go?' He's teasing me now because he can see I'm still a bit awkward.

'Give "us" a go.' There. I said it. The dreaded 'us', and you know what? It doesn't sound nearly as bad once it's out there. In fact it sounds quite nice. Better than quite nice. It sounds comfortable.

Adam stands up and comes to sit next to me. He takes my hand and just sits there, holding my hand and smiling at me. I sit there and look at my long thin fingers resting in his big bear-like paw and I squeeze his hand very quickly.

I know the kiss is coming, the kiss is coming. Shit, the kiss is nearly upon us. What am I going to do? But when Adam bends his head down he's still smiling,

and he very slowly kisses me on the lips then sits back, smiling some more and just looks at me.

'How was that?' he says.

'OK,' I'm nodding my head. 'It was really OK.'

And he bends his head again and we kiss again, for longer this time, but no tongues, alright? Then he sits back and looks at me some more.

'Are you sure about this?' he asks.

'Nope. I'm not sure at all, but can we do it again just to find out?'

This time he kisses me for a lot longer. Short soft kisses on the lips, then the corners of my mouth, then back to the lips. My eyes are closed as I try and familiarise myself with the odd sensation of kissing Adam, and the more he kisses me the more I want to carry on.

And wouldn't you know it, I'm the first one to venture out a tentative tongue, to lick just the outside of his upper lip. He carries on kissing me softly, moving down to kiss the nape of my neck and I think, Jesus, where in the hell did Adam learn to be so good at this?

And then he comes back to my lips and licks mine, and I open his mouth so our tongues are intertwined and you know what? It's bloody nice, this is.

And he continues to kiss my neck, and each kiss moves further down my body, and he gently pushes me back until I'm lying on the sofa leaning against the cushions, and he's half lying on top of me, the lower half of his body kneeling on the floor.

And I open my eyes to see Adam unbuttoning my shirt and slowly kissing his way down across my chest and I have to close my eyes immediately, I can't watch this or I won't want to go through with it. I wouldn't

have the courage, but with my eyes closed I can pretend.

Pretend what exactly? That it's Andrew, that it's David? No, just pretend that it isn't me and my best friend.

This would be better with the lights off, is my first thought. Thank God I tidied the bedroom, is the second.

'Hold on,' I whisper, standing up and wrapping my now-unbuttoned shirt around me. 'Let's go to bed,' and I take his hand and walk into the bedroom feeling as if this isn't real somehow, that this is a dream, or maybe a big joke.

I light a candle which flickers soft shadows on the walls, and then I'm lying on my bed and Adam has spread my shirt so that my body is exposed, and he pulls the fabric of my bra – not La Perla, Marks & Spencer – aside, and he gently starts to suck my right nipple.

Where in the hell did Adam learn to be so good at this?

He moves up and kisses me on the lips and I roughly unbutton his shirt, desperate to know what Adam feels like, how his skin will feel when it's pressed up against mine. I pull it off his shoulders and it catches at the sleeve which Adam tries to undo but fails.

We both laugh, but behind the laughter I can just about see that Adam's eyes are glazed with lust, and eventually the shirt is off and I slip my own off together with my bra.

'You are so beautiful,' he murmurs as he moves down my body, kissing my stomach, unzipping the zip at the side of my skirt before abandoning it and approaching from the other direction.

Sliding my skirt up, moving his hands up my legs,

stopping just as he hits the top of my thigh and then moving his hand back down to my knee. Closer, closer. Back up my leg, a little higher this time. Nearly there. And then back up, closer. I moan.

When in the hell did Adam learn to be so good at this?

Through the cotton of my knickers he teases my clitoris. Moving his fingers from side to side, he just avoids it, and I arch my back and press into his hand.

And then he moves the elastic to one side, and slowly, tentatively touches the spot, and it is like a bolt of lightning going through my body. Starts to rub, gently, wetting his fingers by plunging them into his mouth, licking them, looking at me as he continues to slowly rub.

Rolling my nipple around his fingers with the other hand, rolling and rubbing for what seems like hours.

And then I pull my clothes off fast and furiously, and lie on top of him, feeling my skin on his skin, kissing his big chest, his chest covered with unfamiliar blond hair, and I move down, hovering above the waistband.

His cock is straining to get out, pushing against the worn denim of his jeans, and I unbutton his flies. Big, thick, in my hand, my long thin fingers stroking. Adam lying back with his hand over his eyes, gasping.

Kissing him, engulfing him. How he smells, how he feels, sucking, licking, stroking, straining.

And then it's my turn, as Adam rolls onto me, moves down my body, and I have my hand over my eyes as he laps at my clitoris, sucking, flicking, big broad strokes, small hard flicks.

'Inside me. Inside me. I need to feel you inside me.'

The awkward condom moment (I have some in the drawer in my bedside table), and then filling me up, moving slowly on top of me. Propped up on his arms

looking at me with such love, kissing me with such tenderness.

And afterwards, as he showers me with kisses and whispers that he loves me I prop myself up on one hand and look him in the eye: 'Where in the hell did you learn to be so good at this?'

– Seventeen –

When I was sixteen I used to spend hours daydreaming about the Prince Charming who would whisk me away to a world of romance.

We'd walk hand in hand along white sand beaches while waves crashed around our ankles. We'd lie entwined in Hyde Park, him covering me with kisses while people walked past and envied us our love. We'd go and buy Christmas trees together, laughing and joking as we dragged it up the stairs to our house.

Bloody pathetic, isn't it? I don't need you to tell me that real life isn't like that, that love, even when you find it, rarely echoes the love that we're expected to believe in from films.

And now I have Adam, and the two of us together are a world away from my teenage expectations. Adam and I are friends. We are also lovers. Adam is in love with me and I am not in love with Adam.

But who knows how you are supposed to feel when you are in love? Maybe I *am* in love, maybe I've got it all wrong. Then I think back to Simon, to the way he made me feel, the excitement, the ripping our clothes off, the highs and the lows, and I worry that I haven't got this any more. That I'll never have it again.

I have become a Jennifer Mason, but I'm not sure it's enough.

You want to know what our relationship is like? Much in the way the movies, chick flicks, always tend to splice together a montage of slushy clips to show romance, I will put together a montage of everyday clips to show you how we are together.

Maybe you will think it is love. Maybe you will think it is enough.

Clip number one:
I am at work, head down, busily beavering away on my next script. A voice says softly in my ear, 'I'd like to talk to you about the item on date rape.'

I look up and it's David. Standing way too close for comfort. Invading my personal space. His classically handsome face looks almost distorted at such close sight, and I involuntarily swivel my chair to the side, I am not comfortable with such close proximity.

'Sure. Do you want to have a chat now?'

'If that's OK.'

The phone rings and I go to pick it up. 'Excuse me a sec, David. Hello, *Breakfast Break*? . . . Would you mind if I called you back, I'm in a meeting. Thanks. Bye.'

I swivel round to David. 'Sorry about that. What's the problem?'

The phone rings again and David looks exasperated. 'Tasha, why don't we go somewhere a bit more quiet, get away from these phones.'

I stand up and pick up a notebook, a pen and the script and we head downstairs to the canteen. As we

walk past the other producers and researchers in the open plan office they watch us with disgruntled stares.

It isn't usual for the presenters to request chats with the producers on a one-to-one basis during the week. If they have problems they usually moan to the editor, who then has to call the producer into his office, close the door and gently suggest a few changes.

I know this and the others know this. I know what they are thinking – that David is singling me out for preferential treatment and they are right, and as I walk along I can't help but feel slightly awkward, conscious of the stares, the knives hovering above my back.

Because television is a bitchy place. You may not know this, certainly if you're lucky enough not to work in media, but television is not glamour and fizz, not by a long shot.

I've lost count of the number of times I've been to a party and someone has asked what I do. When they hear those seemingly magic words, television producer, their eyes become large and they say the same thing every time, 'God how glamourous.' But it's not glamourous, it's work, and the bitching and backstabbing are the bonuses that no one tells you about.

And as I walk across the office with David a step behind me, I can already sense the huddles of people, 'Where are *they* going?' I can almost hear them whisper to one another, 'What does he want with *her?*'

We sit in the canteen with our cups of coffee and David asks me who the girl is who is coming in to talk about date rape. He is worried about it being prejudicial, because the case has not yet come to trial and I reassure him we are changing her name and filming her in darkened silhouette, but he knows this, he damn well knows this.

'So how about you, Tasha, how are you getting on?'

'Er, fine.' What *is* he talking about?

'And how's your love life?'

I laugh, 'My love life? What on earth are you talking about, David, why would you want to know about my love life?'

He doesn't even blush. 'Come on, Tasha, you're famous for your men, we're always hearing about your escapades.'

'Who the hell from?'

'Everyone. You're the envy of half the women who work here, you seem to have all the men chasing you.'

Now I blush. 'That's ridiculous, David. Anyway, I might have had a bit of a wild past but I'm settled now, practically married.'

He blanches, but ever so slightly. 'You? I thought you were the archetypal single girl.'

'Even the archetypal single girl is allowed to break her archetype once in a while.'

He laughs but pushes the point. 'Are you really going to get married?'

I shrug. I know the answer to this is no, at least, not to Adam, but I hardly need to share this with David. 'We'll see.'

'But do you think you'd manage to stay faithful?'

'Why David, I'm a one-man woman.'

'Don't you mean one man at a time?'

'You said that, not me.' So he's flirting with me. So what. Now that I'm here I'm quite enjoying it. Jesus, no one's flirted with me for ages and I had forgotten, I really had, the effect I have on men.

Not that Adam's the possessive type, the few parties we go to he's happy for me to wander off and I could flirt if I wanted to, but truth be told there haven't been many men I've wanted to flirt with. But this is quite

nice. I look coyly at David from under my lashes and say, 'Are you the faithful type then?'

He looks at me for a few seconds and says slowly, 'What do you think?'

'I think you have affairs.' In fact I know he has affairs. Suzy, the old make-up girl got the sack when she made the mistake of falling in love with him during their affair.

She started phoning him at home, crashing down the phone when his wife answered, leaving notes in his jacket pocket hoping that his wife would find them, leaving lipstick marks on his shirt, accidentally on purpose.

David thought nobody else knew, but everyone knew, we all knew. Suzy would sit in the canteen in floods of tears and pour her heart out to anyone who would listen – which meant everyone because we all fed off the gossip for months – and finally, when it all got too much for David to cope with, Suzy was called into the editor's office and 'let go'.

'Oh? And what kind of women do you think I have affairs with?'

'I don't know, David, why don't you tell me?'

'Why don't I tell you over a drink tonight?'

I can't do this anymore. The game has turned serious and I want out. 'I'm sorry, David, I can't tonight but another time perhaps?'

'Another time.' He nods, his ego smarting from the rejection, but hopeful for the future nonetheless.

I leave David sitting in the canteen with his cup of coffee and head back upstairs. Jim, the producer of Monday's show sidles up to me and whispers archly, 'Very cosy, Tasha. People might start to talk.'

'For God's sake, Jim, he wanted to talk about an item on the show.'

'Oh, silly me,' he slaps a limp wrist, 'and I thought he wanted to talk about another kind of item.'

'Don't be ridiculous.'

'Well darling, they do say if you've got it flaunt it,' he looks me up and down, 'although in your case I'm not entirely sure what *it* is.' He sighs dramatically and minces back to his desk while I raise my eyes to the ceiling and pick up the phone.

'Hey toots,' Adam's latest pet name for me. Needless to say I haven't got a pet name for him. It would be too intimate, too . . . couply.

'Ad, you're not going to believe what just happened?'

'You've been made the editor of the programme?'

'Nope.'

'Annalise has been shot and while she's in hospital they've asked you to fill her shoes?'

'Nope. Wrong again.'

'OK, you got me. What just happened?'

'David made a pass at me!'

'No! That arrogant shit, what did he say?'

This is what I love about Adam. That he is like one of my girlfriends, that I can phone him all day if I want to and tell him the ridiculous things that happen at work, and that he will always want to talk to me, to share in the gossip, to share my amazement.

So I tell him and Adam says, 'Well I can't blame him really. I couldn't work in the same office as you and not try it on at least once.'

'Yeah well you would say that.'

'Why would I?'

'Because you love me dumbass.' I'm grinning.

'Do I?'

'Yes.'

'So are you going to go for it?' Adam is fitting perfectly into the role of one of my girlfriends.

'Hmm,' I laugh, putting on my most confused voice. 'I don't know. Do you think I should?'

'Well, remember that make-up girl, Suzy. If it all went horribly wrong, you could be out on your ear.'

'But what if I just want some sex?'

'Well if you come home before eight o' clock tonight, I can organise a gorgeous, hunky, muscle-bound man to be waiting for you wearing just his boxer shorts and a dishcloth.'

I laugh out loud. 'A dishcloth?'

'Well he'll have to have cooked you a gourmet meal.'

'And what would that meal be?'

'You'd start with a salad of grilled goat's cheese, followed by salmon steaks and chive butter, with a few new potatoes and mange tout.'

'What's for pudding?'

'*He*'s for pudding.'

'Damn,' I laugh. 'I knew there was no such thing as a free lunch. And by the way, where did he get the muscles from?'

Clip number two:

It's a Sunday morning and I have to find a present for Emma's birthday. Emma is impossible to buy for – what do you buy for the woman who has everything? You buy the cheapest possible thing you can get away with from a designer shop.

A keyring – even Tiffany or Louis Vuitton would be too telling, so Adam suggests going into town to The Conran Shop.

Just before we walk out of the door Andy calls. 'I met *the* most amazing guy last night,' she begins, before telling me the story I seem to have heard a million times before.

And as I listen to her I find myself thinking, thank God I'm not out there anymore. Thank God I don't have to do this anymore. I don't have to spend days and nights sitting by a phone waiting for it to ring. I don't have to worry that someone will go off me once we've slept together because he won't like my body.

But I have to be completely honest with you, a part of me is slightly envious. A very tiny part of me misses it. Not enough to worry about, but nevertheless it's there.

So I sit and listen to Andy and I don't bother giving her advice because she never takes it anyway, and after she says, 'What the hell, I'll call him,' I put down the phone and walk out of the door with Adam.

We climb into the Saab and I pull the mirror down to check my hair.

'You look gorgeous,' he says. 'Stop fiddling.'

'You always think I look gorgeous,' I moan. 'I've stopped believing you. You're like the boy that cried wolf. When I do look gorgeous I won't believe you because you say it all the time.'

'That's because I think it all the time.'

'Even first thing in the morning?' The ego needs feeding.

'Especially first thing in the morning.'

What's so ridiculous about this is that it's true. In all the relationships I've had in the past I've tried to look immaculate all the time. I've managed to look great, even first thing in the morning by sneaking into the bathroom, brushing my teeth and rubbing in some tinted moisturiser.

I've never been relaxed enough for someone to see me *au naturel*. I've never been secure enough to think that it's anything other than my looks that keeps them with me.

Isn't this quite common though? That when relationships take off quickly the attraction is based on the physical. You go to bed with a man after a few dates and you worry about what he will think the next day.

You wake up in the morning and you pray that he begins to like you. That the physical attraction will become a mental attraction too. When that happens, you are incredibly lucky, because more often than not you don't even like the person you are sleeping with and they don't like you.

But Adam knew me so well before we slept together that I have never had to worry he'd disappear. I never worried he would suddenly realise that he didn't like me, because as far as he can see my beauty comes from the inside.

And the funny thing is I feel more beautiful. I've even cut down on the make-up I wear because I don't have to prove so much anymore. I am a woman who is loved, but what are my feelings? Is it security? Is it love? Is it passion? What do *you* think?

We park the car and bustle around The Conran Shop, admiring the furniture and balking at the exorbitant prices. We pick up the gadgets that look so tempting, and then ask ourselves what we would actually *do* with them.

We decide to make a food hamper ourselves, because Emma is a foodie, and what better place to shop than this designer emporium. I hold the whicker hamper and Adam walks around the food section, picking out jars of chocolate truffle sauce, of succulent olives stuffed with anchovies, of olive oil swimming with chillies and peppers.

We fill the hamper, both thrilled with our original present and then we walk over the road to the brasserie for breakfast.

The waiter leads us to the table and instead of sitting opposite me Adam comes to sit next to me, our backs against the wall.

'It's too far away from you,' he grumbles, and he kisses me quickly on the lips. I order coffee, orange juice, scrambled eggs and smoked salmon. Adam orders coffee, orange juice, fried eggs, bacon and toast.

We cover the table with the Sunday papers we've bought on the way, and Adam keeps prodding me to hear a story he's just read in the tabloid.

'I never knew he was having an affair. God, I can't believe he can still get it up,' says Adam in amazement over an ageing politician caught spending the night with a young girl.

And then Adam reads me an article about Simon's magazine, about the rise in circulation, about the scoops they keep getting. Simon. A name I haven't thought about in ages.

'Have you spoken to him recently?' I ask, curious to know how Simon would react, whether he knows about us.

'Briefly,' says Adam. 'I told him about us, I wanted him to hear it from me.'

'Was he OK about it?' Please don't let him be OK about it, please let him be jealous, let this cause him pain. Not that I care about him anymore, it would just be sweet revenge.

'I think so. He even suggested we go to his flat for a drink, said it was time we put the past behind us and were all friends.'

'Is he fucking mad?' I'm outraged.

'That's what I said,' says Adam, grinning.

'Do you think he was serious?' I find this hard to believe.

'Unfortunately I do. I said I didn't think that would

go down too well with you, and he said it was a shame we couldn't let bygones be bygones.'

'What an asshole.'

We sit in silence after that, punctuated with our idle chat about the stories we are reading and then I immerse myself in a feature and when I've finished I look up and Adam is sitting there watching me and smiling. He puts a big arm around me and squeezes me to his chest.

'Have I ever told you how much I love you?'

'Yes. All the bloody time,' I groan, but I'm basking in this love. Oh how I'm basking.

'Oh OK,' he says, removing his arm. 'I couldn't remember, that's all,' and he picks up a piece of toast, taking a big bite as I start laughing.

There's a table in the corner where four girls are sitting. One of them is facing us and I catch her eye. She gives me a wry smile and I recognise that smile. I recognise that smile as the smile I used to give when I caught the eye of a woman who was loved.

A smile that says congratulations. A smile that says I want to be like you. I want to have your relationship. I smile back at her and I reach over and give Adam a huge kiss on the cheek. I ruffle his hair as he looks at me in surprise because I so rarely initiate affectionate gestures. 'I think you're wonderful,' I say and I give him a big smacker on the cheek. He grins happily and goes back to his paper.

Clip number three:

Did I mention that Mel is now living with Martin? Well she is, and it's great and Martin treats her like a queen.

Mel hasn't, thank God, become what I dreaded, she

hasn't abandoned anyone, and nor does she only see me during the day. The first flush of romance swept her off her feet somewhat, but that's what it's supposed to do, and now she's settled down into a proper relationship.

A fulfilling relationship. A relationship where they both love one another.

Adam and I and Emma and Richard – the three couples – have come to their flat for dinner. We are sitting in the living room and I am looking around – this is the first time I have been here – and I am looking at Mel and Martin.

She loves him, I think. She is in love with him, I think. She is passionate about him, I think. I know this because she tells me, they cannot keep their hands off one another, she thinks he is the best-looking man she's ever seen. She has found her lid.

And I look at Emma and Richard, at the way Emma always has to have some part of her body touching Richard's – french manicured fingers resting on his leg, an arm casually flung round his shoulder, a hand running affectionately through his hair – and I wonder why I don't do the same thing.

I look at Adam and think, you are Adam. You are still safe, still reliable, wonderful in bed and wonderful to me. What is it exactly that is missing? Why can I not just settle down in this comfortable security. Why can I not, as Jennifer Mason once said, be content? Maybe I am. Maybe this feeling is so unfamiliar I don't recognise it. Could you be my lid? Could I be your pot?

We move into their kitchen for dinner. Pine, pine, everywhere I look there is pine. Pine kitchen cupboard doors, thick pine floorboards, an old Victorian scrubbed pine table.

A spice rack on the wall, wooden hooks with assorted

pots and pans hanging from them. Clean but well-used. A kitchen that likes to be cooked in. A kitchen that smells like home.

Martin, surprise surprise, is a vegetarian, and the four of us, Emma, Richard, Adam and I, discussed this in the car on our way over.

'But I'm starving,' I said. 'What if it's all brown rice and bloody lentils?'

'If it is we'll stop and pick up some Chinese or something on the way home,' said Adam.

'Vegetarian is very healthy actually,' said Emma.

'Not if you live on pastry, eggs, cheese and bread,' offered Richard.

'Well no, I suppose not,' she agreed, 'but brown rice and vegetables are a fantastic diet, it really flushes out the system.'

'Emma! Please, do we have to?'

'Sorry, darling,' she flushed, and Adam and I exchanged a brief look. Emma again being the subservient woman, not wanting to offend Richard, letting him take charge.

'Oh God, Chinese,' I groaned. 'Oh Christ, you've just started a major Chinese craving.'

Adam chuckled. 'Spare ribs,' he said dreamily, knowing they are my favourite.

'Crispy seaweed.'

'Deep fried crispy beef.' It was Richard's turn.

'Noodles with roast pork,' I added, as my stomach rumbled menacingly. 'Do we have to go? I want Chinese,' in my best little girl voice.

'Yes we have to go, but if you behave yourself then we can have Chinese later.'

'You're not serious?' said Emma.

'Why wouldn't we be?' Adam looked at her in the rear view mirror.

'You wouldn't really eat *two* meals?'

'My woman has a huge appetite.'

'I wouldn't mind if you put on a bit of weight actually. You're looking a bit thin at the moment.' Richard pinched a millimetre of skin on Emma's thigh, unaware that her life, with the exception of Saturday lunchtimes, is spent on a permanent diet, permanently trying to look the very best she possibly can for Richard. Terrified he'll leave her for someone younger, or prettier, or thinner.

But the meal is a delight. A cheese strudel, the cheese speckled with chives oozing out of the puff pastry, swimming on a tomato coulis. An assortment of salads and a home-made tiramisu for pudding. I'm stuffed, and Adam keeps grinning at me across the table as I keep helping myself to more. Grazing. A lick here, a spoonful there. Emma has a tiny portion of everything, and then leaves half of it on her plate, and Richard scoffs as much as I do, happy I think to have found a fellow pig.

And Mel and Martin are a delight. The six of us quickly get over the initial awkwardness, because Martin, Richard and Adam don't know one another really, but they soon become friends-in-the-making. How could they not? How could anyone resist Adam's easy charm, Martin's soothing voice, Richard's well-meaning humour.

Mel whisks Emma and I aside after dinner, to show us a new painting she bought.

'You're so good together, you know,' she says to me. 'Who would have ever thought it?'

'Look who's talking. You and Martin are fantastic.'

'Yes,' agrees Emma, 'you are,' but I can tell she's thinking, why doesn't she say that about us? What's wrong with Richard and I, so I hurriedly add, 'And you,

Emma. You two are the envy of all of us. God, I spent years hoping I'd meet someone like Richard, someone who treated me the way he treats you.'

Her face lights up. 'Really?' Incredulous.

'Really. And Mel's got it now, haven't you, Mel?'

She smiles happily. 'It almost makes all the rubbish I put up with from Daniel worthwhile.'

'What do you mean?'

'I wouldn't be in this relationship if it wasn't for Daniel. It took me ages to realise it but because Daniel was so awful to me, it made me aware of what I was looking for, even though I wasn't really looking.

'But I knew that I would never put up with less than the best. Martin adores me, he thinks everything I do is magical, and that's what I deserve now. That's what we all deserve, and both of you?' She looks at Emma. 'You've got Richard and you're the most perfect couple I know. And you,' she looks at me, 'you've got Adam who is so besotted he can hardly think straight.'

'I know,' I sigh. 'I should be the happiest woman in the world but I still feel there's something missing.'

'Not that old passion thing again?' Emma looks at me curiously.

'Not exactly. I mean our sex life is unbelievable. Seriously, I never dreamt Adam would be such a good lover, and I'm really happy with him. There's something that I just can't quite put my finger on. I don't know,' I shake my head.

'Tash,' Mel says gently putting a hand on my arm. 'Love can be many things. There is no such thing as a perfect love, and what you have with Adam is what most women dream of achieving. You have to wake up and recognise what you've got, how special it is.'

I nod but I don't say anything. I know she's right, I just don't know how to wake up.

The four of us analyse Mel and Martin's relationship all the way home until Adam suddenly screeches to a halt outside a parade of shops.

Richard leans forward, 'Why are you stopping the car?'

'Just popping in to the takeaway to get some Chinese for Tash.'

'But she ate loads,' says Emma, before clapping her hand over her mouth. 'Sorry,' she says, 'I didn't mean . . .'

'I'm stuffed,' I laugh, holding my stomach before hitting Adam playfully on the arm, and we drop Emma and Richard off and drive home to go to bed.

No sex tonight, a few chapters of the book I bought the other day and sleep.

Just as I'm drifting off to sleep, Adam's hand reaches for mine under the duvet and he squeezes it gently.

Now do you get the picture?

– *Eighteen* –

Oh Christ I hate hen parties. A gaggle of women, all pissed, all acting like a bunch of blokes who don't know when enough is enough.

Jilly is one of my researchers and she's getting married. Yup, this little kid of twenty-two is getting married, while I, a sophisticated woman of thirty, am still on the shelf, except I'm not quite as dusty as when we first met.

So here we are, at some Godforsaken dive in the West End, some nasty, tacky, seedy nightclub where Jilly has managed to wangle VIP passes, so we get to sit in an empty VIP lounge overlooking the dance floor.

Half the people here are from work – mostly researchers – and half are her friends from way back when. I'm sure they're sweet, really, but right now they are looking the worse for wear, and I'm not entirely certain I'm going to make it through the night.

I should be drinking. I should have consumed, as the others have, the best part of a bottle of wine over dinner. I should have held the wine bottle, as the others did, and licked the glass rim, taking the bottle deep into the back of my throat and bobbed it up and down, gone down on a bottle.

I should have, as the others did, got progressively

more and more drunk until even the waiters shot our table nervous glances and refused to come over unless they absolutely had to, and when they did they stood there brushing away the women's hands from their crotches, their bottoms.

I should have shrieked with laughter at the clothes the other girls made Jilly change into when we left the restaurant and headed over to the nightclub. A dress made out of a black bin-liner, with pictures of soft willies, cut from soft-porn magazines, stuck all over it, and a hat covered with condoms. In her hand was a huge vibrator, a thick black plastic cock that Jilly is using as a magic wand.

I should have laughed, but I didn't, I wanted to go home.

'Abracadabra,' Jilly slurs in front of the doormen standing menacingly outside the nightclub. 'Abracadabra,' and she waves the vibrator at them while the rest of the girls clutch their stomachs with laughter, shrieking at her antics. The doormen manage a vague smile, and when we produce our VIP passes they stand back and let us in.

'Hen night,' I say with a weary air as we troop past, me being the only sober one there.

'I'd never have guessed,' says the burly black doorman with a knowing smile, and we walk upstairs, or should I say stagger.

I can't be in central London, I think, looking around at the people in the club. Who *are* these people? Where do they come from? It's a world away from everything I know, and I feel so old. The music is deafening and surrounding the dance floor are packs of men, fresh-faced youths on the pull, not talking, just looking, searching around for a woman who might go home with them.

A few brave souls are strutting their stuff on the coloured glass squares that flash every few seconds, women in tiny sequinned mini dresses, crop tops, hot pants, acres of fake-tanned legs and black platform sandals.

I feel so old. The boys, for they *are* boys, stand around drinking from bottles of beer, and Jilly pulls her friends on to the dance floor to jeering from the onlookers.

I wish I was at home with Adam.

I hit the dance floor in a half-hearted fashion, and stand there idly bopping away to the latest chart sounds. I have to look as if I'm enjoying myself, I have to make some sort of an effort.

'You all right?' shrieks Jilly, whirling round to face me. 'Loosen up, Tash, have a drink.' She offers me her champagne bottle and I pretend to swig but in fact only a few drops enter my mouth. I hand the bottle back and Jilly whirls off, straight into the arms of a boy, a boy who fancies himself as a young blade, a boy who pulls Jilly close and immediately puts his hands on her buttocks, all the while looking over her shoulder at his mates and winking.

They writhe together, his hands squeezing her bottom, his crotch pressed against hers, and she pushes him away to tip back more champagne. But he follows her, he thinks she could be a conquest, and within seconds he has his arms round her again, same position.

I go to the bar, find a spare sofa on one side and collapse, chin in my hand, bored to tears.

'Wanna dance, love?' A tall, greasy Italian-looking guy is standing over me.

'No thanks.'

'Mind if I sit here?'

He squeezes in next to me and introduces himself as Maurizio, a twenty-five-year-old waiter who's Italian but was born here. He also drives a Ferrarri. Or so he says. By way of introduction.

'Sorry Maurizio, I'm married,' I say standing up. 'But good luck. I hope you find what you're looking for.' I don't hang around waiting to see his expression, I melt into the crowd and try to find Jilly.

I wish I was at home with Adam.

And then Jilly falls upon me screaming with laughter, and drags me to the front of a tiny stage I hadn't noticed to watch the cabaret. I look around me and see that all the faces pushed to the front are female, eyes bright with anticipation as the music starts and a fireman walks on to the stage.

Oh shit, I knew it, I bloody well knew it. What good would a hen night be without a stripper.

'Which one of you gorgeous gals is Jilly?' Our party screams and all hands point to Jilly, grinning at the fireman, who, it has to be said, is really rather dishy.

He pulls Jilly up on stage and the music starts. Never taking his eyes off her face he undoes his jacket and lets it drop to the floor, gyrating to the music and grinding his hips. If he didn't look such a wanker he'd be quite gorgeous, but his dance movements are more than a little 80s'. In fact, if I didn't know better I'd think he'd come here straight from a gig with the Village People.

His shirt comes off, and then Jilly has to unzip his trousers. I groan, I know what's bloody coming next, don't I? Sure enough, he puts his hands around Jilly's head and forces her face into his jockstrap-covered crotch while he grinds his hips into her face.

He lets her come up for air and she's grinning. She

loves this. Sensible, organised Jilly is pissed as a newt and she's loving every second of this attention.

Need I tell you more? Oh all right, yes the baby oil comes out, yes she shoves her hands down his jock-strap to massage it in (after massaging his pecs of course). Yes the jockstrap does eventually come off and no we aren't disappointed.

There. Happy? When the cabaret finishes I can't cope with this anymore. This is not my scene and all I can think of is getting home, pulling off these bloody high heels and climbing into bed with Adam.

Adam is probably fast asleep now. It's one o'clock and as I sit in a taxi winding its way through London I picture Adam, warm, sleepy, tucked up in bed, and I can't wait to get home and climb into bed with him.

I tiptoe into the bedroom, and unless my eyes are mistaken there's no Adam. Where the hell is Adam? I feel a pang of unease, a small voice saying perhaps he's gone for good, but that's ridiculous, that's the old insecure Tasha talking, the old insecure Tasha who used to worry that every man was going to leave. That's not Tasha who basks in the comfort of her new-found relationship.

But all is explained by the red flashing light on my answerphone.

'Hey Toots, I'm not staying tonight because I don't want to be woken up by you staggering in and throwing up all over the duvet. I've gone back to my flat, yes, my flat, I'd almost forgotten I had a flat, and I'll see you tomorrow. Drink lots of water before you go to bed and take a couple of aspirin. I won't call too early. Love you. Bye.'

I'm smiling as I get into bed. Smiling because he makes me laugh, and because I miss him. I really miss

him, and it's strange sleeping on my own again after all these shared nights.

This doesn't mean I'm in love with him you understand, it's just that I've become accustomed to him. That's all.

'I've been thinking of asking Adam to move in with me.' I exhale loudly, and then inhale more quietly, taking in the soothing smell of the lavender oil burning in the corner of the room.

Louise doesn't say anything, just nods, encouraging me to continue.

'I've got really used to having him around, you know? I know this might seem like a huge step but maybe if I see him more, maybe I'll start to fall in love with him.'

'You're not in love with him?' One eyebrow is raised.

'No.' I sigh deeply. 'There's still this passion thing.'

'Why do you think the highs and lows that you've experienced in the past are so important hmm?'

'That's all I've known.'

'Does that make it right?'

I don't say anything and she continues, 'Does that make you happy?'

'No,' I grudgingly admit, 'but there's still something missing. It's too comfortable.'

'Is there something wrong with comfortable?'

'No. Comfortable is, well, it's comfortable. Comfortable isn't love. Comfortable isn't passion.'

But comfortable is nice. Comfortable has changed me, even in the space of these last few months, comfortable has made me a different person. I've noticed it and my friends have noticed it.

My cynicism has gradually started to disappear, so

slowly I barely even noticed it. But I notice that I'm softer, more gentle, not so quick to judge people.

You must have noticed a difference since when we first met, surely? Yes I'm still full of the sharp retorts, the biting comments, except I'm learning to hold my tongue a little more, and actually, if I'm telling the truth, I don't think of them nearly as often as I used to.

I think that chip on my shoulder has started to go, I think perhaps that I have started to like myself. And in liking myself, I'm learning to like my world. It's not such a bad thing. Is it?

The phones are going crazy at work and I can't concentrate on a damned thing.

'The next time this thing rings I'm going to bloody scream,' I say to Jilly, who's still finding it difficult to look me in the eye after the escapades of her hen night a few days ago.

(For your information the fireman turned out to be straight, single, and desperate for sex. He spent the rest of the night snogging Jilly on the fire escape, and her friends rescued her just before anything serious could happen. What fun and games eh? The wedding's still on, this Saturday. God help them.)

'What?' I scream into the receiver.

'Calm down, it's only me. Bad day?'

'Oh Ad, this bloody phone just never stops.'

'Shall I call you later?'

'No, of course not. I wanted to have a chat with you anyway.'

'Uh oh. I hate those words, it always makes me think of when I was a little boy and my father used to say, "We need to have a talk." I always knew I'd done something wrong.'

I smile into the receiver. 'Well you haven't. It's just

you know how we've talked about spending so much time together, and how you keep forgetting that you have a flat because we never go there?'

'Yes.'

'Well, I've just been thinking that maybe it would be a good idea if you came to live with me.'

There's a silence and I think, oh shit, this isn't a good idea after all.

'Ad? I mean, if it's a crap idea then say so, but it just seems crazy having two mortgages when one of us could be renting out their place, and you spend so much time at mine I thought maybe you should move in. Ad?'

'Fantastic idea! Brilliant! Yes. I'd love to!'

'Really?'

'Absolutely! When can I move in?'

'Whenever.'

'OK, whenever it is. I'll start moving my stuff in tonight. In fact, I can leave work early today. If I start to clear the flat now then next week I'll go to an agent's and put it on the rental market. Perfect!'

We say goodbye and I sit there thinking what have I done. This is a serious commitment. I'm about to make the biggest commitment of my life to a man I'm not in love with. Am I completely bloody crazy or what?

The rest of the day passes all too quickly, and I can't quite believe what I have just done. Calm down, Tasha, I keep telling myself. If you hate it you can always tell him to leave. You can always say you need some space.

You can spend your whole life thinking you want commitment. You grow up with a clear idea of exactly what it is that you want, and yet when you have it, when it's there, attainable, on your doorstep, you change your mind.

Perhaps this is what we need. A dream, a hope for the future, something to aspire to, and perhaps we need to keep replacing this dream with something a little bigger, because when we manage to fulfill the dream, we usually find out that it's not what we wanted in the first place.

Or if it is, it doesn't feel the way we always thought it should.

Sometimes, if you're very mixed up, very stupid or very thoughtless, you screw up the dream just as you get it. You tell yourself you don't deserve it, and you have to start all over again.

I put my key in the lock and the door doesn't open more than a crack. Pushing and shoving I manage to squeeze in, and there on the floor of my hallway are boxes of CDs, of books, of papers.

Clothes are strewn inbetween and as I pick my way through the mess I think again, what the hell have I done. Harvey and Stanley are sitting at the other end of the corridor, watching me belligerently as if to say, 'What on earth are you doing to our home? What's all this *stuff*?'

Adam's left a note: 'Gone back to get some more stuff together. Probably won't be back 'til late, got so much packing to do! Sorry about the mess in the hall, I'll clear it tomorrow. Adam xxx.'

Well where the hell will he clear it to? I look around at the junk, feel slightly sick at the prospect of even more turning up, and then I look around at my lovely immaculate flat with not a lot of storage.

I need a bath.

The bubbles rise high above my body as I lie back, soaking away the worries and drawing out the dirt of London from my pores with a cucumber astringent face mask. My hair's piled up on top of my head, a

glass of wine is resting on the side of the bath, and Ella Fitzgerald is singing from the speakers in the living room.

Mmm. This is lovely. Nothing like a long, hot soak when you're tired and confused, not sure whether you've just done the right thing. I sip the wine and idly watch my cherry red toenails as my feet play with the taps.

And just as I'm debating whether or not to immerse my head in the water, the silent, soothing bathwater covered in bubbles, the bloody doorbell rings.

'Shit!' I say. I'm not going to answer that. But what if it's important? Could be Adam back earlier than he thought, forgetting his key. Could be anyone. Shit! I leap out the bath, wrap a towel around and run down the stairs. Halfway down I realise the face mask is still on. 'HANG ON!' I yell in the general direction of the front door as I leap back upstairs, three steps at a time, and scrub off the mask.

Clutching the towel around me like a talisman I open the door and who should be standing on the doorstep but Andrew.

Yes, *that* Andrew. Andrew who I fancied the pants off. Andrew who I haven't seen since Adam and I got together. Andrew who kissed me. Andrew who's standing there looking absolutely, one hundred per cent fuckable. Still.

And me? I'm standing there looking like something the bloody cat's dragged in.

My hand instinctively goes up to my hair, piled up in a messy topknot but I can't let it down and shake it out, it would be too damned obvious so I grin nervously and rub one foot against the back of my calf. Just checking, and yes, phew, they're shaved. Not a hair in sight.

Why does this sort of thing only ever seem to happen to me?

'I hope I'm not disturbing you?' His sexy drawl is as sexy as ever and it's quite obvious he's disturbing me, he's pulled me out of the bath but I stand there and say, 'No, it's fine.'

What am I supposed to do? Am I supposed to ask him in? Am I supposed to stand there on the doorstep saying, 'Can I help you?' or what? Help!

'Um,' he grins, 'do you think I could come in?'

'Oh God, yes, of course,' and I stand back and let him in, thinking, why doesn't he kiss me hello. Why does his mere presence, standing on my doorstep, in my hall, sitting on my sofa, reduce me to jelly.

I *know* what I should have done then. Really, you don't need to tell me. I should have said something like, 'Hang on a minute, let me just get dressed,' and maybe if I had everything would have been fine. But I didn't, I was so nervous, excited, adrenalin rushing through my body that I didn't think. I just sat down, the towel still clutched round me.

'So Adam's not here then?'

'He should be back any minute.' A blatant lie, but he'll stay if he thinks Adam's going to be here. After all, he's here to see Adam. Isn't he?

'OK, you don't mind if I wait for a few minutes, do you?'

'Not at all. Would you like a drink?'

'A glass of wine would be lovely.'

I come back from the kitchen, snatching a quick look in the mirror in the hallway on my way back and pulling a few tumbling tendrils down from my topknot, and I pour the wine into the glasses.

'Didn't you try him at home?' I am curious. Maybe,

just maybe, he's here because he wants to see me. Maybe he's using Adam as an excuse.

'I didn't bother. He told me was moving in here and I just assumed he'd be here. I was going to ring but I was passing the door so I thought I'd chance my luck.'

He takes a sip of the wine and settles back against the cushions, closing his eyes as he savours the crisp cool flavour and sighs loudly. 'What a day.'

I want him. I want him. I want him. I want him to lean over and kiss me. I want him to rip my towel off and clutch me in his arms. I want to undress him. I want him living here. I want to wake up every morning and be with this man. Oh God, what is happening to me?

Forget Adam, forget everything. I am here in this moment with a man who makes my heart beat faster. Isn't this what I've been waiting for? Isn't this what I've wanted?

Andrew opens his eyes and looks at me. My face, my body, my legs, and I feel myself flushing. 'I'm surprised,' he says, his eyes travelling back up to meet mine.

I frown at him.

'I'm surprised that you look the way you do with next to nothing on.'

'What do you mean?'

'I've only ever seen you looking perfect, I thought you would be one of those women who look great when they're all dressed up but terrible first thing in the morning, or just out the bath with no make-up on.'

'And do I look terrible?' I smile flirtatiously.

'No. Jesus, you look sexy as hell.'

This is it! This is it!

'Look I'd better go.' He's shaking his head.

'Please, stay.' Urgency in my voice.

'You're Adam's girlfriend now. I can't stay, I can't be

in the same room with you looking the way you do now. This is crazy.'

My heart's pounding, pounding, pounding. I'm back on the rollercoaster, high as a kite, flying through the clouds on a torrent of passion.

'We're not doing anything.'

'Yet.' He looks at me slowly and then moves a little bit closer, gauging my reaction, waiting to see whether I move away, but I don't. I move a little bit closer.

He takes my hand and takes a deep breath. 'Adam's my friend, Tasha. I couldn't do this to him.' He shakes his head again, trying to dislodge the thought, remove it, pretend it isn't there. 'But, Christ, you are gorgeous.'

He groans and suddenly he holds my head with both hands and kisses me, furiously, passionately and I think I am going to die with the excitement. I moan as he circles his tongue in my mouth and then we both jerk back in horror.

My front door slams shut. Footsteps running down my stairs. A car door opening and an engine revving. A car, a Saab, roaring off into the night.

Andrew and I look at each other, fear written over both our faces.

'Oh my God,' I whisper. 'Adam.'

– Nineteen –

Don't judge me. Please don't judge me. Not yet, not before I try and explain, try and justify what I did, try and find the mitigating circumstances.

Do you remember a while ago I told you about women who are stupid? Women who don't recognise a good thing when they've got it? Women who screw it up?

And cast your mind back to when we first met. I told you that some women put up with terrible relationships because they don't think they deserve any better. These same women, when they find a good relationship, screw it up because they don't think they deserve it.

Am I one of these women? Oh God, have I screwed up what could have been the best relationship of my life? Or was it the best? Was it just average? Could it only ever be just average because Adam never makes me feel the way that Andrew, in the space of probably ten minutes, just made me feel.

Andrew leaves. I practically push him out the door and neither of us say a word to one another as he walks out. Then just as he walks through the door he turns to me and says softly, 'I'm sorry.'

'Just leave,' I say, shutting the door in his oh-so-

handsome face. Whatever I was thinking, whatever I was feeling has gone, vanished into thin air as I lean back against the wall in the corridor, one hand still on the door handle.

My knees sink slowly to the floor and I crouch there for a while, before sitting down and hugging my knees to my chest. I'm shaking, and I feel very cold, very alone.

I sit there for most of the night, amongst the boxes and books that are all I have tonight of Adam's. Every time a car drives past I look up, praying it's Adam, praying I can explain.

But can I explain? Should I explain? I don't want Adam to leave, but nor do I think I want him to stay. At one point I stand up and look in the mirror and a mass of confusion stares back. What the hell do I want? Do I care? Does anyone care?

At around two o'clock in the morning I start to look curiously at the boxes on my floor. At the parts of Adam's life I've never seen. Perhaps if I open them it will bring him back. Perhaps by sensing he is near he will physically be near. Soon. Or is that what I really want?

I pick up a huge Aran-knit jumper. A big scratchy patterned thing that I've always hated and I hold it close and take a big sniff, smelling Adam's strength, his security, his comfort.

I let it go and open another box, pick up the books, stroke their spines, open and read a few words by Nick Hornby, Irvine Welsh, Andrew Davies.

I read the words and rewrite them in my mind. 'Where does he go, when he's gone? Who can we trust?' I put the book down. He's not here and he can't trust me. How can he? I can't trust myself.

And another box filled with CDs. Billy Joel, Jackson

Browne, Crowded House. My Mr Middle of the Road, I think, and smile sadly as a tear threatens to stagger down my cheek.

And photographs. Dozens of photographs. Here's Adam and Simon, on holiday somewhere many years ago, arms flung round one another as their sun-burnt faces grin broadly at the camera.

Here's Adam with his parents, all of them having lunch in the garden, empty plates with chicken bones, empty bowls on the table. Smiling, happy, Adam's shirt off, basking in the sunshine. I trace my finger down his chest, across his arms. The body I know so well.

And then I pick up a picture of me, a picture I vaguely remember. A picture that I haven't seen for years. I recognise my clothes, beige silk trousers, blue denim shirt, brown loafers and I know I haven't worn these clothes for years. Not since Simon.

I'm sitting in a large airy living room, smiling at something, looking to my left, presumably at someone who is not in the picture. I remember this night. It was a dinner party, three years ago, and I was with Simon. It's coming back to me now. I'm talking to Adam and Simon took the picture. The last time I saw this picture it was at Simon's. How did Adam get it?

And then another picture, a picture I didn't know existed, a picture taken recently. Me again, fast asleep, lying on my side, one arm under the pillow, one clutching the duvet to my chin. I never knew about this picture, Adam must have taken it one morning, caught me at my most vulnerable.

I flip the picture over and on the back Adam has written, 'My Tasha. July 15th, 1996.' I didn't know this picture had been taken, a picture of me taken

unawares that Adam has kept these years, a picture that yearns, aches, sighs for a touch.

At three o'clock in the morning I find myself pacing up and down the flat. He's at home now, I think. He's tucked up in bed. I need to talk to him. I need to explain.

I know what you're thinking, shades of Simon, of driving round to find him in the middle of the night, and I think it too, as I'm driving to Adam's flat, pulling up outside, double parking in Sutherland Avenue and sitting staring. Just staring. For a long, long time.

Thinking about Simon. Thinking about Adam. Thinking about Andrew. Thinking that maybe this was supposed to happen. Maybe I'm not meant to be with Adam.

Thinking about my life. About how far I've come, what I've achieved, and whether any of it really means anything if I'm on my own.

And I sit and I stare, and eventually look up at Adam's windows, blackened windows and I know that I can't ring his doorbell. I can't face him yet because I don't know how to explain. I don't know what to say.

I don't sleep very well. I lie in bed, on my back, eyes wide and staring into space. I think about my relationship with Adam. I think about Andrew. I think about that kiss and I still don't know what to do.

In the morning I go to work on auto-pilot, picking my way through Adam's junk in the corridor, driving to work in the rush-hour, no road rage from me this morning. I drive slowly, calmly, my mind somewhere else.

'You can't do a fucking item on Big is Beautiful,' says Jim, striding up to me with fury in his eyes. 'We're doing it on Monday.'

The lack of communication in this place is amazing. How many times do we ring up an author, a celebrity, a guest and ask them on the show, only to find out they've already been approached by ten different researchers from *Breakfast Break*, all working on different days, all desperate to entice them on to their day, their Monday or Thursday that is 'so much better than all the other days'.

I look up at Jim wearily. I don't need this now, not now. I've been trying Mel all morning and her answerphone at work is on which means she's in a session. 'I'm sorry I can't get to the phone, but do leave your name and number and I promise I will telephone you immediately. Thank you so much for calling.'

I don't need this hassle, I don't need people shouting at me. I'm very close to breaking point so I just look at Jim with tired eyes and say, 'We've been planning it for ages, Jim. I'm sorry, but we're going ahead.'

'Who are you using?'

'Julia Douglas.' I wait for his reaction. Julia Douglas is what you might call a B-list celebrity. She's written dozens of books on being fat and proud of it. She's the number-one model with the agency, 16 Plus VAT, and she's just endorsed a new line of fresh cream cakes.

His reaction is not what I expect. Jim smirks and says, 'Well *love,* you'd better cancel her. We've got Gina Golden.'

Shit, shit, shit! We've been trying Julia Douglas for weeks. Faxing her agent in America, then her publicist, chasing them, waiting for their return calls that never came, and finally being told that sorry, it was a short tour in England and she wouldn't be doing any television.

Gina Golden is a major A-list Hollywood star. She shot to fame as a child with her platinum blonde curls

and big green eyes. She was as cute as cute can be, and her career soared upwards, as has, recently, her weight.

She's in her fifties now. Still beautiful, but a number of loveless marriages has taken it's toll, and she's now huge. Swathed in shimmering caftans, she hasn't been able to play a film part in years.

So instead she's become a businesswoman. She has a line of jewellery, costume rip-offs of designer gems, a line of cosmetics and a line of beauty products.

But she's still remembered as the most beautiful platinum blonde star since Jean Harlow, long since deceased. She's dragged out regularly at the Oscars and the Emmys. No Hollywood function would be complete without the ample form of Gina Golden.

'How the hell did you get Gina Golden?' I'm jealous, but curious.

'Contacts, darling. She wasn't going to do anything but a friend of mine in LA is her personal make-up artist and he talked her into it.'

I shake my head in amazement. Does this gay mafia know no bounds? 'You win. I'll cancel Julia Douglas.'

Jim walks off and then, God knows why, tears start welling up in my eyes, and before I know it I'm fighting to keep down huge heaving sobs.

I know people are watching but I don't care. I lean my head into my hands and my body heaves, black lines of mascara running down my fingers in streams and then I feel an arm around my shoulder.

'Come on, Tasha, it's going to be OK.' David pulls my chair back and leads me out of the office and into his dressing room where he puts his arms around me and I fold into them, leaning my head against his chest and sobbing make-up all over his shirt, but he just holds me tight until I stop.

When you've hit breaking point sometimes you need to be held, and sometimes you need to talk. The odd thing is we tend to talk to the most unlikely people. We talk to strangers in the street, a kind word or a reassuring hand on our arm causes us to open up, causes all the pain to come spilling out.

We talk to strangers, or to people who are not in our inner circle because we don't care and they won't judge. We don't think about the consequences of talking to those we don't know well. We don't worry that they are seeing us at our most vulnerable, that they may take advantage of that. No. Why would we?

David sits me down and disappears, coming back with a cup of tea. He hands it to me silently as I hold it on my lap, lapping over the cup and into the saucer as I start to talk, taking huge great hiccups of breath every few seconds. But I'm calming down.

I talk and I tell David what happened. I tell him about Adam and I tell him about me. I tell him about Simon. I tell him about the rollercoaster. I tell him about Jennifer Mason.

And then when I've finished and I'm just starting to feel embarrassed about the depths of my soul I have just revealed to the presenter on my show, David leans down and strokes my face.

I feel the tears well up again at this sensitivity, this kindness, the way you are always OK until someone asks in a gentle voice, 'Are you OK?' and suddenly you're not.

'You will find someone else,' he says, thinking perhaps he is saying the right thing. 'It feels like the end of the world but time heals all wounds.'

Oh shut up, I think. Keep the clichés to yourself, this isn't about healing the wounds, this is about love, this

is about passion, respect and admiration. This is about which are the two that are enough.

But I smile gratefully for he *has* been lovely, he has held out a helping hand when there was no one else around.

'How about that drink after work?' he says. 'You shouldn't be on your own tonight.'

Typical man, isn't he? He's happy to hold me, to comfort me and to listen to me, just as long as there's something in it for him. But there isn't this time, because the very last thing I need is another man to confuse everything further.

'No,' I say.

'Are you sure?' The sensitive concerned look is on his face again and as I look at him I can't help but wonder where he learnt to do that. From a film perhaps?

'I'm sure.'

He shrugs his shoulders and says, 'If you're sure you'll be OK. Another time perhaps.'

I don't say anything this time, I just walk out of the room and sit back down at my desk, trying to ignore the whispers and stares. I pick up the phone and try Mel again, but it's still her answerphone. I don't leave a message, and I keep trying her all day, but it's a busy day, and she's not there to pick up.

At some point in the afternoon I call Andy. Not perhaps the most sympathetic of people, I know, but she knows me and she knows Adam, and perhaps she can tell me what I should do.

'Bloody hell,' she says when I tell her what happened. 'You've really blown it this time.'

'I know, Andy, I just don't need to hear that right now.'

'Well what do you want me to say?'

I sigh. 'I don't know. I just don't know what I want.'

'Do you love Adam?'

'Yes. You know I do.'

'But you fancy Andrew.' It's a rhetorical question to which we both know the answer.

'It's a bit of a mess,' she says. 'Are you going to talk to Adam?'

'As soon as I've figured out what I'm going to say.'

'Look, why don't you come over later? I'm not doing anything tonight and I'll make something to eat. We can talk about it then, work out what you're going to say.'

'Andy, you can't cook.'

'Yeah, but I meant I'll go out and buy something.'

'OK. If I get hold of Mel can I ask her too?'

'Sure. Do you want me to ask Emma?'

'Mmm. Not sure. I think just the three of us.'

'OK fine. She'll probably be busy anyway, cooking dinner for Richard or organising some cosy dinner party.'

I laugh. 'I'll see you later. And thanks, Andy.'

'What are friends for?' She puts down the phone.

I ring Mel and this time she answers, and her voice is stern. Before I even tell her what happened she stops me. 'Adam called me this morning, Tasha. He told me he walked in on you last night, half-naked, in a passionate kiss with Andrew. I have to tell you that he's devastated. I don't know what you think you're doing but it isn't fair on him. He's too good for this sort of treatment.'

Oh Mel, my Mel, please don't be angry with me, please try to understand.

'I don't know how it happened, Mel, I feel awful. I feel so bloody awful. What did he say?' The tears well up again and the words catch in my throat.

'Oh Tash,' her voice is more gentle now. 'We really need to talk.'

'I know, I've been trying to get you all day. Can I see you tonight?'

'Of course you can. We were only going to the movies so I'll ring Martin now and tell him I'm not coming home.'

I tell her to come to Andy's, and I put the phone down feeling just a tiny bit better. Not a huge amount, but Mel always sorts my life out for me. Mel will tell me what to do.

'It's this passion thing, isn't it?' says Mel, as Andy rushes back from the kitchen, not wanting to miss a second.

'You have this ridiculous notion that there's something missing in your relationship with Adam when in fact he is everything you have ever talked of finding.' I've never seen Mel angry before, and even now the anger is contained, but I can see that she is furious with me, she feels Adam's pain, she doesn't feel my confusion.

'Imagine how Adam felt,' she continues, her voice rising with emotion. 'He walked in and found you with next to nothing on in the arms of his friend. And not only that, this was on the day, the very same day that he was moving in with you. Imagine how that feels, Tasha? Imagine what he is going through.'

Andy leans forward, hanging onto every word. 'Will Adam take her back?'

'Yes, Adam will take her back. He won't trust her, not for a long time, but he's willing to try because he loves her. He really loves you,' she says, looking at me. 'He said he'd even go to couple counselling if it will make you happy.'

'But maybe it's not right with Adam,' Andy offers.

Mel snorts with derision. 'Andy, if it's not right with Adam when is it going to be right with anyone?'

Andy jumps to the defence. 'Maybe it *is* right with Andrew.'

'What?' Mel laughs with amazement. 'With some good-looking bastard who goes around breaking women's hearts? With Andrew who Tasha hardly knows, who will undoubtedly turn out to be a pig?' She turns to me then. 'Tasha, all your life you have had short-term passionate flings. Some of them have felt like relationships, Simon for example, but none of them have been real.

'I've never seen you comfortable in a relationship. I've never seen you relax and be yourself. I've seen you try and become a number of different women, women who you thought they wanted you to be. I've seen you be the doctor's wife, the rock star's girlfriend, the artist's muse. I've seen you change your hair, your clothes, your friends, and there's nothing wrong with that except you've never done it for yourself. You've done it because you've hoped it would make them love you more.

'But don't you understand that *that* wasn't love? That wasn't real? That what you have with Adam, by the mere fact that it *is* so comfortable and natural, is real? That *that* feeling is called love.

'You have to grow up, Tasha,' she sighs. 'Teenagers have crushes. Teenagers go from one relationship to the next and live their lives on that rollercoaster. You aren't a teenager anymore. You're thirty years old and you have a chance of happiness with another person, lasting happiness, happiness that could last the rest of your life.'

'BUT I CAN'T HELP THE WAY I FEEL ABOUT

ANDREW!' I shout, stopping her tirade, leaving both of them sitting there open-mouthed.

'And if it's not Andrew,' I continue in a softer voice, 'then it will be someone else. Not that I'd be looking for it, but in a few years, or a few months or whenever, someone will come along who will be exciting, who I will fancy, and again I will look at Adam and know that I made the wrong decision.'

'I agree with Tash,' says Andy. 'I know it's desperately sad but she's right. It happened yesterday and if she goes back with Adam it will happen again.'

'So you've made your decision.' Mel's looking at me, and it's impossible to read the expression on her face, or the tone in her voice because neither are there. Completely blank.

'Yes.' I nod. 'I don't know whether it's the right one, but I think it's right for me. I need more, Mel. And I also can't help but feel that this is fate. That Andrew was meant to come over last night and it was meant to happen because Adam and I are wrong together.'

Mel rubs her eyes and sits back. 'You know I love you, Tasha. You're my best friend and I'll be there for you, whatever you do, but if you do get together with Andrew, don't expect me to befriend him too.'

I drive home feeling guilty, lonely but also relieved. I can't help it. I can't stand the pain Adam must be going through, but I have to think about me now. I have to stop the pain in the future. I have to stop 'us' now.

But then just as I'm about to put the key in the lock, my front door opens and Adam is standing in the doorway, arms filled with boxes, piled up high under his chin. He stands there and he looks at me, not

saying a word. Just looking with red-rimmed eyes filled with pain.

'We need to talk,' I say quietly, gently pushing him inside. I close the door on the outside world and walk into the living room and sit down.

– Twenty –

What are you supposed to say when you are sitting opposite the man you love, the man you are not in love with but the man you love, and you are feeling his pain as if it is your own.

When you would do almost anything to stop his pain, but the one thing you could give him, the one thing that you know would surely make it go away, is the one thing you just can't give.

I look at Adam and I want to put my arms around him. I want to cuddle him and tell him that it's all going to be OK, but I can't do that. I have to be cruel to be kind, I can't give him a teaser, a taste of what he will be missing in the future because then he will collapse, and if he collapses I don't know what will happen to me. Really, I don't.

So we sit there, opposite one another, in silence.

'What did I do?' Adam whispers eventually. 'I must have done something wrong.'

'Oh God. Ad, you didn't do anything wrong. I'm sorry, it wasn't what it seemed.'

'What do you mean it wasn't what it seemed? What was it then, were you just giving him a friendly kiss? Do you kiss all your friends like that?' He stops, as he

realises what he's just said. No I don't kiss all my friends like that. Just Adam.

'Adam, it just happened, it was one of those things.'

'Things don't *just happen*, Tasha. They happen when you're not happy. They happen when there is something wrong with the relationship, and I have been up all night trying to think what is wrong with our relationship, and you know what the stupid thing is?'

I shake my head but he's not even looking at me. 'The stupid fucking thing is that I can't think of anything. I cannot think of one single thing about our relationship that I would change. I must be stupid, because obviously there's something fundamentally wrong, so what the hell is it? What is it that's missing?'

That pit-stopping, heart-wrenching feeling that is passion is what is missing, but I can't tell him that. Even if I told him that I loved him, that I respected, admired, trusted and loved him, I couldn't tell him that.

Adam starts again, his voice louder, the second person in two days that I have seen lose their temper, the second person who I thought would always keep their head, but then I am inspiring strange emotions in people these days.

You probably hate me by now. I know you're on Adam's side, and I can't exactly blame you, Christ, if I wasn't me I'd be on Adam's side too. But can't you see that it's not fair on him, it's not fair to stay with him until another Andrew comes along.

'I really try and understand you, Tasha. I've been your friend as well as your lover and I really thought I knew you, but you . . . ' he splutters with rage. 'You've really done it this time. You've destroyed the best relationship of my life. Jesus, of your fucking life too.

'And don't tell me it's not because I know that's not

true. Christ, we've been so good together, we've been so happy. How can you blow it? How can you do this to me?'

The questions come in a softer tone of voice, with an air of bewilderment, and I don't know what to say.

'Haven't you been happy?'

'Yes I've been happier than I've ever thought possible.' I go over and sit next to him, and hold his hand gently as he looks up at me with hope in his eyes.

'But something in me is stopping me from accepting things as they are. I love you, I really do, but right at the beginning you knew I wasn't in love with you, I *told* you I wasn't in love with you, and as much as it hurts me to say this, I'm not in love with you now.

'I've tried so hard, Adam.' I can feel tears welling up in my eyes, crocodile tears you might think, but they're not, they're genuine tears of dismay that this hasn't worked out, that I haven't managed to fall in love.

'I've tried to fall in love with you and sometimes I think I have, but a lot of the time I know I haven't.'

'But if you think you have at times, then surely those times will become more and more frequent. I can make you fall in love with me.'

'No.' I shake my head. 'You can't, Adam. Jesus, if you only knew how I wish you could, how I wish I could, but it's not going to happen, and I know that now.'

'What, because of a kiss from a bloke who's supposed to be my friend?' He spits out these last words.

'No. Not because of that kiss. But because I'm not a hundred per cent yours. Because I can't stand the thought of not keeping my options open. Because I still find myself looking around at other men.'

'You bitch.' He says it quietly.

'I'm sorry.' A tear rolls slowly down my face. 'But I

can't guarantee that in the future there won't be other Andrews.'

Adam flinches at the mention of his name, then looks at his hands before saying, 'I don't care. I don't care about the future. I just want to be with you now.'

'I don't know, Adam. I need some time. I need some space.' God how I hate myself for coming out with these words, these clichés that sound so futile in the face of this disaster.

'I need to be on my own for a while, and I think it's a good idea for you too. I think we both need some time. We both need to think about what we want.'

He laughs bitterly. 'I know exactly what I want, you're the one who's confused. And what makes you think I'll wait?'

'You don't have to. You have every right to tell me to fuck off. To say that you never want to see me again. I'll understand. It will hurt me more than you'll ever know but I'll understand.'

He sighs and puts his head in his hands. 'I can't do that. You know I'd never do that. I love you too much.' He starts crying then, and I start crying too. We sit there on the sofa, arms tight around one another and we comfort each other through our tears, and eventually he whispers into my shoulder, 'I'll wait,' and I feel like the biggest bitch in the whole wide world.

Emma phones me early the next morning, breathless with excitement. I rush into the living room to get the phone, and when I hear it's Emma I think she's ringing to say how sorry she is, to ask if there's anything she can do.

But within seconds it's completely clear that she doesn't have a clue what's happened, and I don't tell

her, I don't want to blemish the thrill in her voice, and I've got to tell you, she's practically bursting.

'I'm getting married!'

'That's fantastic!' (That could have been me.) 'When did this happen?'

She's bubbling over and I can almost picture her, curled up in a chair wearing her ivory silk Janet Reger dressing gown, a huge smile covering her face.

'Last night! Richard took me to Le Manoir and he proposed!'

How can you not feel delighted for your friend when she has achieved the one thing she has aspired to all her life. I am truly, truly, delighted, and for a few minutes my own problems recede firmly into the background.

'Did he do something revoltingly naff like drop a ring into a glass of champagne?' The old Tasha rears her head for a couple of seconds. Sorry.

'No,' she laughs, 'he was perfectly old-fashioned. He waited until coffee and then said he had something to ask me. My heart stopped, Tasha, honestly, I couldn't breathe. And then he pulled out a little black velvet box and I was shaking so much I thought I was going to fall off the chair.

'And the ring is beautiful, it's exactly what I wanted.' Emma always gets what she wants and I can picture her now, walking past Tiffany with Richard and idly pointing to a huge solitaire diamond saying she'd like something just like that.

'So what's the ring like?'

'It's from Tiffany!' That *would* be the first thing she says. 'And it's a huge pear-shaped diamond with two smaller diamonds on either side. I love it!' And I know that as she says this she is holding her hand out, splaying her fingers and admiring her rock.

'So when's the wedding?'

'Heaven knows. We rang both sets of parents last night and Mummy's over the moon, so we're all going out for dinner tonight to discuss it.'

You just know what Emma's wedding will be like, don't you. Three hundred of her parents' closest business acquaintances, a wedding for the parents, a wedding that has nothing to do with Emma and Richard.

'There's only one thing I'm absolutely sure of,' she continues, running out of breath. 'I want all of my girls to be bridesmaids.'

I go back to bed smiling. That makes two of us who have got what they want. What, I wonder, will happen to the remaining two?

So I lie there and think about this for a while and then, as I'm drifting off to sleep, my mind starts wandering, as it so often does in those half-awake, half-asleep moments, and I start to think about Andrew, and seeing as we're now so close I'll share my thoughts with you.

My first thought: Actually it's not really a thought, it's a memory. I lie there and press rewind, go back to the night Andrew taught me to smoke cigars. Pause for a while as I remember his words, the look on his face as he told me he wanted to take me to bed, to make love to me, and I shiver at the memory.

My second thought: A memory. Adam was there that night, and he was quiet. He was in love with me then and he knew there was chemistry going on between Andrew and me. What must he have been feeling?

My third thought: I want some deep, lustful, animal

sex. Sex with no strings attached. I need to go on a quest for passion.

My fourth thought: Andrew is the most likely candidate, if, and it's a big if, if he'll still want to know. He is, after all, Adam's friend.

My fifth thought: Adam. A memory. Adam's arms around me, Adam kissing me, Adam inside me. No. Go away. I will not think about this.

My sixth thought: If not Andrew, who?

My seventh thought: David.

My eighth thought: David's perfect, handsome, tele-friendly features. His height, his strength, his fanciability factor. David's arms around me sobbing my heart out in his dressing room. David buying me a coffee in the canteen and flirting, asking me for a drink.

My ninth thought: No. Too close to home. How could I explain that it's just a fling, a quest for passion. What if he refused to accept it? What if he had me 'let go'?

My tenth thought: Andrew.

'Andy?'

'Hmm?' I can tell I have woken her up, that she is still in her bed, has just reached a sleepy arm to the phone.

'Did I wake you?'

'Hmm.'

'Sorry, sorry, sorry, but I need your help.'

'What with?' She's whispering.

'I can't explain now. Do you want to meet me for breakfast?'

'Hang on,' she whispers, 'don't go away.' The phone is put down and picked up again.

'Sorry. I couldn't talk, I had to come into the living room because the man's still asleep.'

'I thought Chris didn't work out.'

'Chris who?' she laughs. 'No, this is a new one, a guy I met last week. Cor, what a night, I can hardly walk.'

'Did you hear about Emma?'

'She woke me up about half an hour ago to tell me the good news. Fantastic, isn't it, and she didn't even have to issue an ultimatum.'

I laugh. 'So you weren't properly asleep when I called, which means you're awake enough to meet me for breakfast?'

'I've got croissants in the fridge,' she grumbles. 'I was planning a nice long romantic breakfast in bed with Mark.'

'All you'd be missing is the sunlight streaming through the windows,' I say, looking out my own window to a dark grey sky threatening rain. 'Please,' I plead.

'Oh OK,' she says. 'If it's urgent.'

'It's on me,' I laugh. 'And you can always leave Mark in bed and bring the papers home. Just think how romantic that would be.'

'OK,' she says. 'Deal. See you in fifteen minutes.'

I pull on my jeans, slip a jumper over my head and jump in the car to go to our local café, and just as I've ordered and I'm sitting at a small round table tucked away in a private corner, Andy walks in. She's wearing her trainers, a black tracksuit, big gold earrings and the ubiquitous Jackie O sunglasses. She orders at the

bar and then turns to look for me. As soon as she finds me she bows her legs and walks to the table moaning and groaning. 'The pain,' she says, 'the pain,' sitting down and grinning widely. 'This is my Hollywood housewife look. What do you reckon?'

'Very Hollywood housewife.'

'That's what I thought. Understated but glam.' She grins happily. 'So what's so important you have to tear me away from a gorgeous man for breakfast?'

'I need your help.'

'You said.'

'I'm on a quest for passion.'

Her eyes widen with excitement. 'That's fabulous. How are you going to do it?'

'That's why I need your help. It's got to be with Andrew, I have to sleep with him. I have to know whether what he makes me feel is real. But how the hell am I going to do it?'

'Just ring him up and ask him over.' She's looking at me as if I'm mad.

'But what if he says no. I mean, for God's sake, he's the reason Adam and I broke up, he's hardly going to go steaming in again.'

'I see what you mean.' We both sit there and scoop the chocolate off the top of our coffees. I lick the back of my spoon and regard my upside-down reflection. I look horrible.

'Are you sure you want to do this?' Andy's looking at me intently.

'Andy! Of course I'm sure. You have always been the one who said hold out for passion, don't settle for anything less. How can *you* be asking whether I'm sure?'

'I don't mean are you sure, I mean, are you sure you're ready for this now?'

No, I'm not sure at all. I'm not sure I am ready to climb into someone else's bed, to feel a body that isn't Adam's, but this is why I need to do it. I need to be reassured that I've done the right thing, and what better way than to fuck a man who is 100 per cent fuckable?

'Ready as I'll ever be.' I grin at her.

'OK,' she says. 'Sometimes a girl's gotta do what a girl's gotta do.'

'So? How do I do it.'

'Presumably you don't want to do it in your flat.'

I shake my head vigorously. 'Too many memories.'

'So what about his flat?'

'Nope. It needs to be on neutral territory.'

'Wanna borrow my car?' We both laugh.

'It really needs to be a hotel. Somewhere that doesn't mean anything to either of us.'

'But how can you get him to a hotel?' And then her face breaks into a huge smile. 'I've got it!' She leaps up, jumps up and down attracting stares from everyone in the restaurant. She sits back down again, 'I've bloody got it!'

Her plan is this: I phone Andrew and tell him I need to talk, the theory being that he already feels so guilty that he won't question what about, he'll assume it's about Adam.

I tell him that I want to meet somewhere where we don't know anyone, somewhere where there's no chance of bumping into anyone we know.

We'll both um and ah for a while and then I'll say, what about x hotel, they have a bar there and it's so out of the way we would never be spotted.

I will reassure him that I have no ulterior motive,

that this is purely a need to talk, and the secrecy is just in case anyone sees us and gets the wrong idea, someone who might tell Adam.

He will come to the bar, and it will be awkward in the beginning. I will tell him that I am worried about Adam. That there is no future between Adam and me. That I am far happier being single.

I will perhaps remind him of the occasions we have met, of the conversations we have had, and perhaps, if I am very lucky, he will draw out a cigar from his top pocket.

We will have a few drinks, and he will light his cigar. I will take the cigar and tell him I have forgotten how to smoke it. I will ask him to teach me again. He may or may not demonstrate once more by sucking my fingers, but this is not important, for by this time our tongues will be loosened by alcohol and I will have no qualms in taking his finger in my mouth and asking him, 'How does this feel? Is this right?'

He will be sitting there overtaken with lust. He will cross his legs to hide an almighty erection, and he will feel as guilty as hell.

But. He also fancies me, and men, as we know, perhaps with a few exceptions, are ruled by their pricks, so it will only take a little gentle encouragement to whisk him up the stairs to the room I will have booked earlier.

He may show a few reservations, but in the lift, travelling up to the room, I will unbutton my shirt and I will be wearing nothing underneath. That will put paid to his reservations.

And once in the room with the door safely locked we will tear each other's clothes off, we will not think of the consequences.

There. She has got it. The perfect seduction. He brings the animal lust, I bring the condoms.

Was ever a seduction as methodical as this?

– Twenty-One –

You'd never believe Emma's wedding is nine months away and of *course* I'll go and look at wedding dresses with her. Just look though, I won't be trying any on. Not now.

Do I still think of getting married? Sure, of course I do, but not with quite the same desperation as I used to. I probably could have married Adam, sorry, *could* marry Adam, but I'm not one of those women who is so desperate they'll settle for second best.

I suppose on the odd occasion I thought about it when I was with Adam. Not so much what married life would be like as the big day itself. To be completely frank I've spent years dreaming of my wedding day. I've got it all planned, except every few months, every few men, I change the dress a bit, the guests at the reception, the going away outfit.

So what's the latest look? It's not something I've thought of for a few weeks, but the latest design came to me a few months ago.

And no, I won't be getting married in a meringue, despite what you may think. My wedding dress will be understated, stunning in its simplicity.

My current favourite is white chiffon. An empire line, beaded bodice with layers and layers of floaty

ivory chiffon. A headdress of flowers, or maybe not, maybe an ivory silk headband. Then again it could be a tiara. Nah, too over the top, I'll stick with the flowers.

My flowers will be lilies, sprays of lilies cascading down, and my bridesmaids will be . . . well, I haven't really planned it but the last time the girls and I discussed our wedding days Emma said if we put her in anything frilled, pastel-coloured or made of shot silk, she'd never forgive us.

And Andy agreed, so the four of us made a pact. Whoever is the first to get married has to dress the bridesmaids in Armani. And if they can't afford Armani then it has to be Armaniesque.

Even Mel agreed, and she wouldn't know an Armaniesque outfit if she trod on one. But she knew we knew what we were talking about so she agreed anyway.

My designer of choice for my wedding dress would be Catherine Walker, but Emma's got there first, except she insists on having a look around, just to get a few ideas.

So here we are, three out of four on a Saturday morning. Emma did ask Mel, but she couldn't make it and I'm pretty damned relieved. I still call her, we still chat, it's still fine, but there's something about our conversations together now that makes me think there's still a problem.

I don't think Mel can forgive me. Not just at the moment, and I understand that, I understand it and I accept it because I know our friendship is ultimately strong enough to withstand this.

But it may not be if she knew I was planning to seduce Andrew. So in some ways it's easier that she's not here today, easier because I won't have to lie to her, or withhold the truth.

So we bundle into Emma's BMW and zoom off to a wedding dress shop, a small designer boutique which Emma won't be using because the designer isn't nearly well-known enough, but she's happy to plagiarise. Aren't we all?

But it is exclusive, you can always tell it's exclusive – or at least it thinks it's exclusive – when you can't go into a shop until you ring a doorbell and a sales assistant answers. And here you even have to make a bloody appointment.

So we stand outside and a worried-looking woman comes to the door and opens it just a fraction. 'Yes?' she says uncertainly, doubtless wondering what four women are doing on her doorstep, they can't all be getting married . . . surely.

Chance would be a fine thing.

'I'm Emma Morris, I've got an appointment?' Why do we always turn this into a question. I do it myself, I go to the hairdresser's and say, 'I'm seeing Keith?' as if there's any doubt.

And the other habit I still have, which I hate, is that I'm always apologising. I'll be standing in the supermarket and someone will step on my foot. 'Sorry,' I say. Or someone's blocking my way walking down the street, and sure enough, that bloody word comes out again.

Am I really so pathetic? Please tell me I'm not the only one who does this.

So Emma poses the question, the woman checks her appointment book and, as if by magic, she opens the door and let's us all in.

'My my,' she says looking at all of us. 'How many here are brides to be?'

I smile back. 'Emma's the only one getting married. The rest of us are aspiring.'

'Gosh, well. I'm sure it will be your turn next,' she looks vaguely at each of us and Andy looks at me and raises her eyes to heaven.

The door closes behind us and suddenly I feel quite awestruck. It's like being in an Aladdin's cave of romance, walls and walls of shiny white silk, tiny little pearl beads, layers and layers of tulle.

And in a glass cabinet in the centre are veils, short veils, long veils, veils on combs. Headdresses, crystal tiaras (Andy nudges me and gestures towards the tiaras whispering, 'Mmm, smart.'), and spun silk hairbands.

'Oh God,' says Andy, heading straight for a dress that looks like once upon a time it might have been worn by Scarlett O'Hara, 'I think I've died and gone to heaven.'

I've never been in a wedding dress shop before, and I can't believe the urge to try everything on. No, I tell myself, I can't do this. What, after all, would be the point?

So I sit on the sofa while Emma collects a handful of dresses and whisks them in to the dressing room. Andy sits next to me, but after a few minutes she stands up with a smile. 'What the hell,' she grins, lifting the Scarlett O'Hara dress off the hanger. 'Doesn't look as if I'll ever be getting married so I may as well know what it feels like now. Are you coming?'

'What the hell,' I grin back, walking over to a dress that caught my eye, a chiffon, empire-line dress that's remarkably similar to the one I'd created in my imagination, the only addition being tiny pink roses all over the bodice.

Andy and I push back the curtain to the dressing

room and Emma, standing there in a perfectly matching set of what looks like cream silk underwear, starts to laugh.

'I knew it,' she says. 'I knew the two of you wouldn't be able to resist it!'

'Just don't comment on my underwear,' says Andy. 'It's the old grey favourites today, and I think there may even be holes in them somewhere.'

I start to unbutton my clothes, and just as I'm about to step into my dress I turn to Andy and say, 'Are you sure it's not bad luck to try on a wedding dress if you're not getting married?'

Andy rolls her eyes to the ceiling. 'My luck couldn't be worse, I don't think this is going to make any difference.'

'I know what you mean,' I mutter back.

Emma is struggling with the dress, layers and layers of stiff white tulle, a proper ballerina skirt, down to the floor, with a plain satin bodice, studded with tiny seed pearls, and Andy and I help her get it over her head, lifting the layers until we find a gap for her head.

I do up the tiny row of buttons on the back and Emma turns to face us as we both gasp. She looks absolutely beautiful, like the fairy on top of the Christmas tree.

She walks into the shop and I can hear the sales assistant oohing and aahing as she walks around and admires her reflection in the mirror.

My turn, my turn. I step in the chiffon number and Andy does up the back. 'Hang on,' she says, 'if you're going to do it, do it properly.' She walks back into the shop and I can hear her whispering to the sales assistant. What *is* she doing?

Moments later she comes back with a floor length veil, a silk headband and medium-heeled satin pumps.

'You are a size six, aren't you?' I nod as I put the whole ensemble together, and I refuse to look at myself in the cramped space of the dressing room, this is a moment I want to savour, I want to keep in my memory for ever. Just in case.

I walk into the shop and the amazing thing is my walk changes. I don't stride as I normally do, I take slow, measured steps, steps that you would make walking down the aisle. Steps that hopefully I will make walking down the aisle.

And Emma, bless her, wipes a tear from her eye. 'You look beautiful,' she whispers in amazement. 'You look absolutely beautiful.'

I look in the mirror and a huge smile spreads across my face. She's absolutely right. I do look beautiful. Even with my everyday hair and make-up, I look beautiful, wonderful, glowing, the best I've ever looked.

'God,' I whisper, 'I never realised white was so flattering.'

I don't want to take this dress off. Ever. I want to live in this dress for the rest of my life. Hell, I even want to sleep in this dress. I don't even think that I recently blew the biggest chance at marriage I'd ever had, I just gaze at my reflection in awe.

Andy comes out next, in her Scarlett O'Hara dress and Emma and I fall about laughing.

'You look incredible,' I say. 'Just a bit . . .'

'Over the top,' says Emma.

'I know,' coos Andy in a deep Southern accent, twirling and looking in the mirror, 'but frankly my dears, I don't give a damn.

'Hang on a minute,' she says, 'I've got an idea.' She pulls the sales assistant aside and whispers something

to her. The sales assistant looks doubtful, but eventually smiles and nods her agreement. 'Back in a minute,' says Andy, gathering her layers and layers around her and dashing out of the door with a smile on her face. She turns round just before the door closes, saying, 'Don't move a muscle, either of you.'

Emma and I swish round the shop, and then Andy runs back in, pulling something out of a white paper bag. 'Tah dah,' she says, brandishing a disposable camera. 'Can't let the biggest day of your lives go unrecorded.'

She insists on first posing Emma and I at the side of the sofa, hand resting regally on the arm, and then, just in case the light isn't good enough, taking us outside.

The sales assistant doesn't mind, this is probably the most fun she's ever had, and she rushes around finding veils and shoes for Andy and Emma.

Finally, when everything's perfect, the three of us troop outside. Andy playing wedding photographer, crouching and leaping around snapping the camera, and the rest of us laughing self-consciously as she tells us where to stand. We take turns, Emma and I, in shooting pictures of Andy, who has sent the sales assistant back inside to see if she has any garters lying around.

God what a sight we make, three brides in full bridal regalia in the middle of the West End. The traffic slows down to look at us and I can see the smile on people's faces.

'When's the big day?' shouts a bloke in a Ford Cortina.

'There isn't one!' Andy and I shout back in unison, watching as he tips his head back and laughs.

'Ought to be, darling, shame to let *that* go to waste.'

We giggle like schoolchildren, lapping up the attention, the admiring glances, the occasional comments on how beautiful we look, and then we troop back inside.

What is this aura around marriage? Why is it still, even in these days of equality, the pinnacle of a woman's achievement. Of course I agree with you, it shouldn't be like this, but somehow as long as you're single, you're not quite good enough, you haven't quite made the grade.

You go to parties, or meet strangers and they ask you, 'Are you married?' and when you shake your head they never know quite what to say.

But a girl can pretend, which is precisely what I'm doing, and as I slip out of the dress I feel an incredible disappointment, but I can't let it show as Emma's getting married for real and Andy, well, everything's a big laugh to Andy.

'Well?' Andy's dragged me to one side of the shop while Emma tries on a few more dresses.

'Well what?'

'Have you called him yet?'

I wince. 'No.'

'Why not?'

'I will, OK? I just have to wait until the right time.'

'Now's the right time,' she says, brandishing her mobile phone like some magic potion.

'Go outside and call him now. Do you want me to come with you?'

'No, it's OK.' Reluctantly I take the phone and stand outside the shop. Digging out my address book I punch his number into the phone.

'Hello?' Shit! I don't know what to say, so I press the red telephone button on the phone and hang up.

'That was quick,' says Andy as I hand her back the phone. 'What did he say?'

'Hello.'

'And then what?'

'I hung up.'

'Oh Tasha,' she moans, 'ring him again.'

'I can't. I'll do it when I get home.'

'Promise?'

'Yes I bloody promise. Shit, I just remembered. What network is your phone on?'

'Network? I don't know. It's a Nokia Orange.'

'Shit, shit shit! That means that if he presses 1471 the number will come up and he may . . .' Before I even finished talking the phone started ringing.

'What should I do?' Andy's looking panicked.

'Tell him you misdialled and you're sorry to have troubled him.'

She does this, but even these few nondescript words are turned into seduction as Andy smiles into the phone and lowers her voice. 'I'm so very sorry,' she purrs, before cutting the call and saying, 'phwooargh, he *has* got a sexy voice, hasn't he?'

I don't bother saying anything. What the hell could I say? It's just Andy being Andy.

But at home, after lots of deep breaths, I pick up the phone and with pounding heart dial his number.

'Andrew? It's Tasha.'

'Hello.' His voice is uncertain. 'How are you?'

'Fine. Well, not so fine really. A bit confused.'

'Look,' he says, 'I know about Adam and I'm really sorry. I feel terrible, I don't know how it happened and I tried to explain that it didn't mean anything, but Adam wasn't interested. I'm so sorry.' His voice tails off lamely as my heart jumps. Andrew the heartbreaker is apologising to me! Maybe he *is* a nice guy. Maybe he's *not* a bastard. Maybe he *could* be relationship material.

NO! Tasha, stop it. You don't want a relationship with anyone, least of all him. He's a fuck. He's the result of your quest for passion. Nothing more, nothing less.

'I know, Andrew,' I say calmly. 'It's not your fault, but I really need to talk to someone about it.'

'You want to talk to me?' He sounds, unsurprisingly, surprised.

'It's just that you know Adam, I need to talk to someone who knows Adam.'

'But I'm the last person you need to talk to right now.'

'No, you're the best person I need to talk to.'

He sounds suspicious, as well he might. Jesus, why are men so stupid sometimes?

'Look, it won't take long, but could you meet me for a coffee?'

'I suppose so.' He sounds reluctant, he sounds like a completely different Andrew from the one who wanted to make love to me, the one who held my face and kissed me passionately. But I keep going. I've made a deal with myself and I have to.

We arrange to meet, and I suggest the hotel, explaining that no one could spot us, that I wouldn't want Adam to know, to jump to the wrong conclusion, and we say goodbye, as I pray that he doesn't ring me back to cancel, he doesn't have second thoughts.

I don't want to tell Louise what I'm doing. Even now, even though you're supposed to be completely honest in therapy, I don't want her to raise an eyebrow, to question what I'm doing, to question why I'm doing it.

I don't want her to know because perhaps, deep down, at some level, I know that sleeping with Andrew is the wrong thing to do. I know it won't solve

anything, but I also know that I'm going to do it anyway.

But Louise believes that Adam is my chance at happiness, that passion isn't important, that we have, sorry, had, the sort of relationship that she hopes all her clients will eventually achieve.

She'd never say that of course, but all it takes is a look, a scowl, a perfectly-placed question to make me realise that I'm wrong, or that what I'm doing is not the, how shall I put it, the correct course of action.

But sitting in Louise's room, sitting in the absolute silence is like taking a lie detector test? I can't lie to her, as much as I want to, because it would be like lying to myself, and the first rule of therapy is honesty. But perhaps I can withhold the truth. Can I? Should I?

'How *are* you?' she says, knowing from my session last week that Adam and I have broken up, that I am confused, that I am still holding out for more.

'I'm OK,' I say, which is what I always say because it sounds too futile to say fine, and 'OK' seems to cover the whole spectrum.

'How has your week been?'

'It's been up and down. I'm missing Adam,' I'm not lying, I am, 'but not as much as I've missed boyfriends in the past. I mean, I'm not crying myself to sleep at night or anything like that. There have been times when I've felt incredibly lonely but I don't think that's Adam particularly, it's not that I want to be with him, it's just getting used to the feeling of being on my own again.'

Louise looks at the ceiling for a while, which means she's thinking, she's thinking of the right question, the question that will probe my innermost thoughts.

Eventually she looks back at me. 'So this break-up is different to all the others, hmm?'

I nod.

'Different because it's not as painful.'

It's a statement rather than a question but I nod anyway.

'So because it's not painful does that mean the relationship wasn't right?'

'I think so. I mean, in the past I've spent weeks crying, up all night wandering the corridors of my flat, feeling so lonely I think I'm going to die, but this time the thing I miss most is Adam's friendship.'

'And how important is that friendship to you?'

God, talk about same old ground or what. But I know how Louise works, she thinks if she keeps on going eventually she'll get through. Sometimes it works. I wouldn't have started with Adam in the first place if Louise hadn't kept banging on about the importance of friendship, how attraction doesn't matter, how none of us has 'a type'.

But just because she's been right in the past doesn't mean she's always right. Does it?

'Next to my girlfriends, Adam's friendship is the most important thing in my life, but I think that's the problem, we shouldn't have taken it further, we should have stayed friends.'

'And how important do you think friendship is in a relationship hmm?'

'Very important, of course it is, but you need other things too.'

'Such as passion?' A sarcastic tone of voice but I choose to ignore it.

'Yes. Such as passion.'

'And where do you think you'll find this combination of friendship with passion?'

I hesitate. Do I tell her? Do I tell her that right now I couldn't give a damn about the friendship, that I've

had friendship up to my ears, that what I want, what I really need right now is passion?

I wimp out.

'I'm sure it will happen sometime, but I think that at the moment I need to be on my own for a while.'

'And what about Andrew?'

Damn, the woman's a witch.

'What about him?'

'Well, *he* could give you passion.'

I shrug my shoulders as if to say, 'So? So what?'

'But he couldn't give you friendship.'

I shrug again.

'Have you thought about that?'

'Yes,' I grudgingly admit, 'he's not relationship material at all, I know that.'

'But Adam was.'

Yes, she's right, Adam was. I don't tell her anymore. How can I? I'll tell her next week, after the deed has been done, after the earth has moved and then I'll tell her it just happened, that it wasn't planned, that he seduced me.

She doesn't need to know it was premeditated. She doesn't need to know about my quest for passion. She only needs to know as much as I want to tell her.

'A fling, with Andrew or any one of the Andrews in the world isn't the answer. You've been through that,' she says, while I look guiltily at the ground. 'You've slept with men in the past to raise your self-esteem and it hasn't worked. You might have felt good while you were in bed with them, but afterwards you always felt terrible.

'You've come too far to do that again. Life isn't always black and white, and sometimes the grey areas are the ones that work best for us.'

What is she saying? Is Andrew a black area and

Adam a grey? I don't know, I really don't know so I just nod as if I know what she's talking about and look at the clock, desperate for the end of the session.

Am I doing the right thing, am I doing the right thing? The thought whirls round my head as I'm drifting off to sleep. But then I lie and think about Andrew's eyes, his hands, the way his mouth feels, the taste of his lips, and I think, yes, you have to do it.

I think about Adam too. About the way we laughed together when we were in bed, how sex suddenly became fun, ridiculous, playful. Of course there were times when it was intense, but most of the time it wasn't.

I think about the time I bought a women's magazine and there was a pullout, 'The Positions You Always Wanted to Try and Never Dared'. It fell out the magazine while I was reading it in bed and Adam immediately grabbed it and read the Kama Sutra descriptions out loud in amazement, showing me every picture and shaking his head in disbelief.

He insisted we try each position. He even drew up a chart, little stick figures in absurd positions, with a day written over each one. On Monday we tried The Large Bee – me on top, facing his feet.

On Tuesday we tried The Knee Trembler, but we had to stop because we were laughing so hard as Adam tried to carry me, inside me with my legs wrapped round his waist. He kept losing his balance, stumbling around the bedroom with me sinking lower and lower until eventually we both fell over.

On Wednesday we tried Putting On the Sock, which I would describe except it's a bit too complicated. Suffice to say it didn't work.

On Thursday we tried The Milk and Honey

Embrace, me sitting on top of Adam, my back to him, and I loved this, but he moaned that he couldn't see my face.

On Friday we gave up and went back to our usual love-making, punctuated with moans of pleasure and occasional soft laughter.

No. I'm not going to think about this any more.

– Twenty-Two –

What I don't need, what I really don't need just as I'm blow-drying my hair and feeling sick with nerves about my impending night of passion with Andrew, is Mel.

But of course the phone rings and it's Mel on the other end, Mel who I love more than anyone, Mel who I don't want to deceive.

We're still going through this, glitch, in our friendship, a tiny rough patch if you like, a time when we're not able to be completely honest with one another, when we feel more like acquaintances than friends.

But it will pass, I know it will pass because it has happened before. I have had arguments with people in the past, and for the longest time I was terrified that it meant the end of our friendship, but time and therapy together have taught me that when you truly care about people, your closest friends and lovers, arguments are important, because they're about being honest with one another.

And arguments always recede into the past, strengthening the friendship if you're lucky, and at the very least adding a new dimension.

And Mel and I didn't exactly argue, she just disapproves of what I'm doing, so, much in the way I held

back from Louise, I'm holding back from Mel. Hey, I still have Andy to confide in. And you.

'Do you want to come over for dinner tonight?' Mel sounds like the old Mel, only slightly more tentative, slightly unsure. And I would love to come over for dinner tonight, except tonight is the night I will be seducing Andrew, tonight is the night I have been looking forward to, and dreading, in equal measure.

'Oh damn, I'd love to but I can't.' Quick, think, think. 'I'm going out with some of the girls from work.'

'What a shame. Oh well, never mind. How are you anyway?'

'OK. Up and down, you know how it is.'

'Mmm. Have you . . . spoken to him?'

'To Adam?'

'Yes.'

'No. I'm still confused, I think it is over, but I don't quite know how to tell him.'

'Maybe that's because it's not.'

'Maybe.' What else can I say? 'So how's Martin?'

'Oh lovely as ever, and cooking tonight which is a treat.'

'I'm sorry I can't make it. Can I call you tomorrow?'

'Sure thing.'

It's a nothing conversation. A conversation of small talk, of inanities that serve to keep our friendship on the straight and narrow, but only just.

So we say goodbye and I look at myself for a long time in the mirror without moving. I move my face so close to the glass that my features become indistinct, it's not me, it's just a series of swimming shapes, and I have to shake my head vigorously to remind myself who I am.

'I am a woman with a mission,' I tell my reflection as I pick up the lipliner and slowly draw pinky brown

lines around my lips, blending them in with a matching lipstick.

I feel like everything is happening in slow motion, like it's not really happening to me. I'm a character in a film I tell myself as I tip my head upside down then whip it back, running my fingers through my hair and scrunching it to give me a wild, abandoned look.

I'm a character in a film with the plot already finely tuned. All I have to do now is follow the script, act the part, listen to the director inside my head.

And when my make-up is ready I open my drawer and pull out my new underwear. My ultra-feminine, frothy, lacy, delicate concoction of matching bra and knickers, and I have a confession to make. I don't believe in spending fortunes on underwear as well you know, but I made an exception in this case.

I bought this on Saturday, at a small boutique that Andy dragged me to, a boutique I'd passed many times but had never thought of going in.

'Sometimes you have to spend the money,' she insisted, shoving me through the front door. She wanted me to buy La Perla, but I put my foot down, and in the end she agreed that the set I chose was stunning, albeit a make neither of us had heard of. It was £100, what a ridiculous price for such tiny pieces of clothing, but Andy kept insisting, 'Think what he'll think when he sees it, and think how you'll feel.'

And when I got home and tried it on, I did feel sexy, the cut was so flattering, high on the hips, swooping down low over the cleavage, pale, pale peach lace, and I smiled. Jesus, if I was a man I wouldn't be able to resist this either. And I thought of Andrew and I smiled again.

Not once did I think of poor Adam who was quite

happy with my once-white-now-pale-grey cotton knickers draped all over the radiators in my flat. Not once did I think how Adam would have liked this underwear, would have revelled in its sheer luxuriousness. Not once did I, in fact, think of Adam.

Nor did I think of the expense of this seduction. £100 for the underwear, £150 for the hotel room, but it will be worth it, I tell myself, blanching slightly, it will be worth it for the best fuck, the best night of passion I have ever had.

I open my cupboard and pull out my seduction outfit. Nothing too over the top, can't have him knowing instantly what's going on. So instead it's a dress, a long floaty dress with a slit up one side that nearly reaches my hips, and tiny buttons down the entire length of the front. A dress that whispers as it walks. A dress that caresses my body yet leaves everything to the imagination.

A toothbrush goes into my bag, clean knickers, a hairbrush, and then I'm ready. A few admiring glances in the mirror and I'm out of the door, running to the car, not quite believing that this day, this night, has finally arrived.

And luck is on my side, a parking spot right outside the hotel, walking sedately up the steps and into the cool, dark, plush interior. No need to check in now, I can do what they do in the films, excuse myself from Andrew at the crucial point and discreetly check in without his knowledge.

So I walk through the hotel, ten minutes late, my heels tap, tap, tapping on the marble floor, and then sinking into thick carpet as I walk into the coffee area.

Large comfy sofas, small mahogany tables, discreetly placed in corners of the room. Whispered conversations, private, quiet, relaxed. And then I spot

him, my heart plummets, and he looks up from his cup of coffee and stands up to greet me.

I smile, suddenly feeling shy. 'Hello,' he says, kissing my cheek. 'You look lovely.' And I relax because this was the moment I had been so nervous about, how would he greet me, would he be embarrassed, would I?

But of course it is Andrew. Shining, confident, good-looking Andrew, and he has probably never suffered a moment of embarrassment in his life, and certainly not over a woman he kissed passionately the last time they met.

I sit down, aware that my skirt has fallen open, the slit revealing a smooth, tanned thigh, and I shift slightly so I am slightly more covered but I note that Andrew glances at my thigh. Again. And again.

He sits back and looks at me shaking his head, and I know what this means. It means I still have an effect on him, it means he knows we shouldn't be here, it means we both know what the outcome of this evening will be.

And I start to feel more confident. Shit, I start to enjoy myself, myself in the role of seductress, and I know I can do this, I can make this happen.

'So,' he raises an eyebrow, still looking at me, 'you don't look like a woman on the verge of a nervous breakdown.'

'Now where would you get an idea like that?'

'You did say you were confused, you wanted to talk. But you don't look confused.'

'Oh really? How do I look?' Flirtatious, leading.

'No,' he says gently. 'I'm not here to flirt.' Damn. Knockback number one, but I won't be stopped that easily.

'Neither am I, Andrew.' My voice is serious, I step out of the role of seductress and into the role of a

woman needing sympathy. 'I wanted to meet you to let you know that it's not your fault. That I know what happened between us should never have happened, but that my relationship with Adam wasn't what it should have been. What happened between us was just the catalyst, and I didn't want you to feel guilty.'

He doesn't say anything, just watches me, waits for what I'm going to say next, but shit, I don't know what to say next, I don't know how to tell him what I'm feeling, and yes, for your information I'm still feeling it.

God, you must think I'm a heartless bitch, but even while I'm lying through my teeth about my relationship with Adam, I'm thinking, I want you, I want to see you with no clothes on, I want to smell you, I want to fuck you. Jesus how I want to fuck you.

And then he shakes his head, to himself and sighs.

'What's the matter?' I ask, leaning forward to check he's OK, knowing that my dress will slip forward and if he chooses to look he'll get an eyeful of cleavage.

He looks. 'We shouldn't be here,' he says.

'Why not?' As if I don't know.

'You know why not.'

'No I don't. Why not?'

'Because Adam is my friend and I've already done enough damage. Because you know the effect you have on me. Because I knew, before I even came out, where this would end.'

Yes! I've done it, I've got him exactly where I wanted him and look, we've only been here twenty minutes. Not even that. Shit, this was much easier than I thought.

'And where *will* this end?' Provocative? Me?

'Where do you think?'

'I think you might be presuming a little too much.'

'I don't think so.'

I raise an eyebrow. 'Why don't we have a drink. What can I get you?'

I stand up and walk to the bar, knowing he's watching me, watching my hips sway as I sashay over, back straight, bottom in, tits out, a woman about to be fucked, a woman no man can resist.

And I walk back to the table looking straight ahead of me, not wanting to meet Andrew's eyes, because I won't know what expression to wear, and as I sit down he takes the drink from my hand, and as he does so his hand touches mine and I swear to God, it feels like a bolt of electricity. I jerk back my hand in amazement. Jesus. This is what it's all about. This is what I've been missing.

'Excuse me,' I say, 'I'll be back in a minute,' and I walk out of the room, hoping to God he won't notice that I've walked straight past the loos and I'm heading to the front desk.

'I'd like to check in,' I tell the clerk.

'Certainly madam,' he says obsequiously. 'And your name?'

I check in, and walk back to the table, slipping the credit card key to the hotel room into my bag without Andrew seeing. A quick glance in a mirror on the way back confirms that my hair is still having a good day and my skin is still matte, no powder needed as yet.

We sit there for two hours, talking about our lives, our feelings, our relationships. I learn that Andrew hasn't ever had a serious relationship, that now, at thirty-five, he's looking to settle down, and I have to constantly push away the lingering thought that it could be with me.

I learn that he has a penchant for blondes, and as I wonder whether he means natural or highlighted, he

looks at me cooly, reading my mind, and adds, 'Real or otherwise.'

I learn that he has many admirers, but being one myself I am hardly surprised, and I learn that he believes his expectations are too high, which is why he has not, as yet, found the right woman.

And then I learn about his fantasies. Believe me, this wasn't on the agenda, but the combination of alcohol – we are drinking ridiculous amounts – and sexual attraction which is clouding the air around us like a thick fog, is leading us to reveal far more than I, at least, had planned.

I learn that his fantasy is to go to bed with two women, one blonde, one dark, and to watch them together before joining in. I learn that he has already had a threesome, but it was with one woman and another man, and he found the whole episode disappointing. I learn that he lost his virginity at sixteen, with a friend of his mother's, and I learn that I am getting more and more turned on as we talk. Shit, any more turned on than this and I'd stick to the bloody chair.

And does he learn about me? Does he ever. He learns that I lost my virginity at eighteen while I was on holiday, with a handsome Frenchman who I never heard from again. He learns that I love talking dirty, that nothing turns me on more. He learns that I have never been to bed with another woman, although occasionally I've wondered what it would be like. And he learns that I, too, have fucked two men at the same time and it was one of the most mind-blowing nights of my whole life.

And as we talk, cocooned together in the corner of this room, we move closer and closer, until we are

almost panting with passion that is fighting so hard to stay contained.

This is what I've been waiting for. This is incredible. This is animal lust. This is what it's all about. This is what I've missed. I want him, I want him, I want him. And now I can have him, I've almost got him.

My hand rests on his leg, my bottom's raised off the chair as I'm leaning towards him, my face inches from his, and just as I finish telling him about my night with two men, he whispers in my ear, 'I have got the most enormous hard-on listening to you.'

I look him in the eyes with a smile and then, even though we're in a public place, I move my hand slowly up his leg and feel his rock-hard cock through his trousers.

He closes his eyes and exhales loudly, as I massage his cock ever so gently, then stop, moving my hand back down his thigh. Opening his eyes again, thickly glazed with passion he says huskily, 'Anyone can see us.'

'I know,' I whisper back, 'doesn't that turn you on? There are men watching us, watching my hand on your cock and wishing it was them. Doesn't that turn you on?'

His eyes are closed again and he nods his head. 'Carry on,' he whispers. 'Tell me what else you'd like to do to me.'

I could tell you exactly what I said, but I won't. I know you've had the details in the past, but this is different, this, in some ways, is more intimate. Perhaps because we don't really know each other, perhaps because this is a foreplay I hadn't foreseen.

What I will tell you is that I sat there, leaning so close I was almost on Andrew's lap, and I whispered in his ear exactly what I would like to do to him, exactly

what I would like him to do to me. And I didn't couch it in erotic words, I used the most basic, base, vulgar words I could find. There, does that satisfy you?

It satisfies Andrew. He keeps his eyes closed while I keep whispering, my voice becoming hoarse with lust, and eventually he opens his eyes and says slowly, throatily, 'I have to fuck you.'

I stand up. 'Follow me.' And he stands up and meekly follows me out the room, holding his coat in front of him to hide his erection.

We take the lift up to the fourth floor, standing behind an American couple, and he doesn't seem the least bit surprised that I have booked a room. Perhaps I am not as clever as I thought.

I slide the card through the sensor outside the door, and it opens into a small, but immaculately decorated bedroom. I wish I could tell you it opened into a wonderful sumptuous suite, I know it would make a better story, but I couldn't afford the suite, and this was the best I could do. And it does. Naturally.

Andrew closes the door, drops his coat on the floor and pushes me back on the bed, shoving his tongue in my mouth, hands all over my body. He pushes the straps of my dress off my shoulders, and roughly kneads my tits, bending down to suck a nipple. Hard. Ouch, this hurts. 'Slow down,' I whisper, 'we've got all night.'

But he doesn't slow down. He pulls my dress off and whips off his shirt and trousers, and he kneels between my legs, completely naked, in all the glory I've been dreaming of for weeks. Months.

Except I'm not really feeling anything. I don't even feel slightly turned-on. I feel nothing other than a vague satisfaction that I managed to pull this off.

This has happened to me before, I think. Shit, this

has happened to me before. You build up a fantasy in your head, a fantasy that involves elaborate detail about the man of your dreams.

You lie in bed at night and spin out long daydreams about what it will be like, when it eventually happens. You try and picture their body, their voice, what they will say to you, what they will tell you to do.

You build the excitement, the anticipation, and then, after you've spent hours planning it, it actually happens. And suddenly, as they kiss you, you find that it's not so exciting after all.

But it has to grow, you tell yourself, because this is your fantasy come true. That feeling of lust will come, you think, because it has always come to you in the past, while you have been lying in your bed alone and planning this very moment.

But that feeling of lust doesn't come, or if it does, it's a flicker of the feeling in your head. It's too late to stop this, you think. I have to go through with this because you have talked yourself into a situation and it is too late to get out.

So you do go through with it, and it is far less than earth-shattering. It is not even earth-splintering. You find yourself going through the motions of sex, feeling nothing whatsoever other than boredom.

And afterwards you lie there and tell yourself you will not do this again. You will not spend hours creating a fantasy of perfect sex with a perfect man, unless you haven't a single chance in hell of getting this man, because you will always be disappointed.

And because this has happened to me before, I suddenly realise what the outcome will be, and that I don't want this to happen to me again.

I watch Andrew as he gets off the bed and walks over to his coat to get a condom – did he know this was

going to happen or does he always carry condoms in his inner pocket just in case? – and I know as an absolute certainly that I can't do this.

If this were to happen, it would be a meaningless fuck, and suddenly I don't want a meaningless fuck anymore. I don't want the intensity of fucking someone you don't know and don't care about. I want the laughter, the security, the warmth of making love. I want to make love with Adam.

I don't want you, I want Adam. I don't want your body, I don't *know* your body, I don't know what to do *with* your body, and you certainly don't know what to do with mine.

And for the first time since Adam and I broke up, I miss him. I really, really miss him. A physical pang hits me, and I suddenly realise what I've got. What I had. What I could have again if it's not too late.

But shit. Andrew's coming back. How the hell do I get out of this? Do I just fuck him and get it over with, or do I tell him now? How do I tell him, what do I say?

'Oh God,' I groan, just as he climbs back on the bed.

'What's the matter?' My groan was quite obviously not a groan of passion.

'I can't do this. I'm so sorry, but I can't do this.'

'You *are* joking.' But he knows I'm not, at least his erection does, it's wilting by the second.

'No. I can't, I'm just not ready for this.'

'I don't *believe* you,' he says, his voice cold. 'You lure me here on some pathetic pretext of wanting to talk, and you sit downstairs talking about sex, obviously seducing me, and now, at the eleventh hour, you decide you can't do this? Have you got a fucking problem?'

He stands up and gets dressed, not saying a word, while I lie on the bed, curled up in the foetal position,

half under the duvet with my head pressed into the pillow.

He still doesn't say anything, just walks out, slamming the door behind him. Thank God, thank God he's gone. I want Adam. I cradle myself as I lie in this big double bed, rocking backwards and forwards as the tears finally come.

Huge great heaving sobs. I want Adam. I miss Adam. I love Adam. Tonight wasn't passion, tonight was nothing. I don't care about passion anymore, I care about Adam.

They say you never know what you've got until it's gone, and I always thought that was ridiculous, a load of bullshit. I never thought it would happen to me.

But it's happening now. 0171 266 6431. Where are you, Adam? I don't know what I'll say to you, I just know I have to tell you. Where are you at midnight when I need you.

Oh God, he couldn't be with anyone else, could he? A flash of insecurity, of panic, but no, he couldn't, it's Adam. Pick up the phone.

It rings three times and then his machine picks up. 'It's me, can't get to the phone, so do your stuff after the bleep.' Where is he? It's midnight and where is he? Why isn't he there for me to tell him I love him. I can't leave a message, it's too impersonal, so I just put the phone down and I cry, and cry and cry.

In case you're wondering what's going on inside my head, I'll tell you. I think I have just discovered what love is. That love can be passion, admiration and respect, but that passion comes in many forms. That passion doesn't necessarily have to be heart-wrenching or gut-clinching. That passion can be comfort, safety and security. That passion can be trust, friendship, familiarity.

But whatever it is, for the first time I am completely sure that I have it with Adam. But Adam is not here, and lying here alone, curled up with tears streaming down my cheeks, it has to be the loneliest night of my life.

– Twenty-three –

Louise hands me the bill, folded neatly in half, and says, 'Look at it when you leave.'

She comes over and puts her arms around me, hugging me tight, the first physical contact I have ever had with her, and when she releases me there are tears in both our eyes.

'You've done it,' she says with a smile, 'you've done it.'

This is it, I can't believe that this is really it, that I've finally finished this journey that seems to have taken so long. Christ, it hasn't been easy, and I'm not even sure I want it to end, there's something so comforting about this space, this time for myself, this process of self-examination.

But I knew it was over, I had learnt as much as I was going to, and Louise knew it too. She knew it when I told her about Andrew, about the night of passion that never was, about the truth and strength of my feelings for Adam.

I look at the bill when I reach my car, and my very first thought as I read her words is, Jesus, bit naff, isn't it?

'Good luck, Tasha, and thank you for sharing your

life with me, for teaching me so much. It has been a privilege to know you, and I'll miss you. Louise.'

But my first thought doesn't last very long. My second thought, or perhaps feeling, is pride. I sit in my car and look at the words, and feel incredibly proud of myself for making it, coming to the end of this journey.

We never think we have things to teach other people. I always saw myself as a pupil, trying to learn how to make the best of life, looking at others, trying to emulate them, to do as they do, to have what they have.

But Louise, with all her degrees, her knowledge, her wisdom, has learnt from me. God knows what, but I believe that's true, I believe that despite our professional arrangement, I have somehow touched her life, because she's hardly going to lie to me, is she? What would be the point.

And Christ, has she touched mine. Changed it. Made me understand why I am the way I am. It may sound trite to say I was half empty when I first went to see her, and now I'm full, but that's exactly how it feels.

I do honestly believe that people enter our lives for a reason. That everyone who we meet, who forms an impression, has something to teach us. Everything that happens to us is an experience, and because of that it can never be bad. An experience can only be good because it all serves to shape the person that we are, the person that we become.

I forgive my parents, knowing now that I can't blame them, as I did for so many years, for screwing me up, screwing up my relationships. I've learnt that they were doing the best they could with the knowledge they had, and that that is enough.

I forgive Simon, despite breaking my heart, because if it weren't for Simon I wouldn't have slept around,

wouldn't have learnt that that isn't the answer, and most of all, I wouldn't have met Adam.

I even forgive you, dear reader, for your feelings about me when we first met. Don't think I didn't know how you felt, your animosity, your occasional hatred, but I hope you've learnt from this too. I hope you've seen something of yourself in me, I hope that you too realise that I was doing the best I could, with the knowledge I had.

Christ, stop me before I become slushy, this isn't sounding like me at all. But then again, maybe it is, maybe it's the new me. Nah. Maybe not.

Seven messages on my machine. My heart skips a beat, maybe one of them is from Adam. I called him the morning after the night before, as it were, but he wasn't in, and I didn't leave a message.

I called him that night, and he wasn't in, and I didn't leave a message. For three days I kept calling, and eventually I left a message. I told him that I needed to talk to him. I told him that I needed to see him. I told him to call me as soon as he got in, it didn't matter what time it was.

He didn't call.

The messages are from the girls. Four from Andy, 'Where *are* you? Call me,' one from Mel, one from Emma, and finally . . . finally, one from Adam.

'I'm sorry, I've been away for work. I'm at home, so give me a call when you're around.'

God it's weird hearing his voice. Not that it's been that long, but his voice sounds different, familiar, but different. The affection is missing, replaced by a

curtness, and I sit there and replay his message six times. Definitely curt, but Jesus, can you blame him?

I call back immediately, and he picks up the phone.

'Hi, stranger.'

'Hi,' he says, then more guarded, 'hello. How are you?'

'I'm fine, Adam. How are you?'

'Fine. Working hard.'

'Ad, I need to talk to you.'

There's a silence. 'Ad?'

'I don't know, Tasha. I've had so much time to think and I'm not sure there's anything left to say.'

Oh God no. This wasn't supposed to happen. He said he'd wait. He's supposed to be over the moon, he's supposed to want me back. Please, I plead silently, please God, let him want me back.

'I know how you must be feeling,' I start, talking very slowly, not sure of how to express myself, but sure that I don't want to say too much on the phone, sure that everything will be all right if he sees me, remembers how much he loves me. 'But I've been thinking too, and so much has happened and so much has changed, too much to go into on the phone, but we have to meet.'

Another silence.

'Please.'

'OK,' he says finally. 'When?'

'Tonight?'

'I'm sorry, I can't make tonight. What about tomorrow?'

He can't make tonight? What is this, he's supposed to be missing me so desperately he can't wait to see me. Oh shit, this is my penance, isn't it, this is what I get for behaving like such a bitch.

'Tomorrow's fine. Do you want to come over? I could make something to eat.'

'No,' he says emphatically. 'I'd rather meet somewhere.'

OK, I know this game. I understand about neutral territory, and I understand that he does not want me to have the upper hand, so we arrange to meet at a café in Maida Vale. Not dinner, too formal, but coffee. Coffee that could take half an hour, or three hours, depending on what it is I have to say to him.

I put the phone down and I'm shaking, so I call Mel, Mel who I've been avoiding since this whole fiasco began. Mel who I've wanted to talk to so badly, but I wasn't sure how she'd take it, how she'd judge me.

But right now I need her, I need to explain, to tell her she was right.

'Mel? It's me. I know we're all meeting for lunch, but can you get there earlier? I need to talk to you.'

She's there when I walk in, sitting at our usual lunch table, by herself, looking safe and familiar and lovely, and when she sees me she smiles, her lovely Mel smile and I know that she's forgiven me, that she knows it's all going to be OK.

And as I walk over she stands up and she gives me a huge hug. 'You've got something to tell me, haven't you?' She smiles, breaking away and sitting down.

'Oh Mel,' I sigh and shake my head, 'you were right. Why didn't I listen to you. I love him, Mel. I love Adam. I needed to go through this, I wouldn't have realised if it hadn't been for Andrew, but Jesus, he's the most important thing in my life and of course I have passion with him, I just didn't realise it.'

'I'm so happy for you,' she says, and she means it. 'But what made you realise?'

'I will tell you, but you have to promise not to be angry with me.'

'I promise.'

And I tell her about the quest for passion, the fuck that never was, the exhilaration and desperation when I knew for certain what love is. And she doesn't say anything, she just listens as it all comes out in a torrent and when I've finished she looks at me very seriously and says, 'You must never tell him.'

And I nod because I know she is right, I know that it would hurt him beyond redemption, that if he knew what I had done there would be no going back.

'Will he have me back?' I ask her, because even though I know she won't have the answer, I need to be reassured.

'He loves you,' she says, 'but you have to realise that right now he doesn't necessarily trust you. You need to prove to him that you are trustworthy and that may take time, but yes, I think he will have you back.'

The others arrive, Emma first, then Andy, and within minutes we are shouting across the table, giggling like schoolgirls, each wanting to be the first to tell their stories.

Emma reaches into her Gucci bag and pulls out a selection of bridal magazines. 'Most of it's pretty disgusting,' she giggles, 'but I've got a few ideas from them and I wanted to know what you think.'

She spreads them out on the table, and being the girls that we are, we ooh and aah at some of the pictures, and shriek with horror at others.

'That's the dress I want,' says Andy suddenly, pointing at a dress that's so tight it's more of a condom than a wedding dress.

'You getting married? I don't somehow think so.' I say.

'You never know,' Andy suddenly blushes, 'you just never know when you'll meet the man of your dreams.'

'Andy, you meet the man of your dreams every week.'

'Yes, well.' She doesn't say anything, and we all look at one another.

'Andy?'

'Mmm?'

'Who is it this time?'

'I know,' I shout. 'His name's Mark.'

'Tasha,' she hisses, before saying modestly, 'his name is Mark, he's forty and he's an accountant.'

'An accountant?' We all look horrified. 'You? With an accountant?'

'What's wrong with that?' She looks seriously pissed off.

'Nothing,' I say hastily. 'It's just it's, it's so unlike you.'

'Well, maybe it is but he seems really nice, and he's nice to me, so I'm taking it slowly and we'll see what happens. It's too early to think about the future.'

I'm speechless, I'm truly, truly speechless, and it seems, from the deafening silence that follows this speech, that everyone feels the same way.

Andy has always vowed never to go out with a lawyer or an accountant. 'Oh please,' she'd always joke, 'too boring.' Andy has never described someone as 'really nice'. They have always been gorgeous, or divine, or drop-dead handsome. Andy has never, *ever*, taken it slowly, nor said it's too early to think about the future.

Maybe she knows, I think. Maybe it's true what they say, those married friends of mine who are so happy, that you don't know how you know until you meet them, but then you always know.

Maybe for some people it does happen instantly, and perhaps this is why Andy is being unusually reticent. Maybe for others, others like myself, it takes time to realise that you have found what you have been looking for.

We don't pursue Mark, Andy obviously doesn't want to talk about it any more, and we move smoothly onto other things. We talk about men, naturally, about work, about emotions, about people, about life.

And right at the end of our lunch, when we're leaning back in our chairs, clutching our stomachs and once again moaning that we've eaten too much, we talk about passion.

'I've been thinking about this a lot recently,' says Andy, looking first at me, then at Mel. 'I think you're both right, and I think I was probably wrong. I still don't believe that you can live without it, I still maintain that admiration and respect aren't enough, but I do now think that passion can grow. That sometimes it grows where you least expect it, and when that happens it endures far longer.'

She looks at me and smiles, and I smile back. We hold each other's gazes for a very long time.

For someone who usually spends hours getting ready, I can't believe I'm dressed, made-up and ready to go with half an hour to spare. I have to take my mind off this, off my evening with Adam, what am I going to do for the next half hour?

Television. I sit and channel surf, because I can't bloody concentrate on a thing, but at least I can look at pictures rather than think of what I'm going to say to Adam.

I am so nervous, but so excited. I'm going to see the man I love, and I'm going to tell him that I love him

and everything's going to be OK. Better than OK. Magnificent. A happy ever after.

Time to go, I drive to the café in a haze, and then I walk in and he's not there, but I'm early so I take my cappuccino and sit down at a table near the front. Don't want him to miss me, I want to be the first thing he sees when he walks in. My Adam, my love.

God, will you listen to me? I can't believe what I sound like, so slushy, so soppy, so unlike me. What is going on? Yes, sure, I was like this with Simon, but I never believed Adam could make me feel like this.

I mean, he was always the one telling me he loved me. I never said anything back, other than the occasional 'I know.' And I thrived on being adored, I never felt I needed to give anything back.

I've always believed that in relationships one is always the lover and one is always the loved. It can shift all the time, but there will never be two lovers at one time, or two loved. In the past I have always been the lover. Always and without exception. Until Adam, when I was the loved. Always and without exception.

And now it has shifted and again I am the lover, but not the insecure, needy, jealous lover of my old relationships. I am the lover, but a strong, secure and comfortable lover. A lover who is proud of what she is. Who wants to show just how much she can love, how much she is capable of.

For God's sake, Adam, where the hell are you?

And then I see him, parking the car, looking up and down the road as he crosses, walking in, and my face lights up. I expect his to do the same, and I could swear I see a flash when he first sees me, but then it blanks over and he walks slowly over, cool, calm and collected. Nothing like the Adam I know. The Adam I thought I knew.

I have to hold myself in check, because this wasn't the way I planned it. I thought he'd walk in, see me, and we'd run into each other's arms like in the movies. Still hoping for that Hollywood love affair, but this isn't anything like that. This is wrong. This isn't what's supposed to happen and I'm thrown off guard.

The words I was going to say, something along the lines of, I love you, I miss you, I want to be with you for ever, those words that were to be spoken while watching his face light up seem wholly inappropriate now, and I've got to be honest here, I'm stuck.

'Hi,' he says. 'You look well.'

'Thank you. So do you.' He's not supposed to say I look well, for Christ's sake. He's supposed to say I look beautiful, gorgeous, adorable.

'So,' he says finally, jauntily, not a shadow of the Adam I last saw, the Adam that was in pain, that cried into my shoulder and told me he'd wait.

'So,' I say back, not having a clue what to do. 'So how's work?'

'Oh fine, fine. Been working really hard, it's going well.' That breezy tone again, and I can't help myself, the whine that comes out in my voice, 'Where've you been? I've been calling and calling and you haven't been there.'

'Oh out and about. You know how it is.' No, I don't know how it is actually. I know you, but I don't know what this is about. Where does this tone of voice come from? When did you learn to be so breezy? When did you stop caring? Have you stopped caring?

'So how's Andrew?' he says finally, after we both sit there stirring our coffees and wondering what the hell to say next, how in the hell we're going to break the ice.

'I haven't seen him, Adam. I don't want to see him.'

'Really?' he says with a heavy dollop of sarcasm. 'That wasn't the way it looked last time I saw you two together.'

'Jesus, Adam. What *is* this? The last time I saw you, you told me you'd wait for me, that I could have time, and all I've thought about since then is you, and I've come here today to tell you that and it's like talking to a stranger. You're acting like a total bastard.' Oh shit, oh shit, here come the tears. No. Go away, don't roll down my cheeks, I don't want him to see this. Thank God. They've gone, but not before he saw my eyes swimming in them.

His face softens. His voice softens. 'I'm sorry. I didn't mean to be like this. I was in so much pain when I last saw you, and after that I got angry. I was so furious with you, at the way you had treated me, and I'm still angry. I still can't quite believe what you did.'

My voice catches in my throat. 'You mean you're not waiting for me. It's over, isn't it?'

Adam doesn't say anything, and while he sits there sighing I start to feel so sick I have to physically put my hand on my stomach to settle it.

'I don't know anymore,' he says, sighing again. 'A lot has happened in the three weeks we've been apart. When I moved my stuff out, when we talked, I did think I would wait. I thought you were worth waiting for. But now . . .' He tails off, shrugging.

Do I tell him how I feel? Will that change anything? Will it matter to him?

'Ad,' I say softly, hoping that the familiarity will remind him of what it was like, being with me. 'Ad, I've been a complete bitch to you. I've acted appallingly, but in some sick sort of way we needed this to happen because I needed to realise how much I love you.' I stop, formulating the words in my head before I say

them, testing them on my tongue before they leave my lips. 'How much I'm in love with you.'

He looks up at me, confusion in his eyes. Yes, this is the first time he's heard the words, but I'm not sure it makes any difference now. I'm not sure it isn't too late.

'I have never been happier in my life than when I was with you,' I carry on. 'But I had this ridiculous notion that there was something missing. But since we've been apart I've realised that there isn't anything missing. That what I have with you is all I ever wanted. God, Adam, this is so hard for me.'

'You don't realise what you've got until it's gone,' he says softly, almost to himself.

'Yes, that's exactly it. I didn't realise, and now I do, and I just want to be with you.'

'It isn't as easy as that.' He sighs again, and runs his fingers through his hair, and the thought strikes me from nowhere, a thought so terrible that I almost can't believe it, but it's out there, before I have a chance to think it through, the thought is out there.

'You've met someone else.' It comes out in a whisper, and Adam does the worst thing he could possibly do. He doesn't reply, and I feel as if my entire world is collapsing about my ears.

'You've met someone else.' I repeat it, because I can't quite believe it.

'Not exactly.' He stops. 'But sort of.'

'Who is she?' I really don't want to know, but I have to.

'Someone at work.'

'How do you feel about her?'

'It's not what it sounds.'

What does he mean, what does he mean?

'What is it then? Tell me.'

'It's Cathy.' Cathy. I rack my brains, who is Cathy?

And then I remember, she's a design assistant at work, an assistant that Adam rarely spoke about, other than to mention that she had a crush on him, and that it was sweet.

And I ignored the threat because it wasn't a threat. She's only young, what? Twenty-two? Twenty-three? And Adam was too in love with me to even look at another woman, or so I thought.

'Young Cathy?' I'm looking at him with horror.

He nods.

'But you were never interested in her, she's far too young for you.'

'She's not that young, she's twenty-four.'

'So, you're going out with her? You're sleeping with her? What exactly is the relationship between you?'

'We went out for a drink last week, we'd been working late on a new project, and we ended up getting very drunk, and she told me she'd always fancied me.'

'She's not that young then, if she's forthright enough to make that sort of confession.' Bitch.

'No, she's not that young. And I'm not really sure how it happened but she ended up back at my flat,' oh shit, I don't want to hear this, I don't want to hear that Adam made love to someone else. Please tell me you didn't, please tell me you changed your mind, you couldn't go through with it. Lie if you have to, just don't tell me you slept with her, 'and we ended up in bed.'

He looks up at me then, guilty, expecting, perhaps, an onslaught, but what can I say? Adam has slept with someone else. I had the bloody decency to pull out at the last minute, but he didn't. There is nothing to say, and the silence seems to stretch out and out and out.

'I felt terrible the next morning,' he says, as if it's some sort of consolation, which in a very tiny way it is.

'I didn't want her to be there, I didn't want her in my bed.'

'But I suppose you fucked her again, just for the hell of it.'

He flushes.

'I thought so. So what's happened since then?'

'That's just it. Nothing has, but she keeps asking me when she can see me, and I really don't know how I feel about her. She's very sweet, but I'm not sure I'm ready to get involved.'

Are you ready to get involved with me? Despite feeling absolutely sick, I still want you, Adam, I forgive you.

Adam has to do this. He has to absolve his guilt by sharing it with me, unloading his burden. I am stronger than Adam, and whilst I never fucked Andrew, never allowed him to enter my body, it's still my secret, a secret I won't share with him because I don't believe he deserves any more pain.

I think I deserve this pain.

'If it's over, Adam, and you still love me, then we can put it behind us. I didn't want to hear about it, but you needed to tell me, and now you have I can just accept it and move on. We can move on. Together, if that's what you want.'

'I don't know what I want, Tasha. Yes, I still love you, but I couldn't take this hurt again, and I don't know whether I can trust you any more.'

Thank you, Mel, thank you for warning me so I know what to say.

'I understand that, Adam, and there's nothing I can say to make you trust me, but if you give me time I can prove it to you.'

'Time.' He nods slowly. 'If there is a chance for us, and I'm not saying there definitely is, but if there is, I

need to take things very slowly. We can't just take up from where we left off.'

'I understand that. That's fine. That's what I want.' I breathe a sigh of relief. Thank you God, for giving me a chance. 'So where do we take it from here?' I want him to say he'll see me later, he'll come over, he'll stay the night, and suddenly I want to rip his clothes off and squeeze him tight, cover him with kisses, smother him with passion. With love.

He stands up and takes some money out his pocket to pay the bill, and then he looks at me, leans down and kisses me, half on the lips, half on the corner of my mouth.

'I'll call you,' he says, and walks out of the door.

– Twenty-Four –

It's been four days and he hasn't called. Every time the phone rings at home I dive on it, and every time it hasn't been Adam. The girls know it, they apologise for being them, for being the cause of the listless tone in my voice.

I get in from work and the first thing I do, before cuddling the cats, before dropping my bags, before running up to the bathroom, is to dial 1471, just in case he called, and didn't leave a message. But the last number received is never Adam's.

And every evening, while I'm staying in just in case he decides to call *that* evening, I pick up the phone on the hour, every hour, just to check it's still working.

At work I sit at my desk, surrounded by sheaths of paper, piles of videotapes, and I sit there and stare blankly into space, unable to concentrate for longer than three minutes at a time, glancing at the phone every few seconds, daring it to ring, daring it to be Adam.

'Anyone call?' I ask Jilly repeatedly, even if I've just left my desk for a moment, and she looks at me as if I am mad for she knows how much I hate the phone, and her answer is always yes, but it's never Adam.

We always want what we can't have, and here it is,

living proof. I always wanted the food I wasn't supposed to have, the chocolate, bread and biscuits when I was supposed to be on a diet, and now my craving is Adam.

I think of him everywhere I go. I think of his smile, his laugh, his big strong arms, and occasionally I think of those arms around Cathy, but past is past, I tell myself, and I stop those thoughts before they become too painful, and I wait.

When you're an impatient person waiting five minutes for something that you want feels like a lifetime and I honestly don't know how I'm coping with all this.

One afternoon I get back from lunch, and a yellow Post-it note is balancing precariously on the top of the handset on my desk, with scribbled writing that I can only just make out. 'Call Jennifer Mason,' it says, with a phone number I don't recognise.

I know I know this name. I just don't know where from, so I cast it aside and get on with my script. But all afternoon I keep glancing at her name, knowing that she is somewhere in my memory, and eventually I dial her number, and the minute she picks up the phone I recognise her voice.

'Remember me?' she laughs. 'The passion junkie?'

'Of course I do, how could I forget, you're the woman who changed my life.'

'That's why I was calling. You never told me what happened to you that day we spoke on the phone, but I kept imagining you were in a similar situation, and I was watching the show the other day and saw your name on the credits. I started to think about you and I was curious so I called.'

What a lovely thing to do. What a lovely woman.

'I've got an Adam too,' I say, and we both laugh. 'He

was my best friend, and he fell in love with me but I wasn't sure. After I spoke to you that day I still wasn't sure, but I decided to give it a go.

'And then I screwed it up. I thought there was something missing, I thought we didn't have passion, so I left him and tried to find passion elsewhere, except what I thought was passion, wasn't.'

'And now?' She prompts me gently.

'And now I've told my Adam how I feel, that I want him back and he's thinking about it. But you know the strangest thing? I was a total passion junkie until Adam, just like you, and then it became incredibly comfortable but now, now that I'm waiting for him to come back, I feel like I'm back on that damned rollercoaster.'

'I know,' she says. 'I remember that happening to me when I fell in love with my Adam, but it does settle down. If friendship is the most important part of your relationship, the rollercoaster starts to even out, trust me.'

'I always wanted to thank you, you know,' I say, suddenly knowing that this is true. 'I used to think about you all the time when I first started having a relationship with Adam, I used to wish I was like you.'

'What a nice thing to say! And now you are,' she says, and I can hear the smile in her voice.

'Not yet, not quite, but I hope I'm getting there.'

'And how does it feel right now?'

'Like hell!' And we both laugh. I thank her for calling, and just before she puts the phone down she says, 'Don't forget to invite me to the wedding.'

For the first time in four days I feel calm. A short phone call and I feel that everything's going to be OK.

And isn't it just always the bloody same. The minute you stop worrying about something, the minute you

stop thinking about it, it happens. When you least expect it.

Tonight I'm staying in again, and yes, I still dialled 1471, but tonight the phone seems to have become a little less threatening, a little less menacing, a little bit more of a friend.

I pick up the phone to dial the Chinese takeaway – nothing like spare ribs, lemon chicken and egg fried rice to take away the misery of being on your own, and as I'm ordering, giving them my address, call waiting starts bleeping.

Do I finish ordering, or do I take this call? 'Hang on a sec,' I say to the Chinese man on the other end of the line, while I press recall 2, praying that it works, that this time I don't, as I usually do, say a tentative hello to the person I've just been speaking to.

'Hello?'

'Hello.' It's not the Chinese man, it's Adam. Thank God, it's finally Adam. 'What are you up to?' he says, casually, as if I'm just a mate, an old friend.

Whatever it is I'll cancel it for you, Adam, I'll go wherever you want me to go.

'Nothing much. Why?'

'No reason. Look, are you free tomorrow night?'

Tomorrow night, tonight, any night. I'm free.

'Would you like to go out for dinner?'

'I'd love to.'

'OK. How about if I pick you up at eight thirty?'

'Fine. I'll see you then.'

'Great. Oh, and Tash?'

'Yes?'

'Dress up.'

I put the phone down and it rings instantly, the Chinese man waiting patiently for me to come back to

him, but you know what? I'm suddenly not hungry any more.

I have been out with Adam, I have slept with Adam, I have laughed with Adam, I know all his secrets and he knows most of mine, but I am so nervous I can't think straight.

Dress up, he said. Dress up how? Does he mean long chiffon, or does he mean black jacket and little black skirt? Which is the most flattering, which is his favourite, which is guaranteed to win back his heart?

Ah ha! A camel-coloured trouser suit. Smart, sophisticated, sexy, but not too obvious. A whisper of cleavage, the swish of the trousers as I walk. Shoes in white and camel, exactly the same shade, tiny pearl earrings. I hang the clothes on the cupboard door and stand back to survey. Perfect.

And soaking in the bath, even submerged underwater to wash my hair, I can't stop smiling. And putting on my make-up, blow-drying my hair, I can't stop smiling.

Mel phones early evening.

'Hi sweetie, I'm just ringing to say good luck.'

'Oh Mel, I'm so excited, but I feel so sick, what if he's just taking me out to tell me it's all over?'

'I don't think that's the case,' she smiles, 'and there's no reason to be nervous. It's only Adam.'

'So why do I feel like a teenager, like this is my first ever date?'

'Because it *is* a first date. It's you and Adam getting to know each other again.'

She is, as always, right, and I'm pacing the flat when the doorbell rings, on the dot of eight-thirty.

Calm, calm, calm, I tell myself, checking my reflection, taking long, slow, measured steps down the

corridor. Standing by the front door, with one hand on the handle, taking deep breaths. Composing my features into a smile of welcome, a smile of anticipation, a smile of hope.

I open the door and we stand there, Adam and I, facing one another and grinning, neither saying a word. In one hand Adam is holding a large bunch of white roses, my favourite flowers, and he hands them to me, still grinning, and comes in.

'Thank you, thank you!' I run to the kitchen to cut the stems, put them in water. 'You didn't have to! And they're my favourite!' Tasha, shut up. Stop behaving like an over-excited schoolgirl. But I am over-excited. I can't help myself. Adam's back, he's in my flat.

I turn around and see Adam hovering in the doorway, looking uncomfortable, and I think of how he used to be when he was here. How he would plant himself in the kitchen, feet on the table to read the paper, and how he always looked so at home here.

But now he doesn't, and in a flash I'm not so sure. I'm not so sure that everything is going to work out.

'Shall we go?' he says softly, when the flowers are perfectly arranged and the vase has been put on the hall table, and I am still babbling away about absolutely nothing, desperate to fill any silence that might exist between us.

We walk out, and as we cross the road Adam puts his arm around me, so lightly that I can hardly feel it, just to steer me over, to make sure I'm protected, that nothing can happen to me.

And we reach the car and as he opens the door for me, as I climb into his car, I look up at him and he smiles, and suddenly I know that everything is going to be OK.